RIDE, SALLY, RIDE

(SEX RULES)

DOUGLAS WILSON

canonpress
MOSCOW, IDAHO

A novel about true love, the sexually demented,
and the crack-up of the United States.

A comedy of manners in a world without any manners,
that world being a sexual dystopia in the very near future,
a time in which Asahel found his way
into and out of the vortex.
And Stephanie did, too.

Let me say it one more time y'all
All you want to do is ride around Sally, ride, Sally, ride
All you want to do is ride around Sally, ride, Sally, ride
~ Wilson Pickett, "Mustang Sally"

Published by Canon Press
P.O. Box 8729, Moscow, ID 83843
800.488.2034 | www.canonpress.com

Douglas Wilson, *Ride, Sally, Ride: Sex Rules*
Paperback edition copyright © 2020 by Douglas Wilson.

Cover design by James Engerbretson.
Interior formatting by Samuel Dickison.

Library of Congress Cataloging-in-Publication Data is forthcoming.

20 21 22 23 24 25 26 27 28 29   10 9 8 7 6 5 4

This book is dedicated to Darren Doane,
who had the great idea for the central hook.

This is as good a place as any to insist that all the characters in *Ride, Sally, Ride* are fictional, and I made them all up out of my own head. Any resemblance to any real people, living or dead, is their own darn fault. If they quit acting like that, the resemblance would cease immediately, and we wouldn't have to worry about it.

CONTENTS

EXPLANATION

AS ONE IS CLEARLY NEEDED

First, a note about the subtitle: The unassuming phrase *sex rules* admits of two basic meanings. One has to do with the customs or mores of a particular society, including even the decadent ones. As in, "What are the sex rules in Toronto?" This is a matter of mere etiquette and custom, and not morality. Expecting sex by the second date can be a custom, and in certain places, it is, but there is nothing moral about it. It would nevertheless be one of the "sex rules" for that place.

So the second and more foundational sense of the phrase refers to the binary realities that were embedded in the world at the dawn of creation. Sex, the way God established it at the very beginning, rules.

This is a story about both senses, and what happens when they collide. The ancient poet Horace put it with some force when he said *Naturam expelles furca, tamen usque recurret,* which puts the whole thing into a shoebox: "You can drive nature out with a pitchfork, but she will keep coming back again."

AN OVERTURE

TO THE WHOLE AFFAIR

Asahel Hartwick did not really intend to be the reason for the crack-up of the United States. When that finally happened, the country fragmented into two, and then after that, into four pieces, and then back into two. But the fact that Asahel (known as "Ace" to his family and friends) did not intend this outcome was largely irrelevant. Intentions were, by the last stage, largely beside the point.

Whenever something like this happens, as it has from time to time in the annals of geopolitics, any competent historian can, after the fact, show how the subsequent events that proved so momentous, and which crept up on everybody from behind, and which virtually no one predicted, were in actual fact some kind of inevitable. The whole thing was going to happen, somehow, someway. This kind of inevitability is a strange creature of time, being only visible from the rear and never from the front. Historians can see it clearly, but prognosticators, for some reason, cannot.

So I have gathered my notes all together, and am about to regale you with a number of events in Colorado, events that eventually and inexorably led to a national crack-up. Asahel was the spark in a room full of fumes, and that is why there was an explosion. But whenever any room is full of fumes, and an Asahel fails to materialize, any competent historian will always tell you that some other guy would be along shortly, and he would be the guy flicking the lighter. Had Martin Luther decided not to post his theses on that church door in Wittenberg because it was raining out, and he was just getting over a cold, then perhaps a fellow down the road named Johannes Becker would have done it. And we would today be casually referring to Missouri Synod Beckerians.

I point this out because while Ace Hartwick provided the occasion, he had nothing to do with the fumes. The fumes were there and well in evidence long before he was born.

CHAPTER 1

A PHINEHAS MOMENT

SETTING THE STAGE

The Cherry Creek neighborhood of the Denver area had been one of the swankiest for many decades, and the troubles of 2024 had only accelerated the coagulation of the swank. After the legalization of pot in the years before that, the downtown area of Denver had gone rapidly to the dogs—and by "the dogs," the reference is not to show poodles owned by rich ladies or anything refined and decadent like that. Rather, the dogs that everything had "gone to" would be more like the mangier packs that roam in and around the landfills outside Manila, the kind that would eat dead vultures and call it a treat.

And yet the swells of Cherry Creek had reacted to all of that deterioration with characteristic aplomb.

These were largely the kind of people who were directly responsible for the insane policy decisions that had led to downtown sidewalks being covered with feces and needles, but because they would rather be dead in a ditch than live in a place like that *themselves*, they quite naturally arranged for other people to have to live there. Such an arrangement seemed more fitting somehow.

These elites were really good at a few things. Their long-practiced art form, made up of a mysterious heap of closely guarded secrets of never having to deal with any of the consequences of any of their decisions, had really had an astonishing run. If success can be defined as retaining influence and power despite a long string of unbridled disasters and failures, the ruling Colorado elites were a success story for the ages.

In the Troubles of '24, when the whole country had shuffled the cultural and political deck, there had also been a drastic reshuffling with regard to all the ministries that had previously been congregated in Colorado Springs, just to the south of Denver. At least half of those ministries had relocated to states where their ministries would be able to remain legal, and where their newsletters would not be immediately prosecuted for hate speech. The remaining ministries had made the necessary accommodations with what they called "the new realities," and had tripled their budgets for "legal staff" in order keep up with the never-ending directives from the Colorado Human Rights Commission. These directives were, in the words of the legal counsel of at least half the remaining ministries, "demented," but these sentiments were only expressed in executive session, and even then pretty rarely.

Benson Hartwick was a senior staff member of one of these remaining ministries. He served as an elder in a Presbyterian church (ECPPA), one that still had the remains of a sort of evangelicalism about it. One could still detect, from time to time, something that resembled orthodoxy coming from the pulpit.

And, as it also happened, Benson was a most notable resident of Cherry Creek, having served three times as the secretary for that neighborhood's association. So while he did not feel directly responsible for the sunlight that was bouncing off his very green front lawn at this particular moment, he did feel a sense of proprietorship, and a modest but not unseemly glow of pride. The lawn was so green that if green had a word in its semantic family like red does—that word being *vermilion*—only that word and no other would have sufficed. Well, maybe the green equivalent of *incarnadine* might have sufficed, if the light was good.

The day was quite fine, and the sun had been working diligently away at it. In the warmth of that sunlight, there were some bees and other assorted insects fooling around in the flower bed that ran around the house, and a couple of birds were off in the trees yelling about something, while their feathered neighbors chucked and chattered in the language of their normal business. But the relative disquiet of the suburban fauna did nothing to molest the peace—a peace that passeth understanding—that enveloped Benson Hartwick.

He was masculine in all the stereotypical ways—he was tall, and he had a jaw that jutted out, but not by *too* much. He also had a long-suffering wife named Roberta, who allowed him to make unilateral decisions while telling himself (and any others who would listen) that "we" had come to the decision after a season of extended prayer. Most of the time Benson more than half believed it himself.

When it came to the jargon of servant leadership, no one could even get near him. And he was also fearsome on the racquetball court—at will he could place a ball no more than four inches above the floor from any given position. He had come to believe that his ability to place the ball in just that way was just as good as taking responsibility for the state of his marriage and family, which, he assumed quite wrongly, was in a decent state.

As Benson was looking out over his emerald and practically perfect lawn, a beat-up 2020 pick-up truck shuddered to a stop on the far side of their capacious driveway. The side mirror didn't actually fall off, but it was obviously thinking about it. Benson's son, Asahel, jumped out and came around the front of the truck, sticking his ball cap in his back pocket as he came. Ace was grinning like something wonderful had just happened, but he always looked like that. Despite everything, he was a cheerful sort, and a very happy twenty-year-old. And despite the superficial perfections of his suburban life, he had a quick mind and a quicker grin.

He also had a temper that had nearly gotten him expelled from his private Christian high school a few years back. This, given the lax discipline policies of that particular school, would have been quite a feat had he managed to accomplish it. He knew that his picture-perfect family was "really messed up," as he quietly put it to himself, and the one thing that was keeping him at home—as he was heading into his third year of college—was the intellectual ballast he was taking on from a dark website that specialized in getting nineteenth century theology into the heavily censored blue states.

He called it ballast, although—truth be told—if anyone in authority knew about what he was reading, if Ace had been silly enough to tell anybody about it, they would say he was in the process of being "radicalized." What it actually consisted of was pretty tame, sane, and mildly orthodox stuff written in another era, long before the continent-wide opium dream had started.

Ace had sandy blond hair, and was two ticks on the good side of having a medium build. But he was muscular and athletic, and had actually beaten his father in racquetball exactly one time. That had not been a cause of friction between them as they both agreed that it was a matter of uncommon luck, coupled with the fact that Benson had been playing left-handed. Ace's hair was always tousled, although close cut on the sides, and he had a hard, industrious, diligent look about him. He was nearly always cheerful, but people who knew him well thought of him as taut and coiled.

He walked briskly toward the house.

Meanwhile, a couple of gated communities over, this one not nearly so posh as Cherry Creek, but every bit as gated, Jon Hunt stood on his front porch looking out on the same sunny day that was apparently blessing Benson so much.

Jon had at one time been an attorney with a high-flying Denver firm, but he was now semi-retired. He filled his time up

reading theology and doing *pro bono* work for the now exiled
Christian Legal Defense. He had been a courtroom barracuda
professionally, but had retired from that particular line when
he became a Christian about five years before this particular
sunny day. His conversion was almost the direct result of his
wife leaving him for another woman. In the years since, he had
come to believe that it was a treatment he had richly deserved,
and was surprised only by the fact that it had taken his ex-wife
Victoria so long to get up enough nerve to do it.

He was waiting on the porch for Stephanie, his daughter,
who had gone out for coffee with a young man named Lionel.
Stephanie attended the same university that Ace did, although
they shared no classes. She had decided to live with her father
after the divorce for various practical reasons, but she had come
to see such a change in him after his subsequent conversion that
she was now hanging around to see what might happen next.
She was not a Christian, but she was thinking seriously about
it. Up to that point in time, all her intellectual energies were
occupied with libertarianism. This was, in the eyes of the state
of Colorado, as unwelcome as all get out, occupying a spot right
between *Calvinism* and *cannibalism*.

Jon's thoughts turned to Lionel, who was bringing Stephanie
back from their third and—unbeknownst to Lionel—last coffee
date. Stephanie had accepted the invitations initially because Lionel was the head of the college and career group of his church,
the same Presbyterian church that Benson Hartwick attended.
Stephanie's father was a Presbyterian also, but as his church
met in the basement of the pastor's house, and because he had

affectionately called it Taliban Reformed, she thought she should begin her inquiries into Presbyterianism by talking with someone who was a bit closer to her in age, and perhaps a *tad* more mainstream. From her discussions with Lionel she had come to believe that being mainstream was perhaps a bit overrated.

She was getting out of the car now, and Lionel waved as she walked up the drive. He did not see if she waved back—she did not—because he had seemed to be distracted by his own hand. The sunlight had glinted off his ring.

Stephanie had jet black hair, cut in a page boy style, and a spray of freckles across her nose. She was willowy without being skinny, and she managed to be well-proportioned without being in any way a hazard or public nuisance. She was a pretty girl, but there are different kinds of pretty girls in this world of ours. Some women are just plain gorgeous, and they don't really know how to turn it off, but Stephanie was not like that. She was entirely secure without any make-up, and was routinely described as "that pretty girl," but whenever she decided to put on the Ritz, the effect was to summon up an oceanic goddess of beauty *de profundis*. And if she smiled at anything male while done up like that, he would probably be in the ICU for at least a couple of days.

She ran up the front steps, and kissed her father on the cheek. "Hello, crazy legs," he said. "How was it?"

"Ugh," she said. "I'll tell you over dinner. Let me just say that his idea of a church that is culturally engaged runs along the lines of *monkey see monkey do*. And what he knows about the Old Testament wouldn't fill a shoe box. I asked him about something in Deuteronomy, and he said, 'Ah, yes, the Pentatooch.' And he wasn't kidding either."

With that, she went into the house.

* * *

When it came to the United States of America, the lines on the map were all still in the same places. Whenever the weatherman was describing the Arctic Express blowing down out of Canada, the long-familiar shape of America was still right there on the flickering screen, welcoming all that snow, and the spring to follow.

That facade had been diligently maintained by all the authorities for just over a decade now. There were still technically fifty-one states—Puerto Rico being admitted in the barfight that some called the year 2022—but knowledgeable observers knew what a facade all of it was.

At the same time, most everyone else—whether a knowledgeable observer or not—knew that the unity of the "United" States was *something* of a facade. But they didn't think about it much because they had just gotten used to it, and since there had been no active shooting war, it was somewhat easy to adjust to the new normal.

The rock that had been dislodged at the top of that particular geopolitical avalanche was the repeal—although there had been considerable debate over whether it actually *was* a repeal—of the infamous Roe v. Wade decision. That had happened in 2023, and while it had been accompanied by a great montage of jesuitical reasoning that claimed in the footnotes that it was *not* a repeal, the net effect was that an Alabama abortion ban had been upheld. Numerous states followed immediately, with nearly identical language, and immediately there had been in effect two Americas.

There was the northeast Atlantic coast America together with the left coast America. The farthest inland that this America got was Ohio on the one side and Colorado on the other. The quickest identifiers for a particular state were how strict their laws on abortion were, and how loose their laws on the use of recreational marijuana were. And homosexual marriages could also be a marker—most of the heartland states had used the language of the Roe-reversal case, adjusted the language to fit, and dispensed with that travesty as well. About three red states were still embroiled in this process, while the blue states were opening themselves to more and more novel configurations of marriage.

And so it was that 2024 had been a banner year for U-Haul—three times the annual business they had ever had before or since. A *lot* of Americans had gotten an eyeful of what all the pundits were still formally denying, and they had decided to reshuffle to areas more conducive to their values. This accelerated the political processes that had been underway in all those various regions anyway. The red states got a lot redder, and blue states got a lot poorer. The blue states also lost twelve votes in the Electoral College, and counting.

The result was that in between the America of the coasts was heartland America. Oil and agriculture were huge, and pipelines, trucks, and river traffic all flowed down to Louisiana and Texas, and out to the world through the Gulf of Mexico.

The remaining threads tying the Union together were fraying, and many of them had already snapped. California had taken the first formal steps, as required by their constitutional amendment, to secede from the Union. Leaving the Union slowly was thought to be a decent approximation of due process. But a number of the heartland states were only technically still in. More than a few citizens of the more inflamed states—that is to say, the border states—believed that in the years following the Trump presidency, there had been more than one political assassination conducted in one state as ordered by the governor of another state, some of them by drones. This conviction was held by the nutcases who were conspiratorially-minded, by the relatively few people involved in the assassinations, and by a handful of others.

The heartland states were held together by an odd alliance involving three groups. The first was the free market guys, wanting to sell oil to the world and anything else the world might want to buy. The second group was the social conservatives—marked well by hostility to abortion, pot, and porn. The third group was actually a smaller sector created by an overlap between the first two, specifically the social conservatives who were selling a lot of oil. This group was a mere handful of men who served as an informal liaison between the other two groups.

And such was the disarrayed state of things all around the nation while Ace, momentarily unaware of most of it, said hello to his father, went into the house, and got a glass of water from the fridge.

THE MEETING

The moving van had been parked in the driveway across the street from the Hartwicks' all morning, and the usual objects that attend such disheveled circumstances were scattered all over the lawn. The piles of boxes were making their presence felt, drawing the attention of passing motorists. New neighbors were moving in, but it looked like they were making heavy weather of it.

Benson Hartwick, as the soon-to-be neighbor across the street and the ever-eager evangelist, had called his wife from the office—he had noticed the van when he was first headed off to work that morning—and asked her to make a platter of cookies to take over. He had already rearranged the schedule with his team so he could go home at noon. Then he and Ace could go across the street and volunteer to help with the unloading.

In addition to his college hours, Ace worked at the recycling plant, and Benson had asked him to arrange for a few hours off that afternoon. As the final stage of the plan, Roberta could come across with the fresh-baked cookies, and the Hartwicks could make their "welcome to the neighborhood" official.

The new neighbor was named Steven Sasani. When the two Hartwicks arrived, he welcomed the help with a great deal of enthusiasm. "*What* a nice gesture! This is *so* thoughtful. We are really eager to get to know *all* of you better. Sally will be out shortly—she's still getting herself ready."

Sasani was a slight little man, just on the healthy side of scrawny, the kind of man who filled all his moments with quick twitches and sudden movements. He had a small cookie duster mustache, was bald on top, and was wearing a blue polo shirt and the kind of slacks that had gone out of style twenty years before. He seemed affable enough, and continued to be *very* grateful for the help.

With a great deal of back and forth, toing and froing, multiple boxes were carried in. After about forty-five minutes of that, Benson and Ace came in through the front door with the last of the boxes. Their presence and involvement had caused enthusiasm for unloading the truck to pick up considerably.

And there, when Benson and Ace came in with the last load, sitting on the couch—the couch that the two had carried in just a short time before—sat a life-sized doll thing. It was a newer model sex android, from the looks of it, although she was completely dressed. She was decked out like a suburban housewife, a blue bandanna on her head just like it was moving day, and she was staring vacantly, straight ahead. Her lips had that come-hither pout, that sexy look, like she had just been hit in the mouth with a brick.

Steven was sitting next to her, holding her hand and stroking it. "Everyone, this is Sally. We were just chatting in the back room about how thoughtful you all are being. This is not at *all* like Arkansas. People there were *so* judgmental. It got so bad that we finally had to get out—at least if we wanted to stay sane. But it looks like we landed on our feet, right, Sally?"

With that he reached back and touched something on the back of her neck. And Sally said, still looking straight ahead, and with her mouth moving *almost* naturally, "I can talk dirty in Spanish." Steven laughed easily, readily, with no trace of self-consciousness. "Such a kidder. Always a laugh riot. I can't wait for you all to get to know her better."

The macabre juxtaposition of Steven and Sally there on the couch was hard for Ace to take in. Sally was a knock-out, or at least she was a sex android manufacturer's idea of a knock-out. There was something creepy about her, but still you got the drift. If she had not been a sex doll, and had been a living person, she *would* have been a knock-out. And further, taking it another step forward in logic, she would not have been the kind of woman who would have been sleeping with the likes of Steven Sasani. And yet there *he* was, sitting with a facsimile of the unattainable.

And so that was how it came about that Benson and Ace just stood there staring, and Roberta was also staring, having just arrived, standing right behind them, plate of fresh-baked cookies in hand.

THEY OR HE?

Benson Hartwick closed their front door behind them. "Well, this is an interesting situation, and no mistake," he said. Roberta nodded in agreement.

"*Interesting* is not the word I would pick," Ace said. "Perverted is more like it. Or maybe demented."

"Now of *course* we differ with the choices they are making," his father said. "But we really need to have them over."

"Dad," Ace said.

"Yes?"

"What do you mean choices *they* are making? What do you mean by having *them* over?"

"Well, you know what I mean. This is just the usual muddle about pronouns. Things were certainly simpler when I was a kid. I still haven't gotten used to the pronouns. But one thing hasn't changed over all those years—and that is the fact that they need Jesus."

"*They* need Jesus?"

"Well, right. Isn't that obvious?"

Ace snorted. "They don't need anything because *they* aren't over there. *He* needs Jesus, I will give you that."

Roberta had followed her husband dutifully for many years, and in most instances it looked pretty good to the general observer. But she really wasn't so sure about this one. She looked at her son like he was starting to make sense to her. Perhaps Benson saw that, or perhaps he just felt it in the air, so he turned to Ace with that decisive look he sometimes got at random times, and said this:

"Son, I appreciate the fact that you have been reading and studying a good deal. And your mother and I do fully support your desire to go into the ministry. We love your zeal and we can read the passion of your heart. We love and *affirm* the passion of your heart. But—and I have cautioned you about this before—knowledge of theology is *no* substitute for a passion for the lost."

"Dad, this is not really a theology issue . . . well, okay it is. Everything is. But not *theology* theology. This is more like 'how-not-to-lose-your-sanity theology.' This is 'how water isn't dry' theology."

Benson's decisive glint looked as though it had hardened as he looked at his son again.

"We need to have them over. And that's it."

REALLY LISTENING

So it was the mother of all awkward dinners.

Steven and Sally Sasani sat on one side of the table, and Ace was sitting straight across from . . . their company. Benson and Roberta Hartwick were at each end of the table, and Steven Sasani was happily carrying most of the conversation. He seemed, and Ace couldn't comprehend how he *could* seem, totally at ease.

There had been some discussion in the kitchen, conducted in hot whispers, about how they were supposed to serve up the plates, but Steven had stuck his head in. Apparently he had needed to deal with this sort of thing before. "Not very much for me, thanks. I am sure it is delicious, but I am such a light eater . . . great, thanks. That looks *perfect.*" As it turned out, he didn't need a lot on his plate because he helped himself liberally to Sally's plate, which contained ordinary portions. He packed all of it away.

All through the dinner, in between regaling them with stories about backwoods Arkansas, and how the rubes and corn-pones there would behave in unseemly ways, Steven would say things like "Try some of your broccoli? You took too much?" And he would reach over to his partner's plate and help himself, and then say, "You are so right, dear. This is the freshest broccoli we have had in some time!" Thankfully he didn't try to put any food in her mouth. But he did comment loudly how delicious the food was, and how much she *had* to have eaten.

Ace kept looking at his father, hoping for some sign that he was going to crack. An acceptable indication, in Ace's book, would be something like standing up and throwing dishes and platters. Anything like that would be a sign that sanity had returned. But nothing—Benson was serenely listening to Steven, nodding at all the appropriate times, and making sure he made periodic eye contact, such as it was, with Sally. But Ace was on a slow boil, and wasn't sure when he was going to foam all over the stove—but he was pretty sure that he was going to.

Suddenly that moment appeared to him to be imminent, and he knew he had to get out of there. He had had more than sufficient amounts of lunacy for one modest suburban dinner. "I have a lot of homework," he said, which was true enough. He got up and excused himself, cleared his place, and headed off to his bedroom. But he had to spend some time reading his Bible before he could even calm down enough to think about his textbooks. For some reason, his Bible had flopped open at the account of Phinehas and his spear. Ace read through it listlessly, and then shut his Bible abruptly.

An hour later, his father tapped on the door. "Come in," Ace said, standing up. He threw his pencil down on the desk.

"Son, your mother and I have been talking . . ."

"So *they've* been gone a while?"

"Yes. They left about half an hour ago."

Ace ran his hands through his hair. "Did he carry her under his arm? Fireman's carry? What?"

"Son, I know you're upset . . . but we all have to remember that each one of us has a Sally inside of us. Whenever we point a finger, the other fingers are pointing back at us. The answer is always Jesus."

"Dad, I agree the answer is Jesus. But what I object to is turning Jesus into part of the problem. Especially *this* kind of problem. My difficulty is not with the answer, which is Jesus, but rather with the question."

"Ace, after you left, we had a glorious opportunity to present the gospel. And I got a sense that they were really *listening*. How can you have a problem with that? Do you see why I am worried that your interests in theology are getting in the way of a practical love and concern?"

Ace buried his face in his hands for a moment, and then looked up. "Dad, what if he goes home and prays the prayer? And suppose he then comes over to tell us that *she* did too, and that he wants Pastor Rodriguez to baptize her? About the only thing that could make things worse at that point would be if Pastor Rodriguez said that he *would*. And given that stinker of a sermon three weeks ago, he might just do it, too."

THE CROSSROADS

Two days later, Benson and Roberta were off to their senior couples' Bible study, and Ace was spread out at the dining room table, doing his homework as was his custom. There was a knock at the door, and when Ace opened it, Mr. Sasani was standing on the porch, mildly agitated. Maybe even rattled.

"Asahel! I am so glad you are home."

"Mr. Sasani . . . what is wrong? Anything wrong?"

"I just got a message . . . I mean . . . I have to drive downtown to pick up a package at FedEx Freight, and I think I will be gone about forty-five minutes. There was some problem with the shipment. Would you mind looking in on Sally while I am gone . . . new city, no friends yet, she is kind of frightened . . . I left the door unlocked."

"Gosh, I don't know, Mr. Sasani . . ."

"Asahel, I know I can depend on you. What would be the *right* thing to do?"

Ace's resistance collapsed, but it was not because of the pressure coming from Mr. Sasani. The pressure was coming from another quarter entirely. "You sure you want me to do the right thing?" he asked.

"Absolutely. Thank you," Mr. Sasani said. "Thank you. *Thank* you. I knew I could count on you, Asahel." And as he turned away, Ace was pretty sure he saw him leer.

After Mr. Sasani's Volvo disappeared around the corner, Ace walked slowly across the street, just like he said he would, hands in his pockets. *Might as well get this over with.*

He walked into their house, and noticed that no lights were on, except in the back of the house. He followed the light down the hallway, and looked in on what had to be the master bedroom. Sally was propped up against the headboard, blindfolded and topless.

About ten minutes later, Ace was driving through the evening to the recycling center. It was closed now, but he had a key. A couple times he looked over at Sally, who just sat there, decked out in one of Ace's old tee-shirts, one that said *Christian Youth Jubilee* on it.

"So this is the way that sanity can come to seem like madness," Ace said to himself. "And I need to do something crazy just so that I *don't* go crazy." He hit the steering wheel with the palm of his hand.

Five minutes later, he pulled into the center. He walked around to the passenger side, and picked Sally up. She was lighter than a bio-woman would have been, but still not all that light. The place was deserted, and he walked slowly through the bins toward the giant compactor in the back. He trudged slowly up the concrete steps that emptied out on a landing over the big container. Standing on the lip of the landing, he stood Sally up, holding her up by the neck. Pausing for just a moment, he took a couple of deep breaths and pushed her in. He felt his hand brush against something on her neck as she went over. She went end over end, and landed flat on her back.

Ace stood there for just a moment, and then he heard a voice, wafting up from below. "Uhhh. Do it again. Uhhh. Harder, harder."

As Ace walked over to the switch that would activate the compactor, he was nodding his head slowly, and very deliberately. Her voice was fading, but against the dead quiet of the late evening recycling plant, he could still hear it plainly. "Ride me, ride me," the plaintive voice was saying.

"Okay," Ace said, "ride, Sally, ride," and he flipped the switch. When that cycle was done, he dumped a massive load of tin cans on top that he had not gotten to earlier that day, and crushed them also. The doll was now buried at the center of an enormous crushed rectangular block of metal.

THE RIGHT THING

Ace got home about five minutes before his parents did and seated himself at the dining room table again, working on his homework, right where he had been when they had left. A few minutes after that, there was a furious pounding on the door. Mr. Sasani was standing there, angry and distraught.

"Where's Sally?" he spit out.

Ace just stood there, and said nothing.

Mr. Sasani yelled at him again. "Asahel! What did you *do* with her?"

"You asked me to look in on Sally and to do the right thing. So I did. I think that's all I need to say."

Mr. Sasani turned on his heel, and scurried across the yard, punching at his cell phone. Ace heard him say, "Police?"

Fifteen minutes later, the kind of quarter hour that seemed like five minutes, a couple of cops showed up at the Hartwicks' door. Roberta was the one who answered it, and she invited both of them to step in. One of them, a short, burly man, asked for Asahel.

"Excuse us, young man, but your neighbor across the way says that he believes you kidnapped his wife. Do you know anything about this?"

Roberta had figured out pretty quickly the rough outlines of what must have happened, but out of long habit she had said nothing. Benson was standing in the background trying to calculate what he thought, and wasn't doing too well. He had no categories. He was a decent and well-meaning man in the main, but he was a good man without categories. And a good man without categories is sometimes not a very good man.

Ace stepped back out of the doorway. "You are free to look through the house to see for yourself. But you shouldn't actually be looking for a *wife*—I believe he is referring to his sex doll."

The cops were startled a bit by that little fact, but walked briskly through the house, checking every room. "Is there a basement here?" one asked. Ace shook his head. The other one leaned in a bit and whispered. "Would you mind walking across the way with us and having a little visit with Mr. Sasani?"

"Sure thing."

"Before you go," Roberta said, "just one thing. You gentlemen need to ask Mr. Sasani why Sally couldn't call herself, if she were in some kind of trouble."

Benson started to shake his head as though he did not want Roberta saying anything, but then he suddenly stopped. He had the demeanor of someone who had just dropped something, and had a hundred little pieces of something to pick up, and who didn't know where to start.

As the cops started to move toward the door, Benson suddenly asked them, "Can I speak to my son for a minute?" They nodded and Benson pulled Ace into the hallway that ran alongside the living room.

"Ace," he whispered, "If you had a sister, which your mother and I prayed for often, would you have been the kind of older brother who destroyed his sister's dolls? Would you have been *that* person?" He spoke with the finality of someone who had just discovered a slam-dunk argument.

Ace shook his head. "That's not the set-up, Dad. It would have to be a brother, not a sister. And if he had been having sex with his doll, I would not have needed to smash it. *You* would have."

Benson pulled back as if he had been slapped in the face, and he stood silent for a moment. "You're right," he said after a minute. "I *would* have." His eyes started to clear for a moment, but then they fogged again, almost immediately. Life in Colorado was far more difficult than it had been for his great-grandfather, who had arrived in that beautiful state when things were closer to normal.

Ace rejoined the policemen, and they headed out the front door. As they walked over to the front porch across the street, Ace saw that Mr. Sasani was seated on a large cardboard box, the one he had apparently picked up at FedEx Freight, and he was weeping as though his heart would never be the same. He seemed to be the kind of man who would never love again, but the end of the box was opened, and there was a second box inside it. That box was labeled "Veronica the Nurse."

CHAPTER 2

WOKE PROSECUTORS ARE THE WORST

FIRED. ARRESTED.

The following Monday, the police seized the surveillance video at the recycling center. The next morning, Tuesday morning, Ace was fired from his position at the center. And shortly thereafter he was arrested at his home.

However, before the arrest happened, we probably ought to note that there were some aspects of his firing that were of some interest to Ace. He puzzled over it a great deal afterward. His boss, Dave, had him load up his possessions from his desk there at work, put them all in a box—there weren't very many of them—and then Dave personally walked him out to the front gate which emptied into the parking lot. In many ways it was just a traditional firing.

They walked in silence, and Ace wondered why on earth Dave was escorting him out instead of just sacking him and being done with it. But when they got to the edge of the parking lot, Dave astonished him greatly when he broke into gestures and started yelling at him.

But while he was yelling, the words he was saying conflicted almost entirely with his angry expressions and with how he was punching the air. "Ace, you are by far and away the *best* employee I have ever had! I hate to do this to you, but I have a wife and three little kids, and we are barely making it as it is. I just had all these cameras installed last year, and so I know where they are, and what they can pick up, and I am doing it this way so I can prove to some bureaucrat that I was giving you one last chewing out before you were gone. You can't be too careful these days."

Ace nodded, trying to look abashed. He looked down at the pavement and shuffled his feet.

Dave took a deep breath, and started in on him again. "I just wish I had your guts. I wish a lot more people had your guts. Colorado used to be a wonderful place before . . ." He stopped himself. "No sense going down *that* road," he said, breathing heavily.

Ace nodded again. "I have enjoyed working here," he said. He then thought he should put up his hands in a gesture of modest protest, so he did that for a moment, and then took them down again.

With that, Dave erupted, turning red in the face and gesticulating wildly. "I think the world of you. I will pray for you. May God bless you richly. I really will pray for you. Promise."

When he was done shouting his strange benediction, he flipped Ace off with both hands, turned on his heel, and marched back through the gate to the recycling center.

OLSEN GONE

Although the Thursday morning two days after Ace's arrest was a beautiful one, Connor Connorson was not to be found out in it. He lived in the same general area of Denver as did the Hartwicks and Hunts, but he was currently down on his hands and knees in his study, swearing at an uncooperative router. He was a graduate of Duke Law, and had graduated with a burning desire to save the nation, and possibly the world. He was one sore wokescold attorney, and he shared this vision for justice, and his bed, and his house, with one Henry Baker, a fellow attorney, and his lover since their time at Duke together. The two of them worked for the prosecutor's office. Their boss, Ted Olsen, was an old school liberal and Democrat, meaning that his was a liberalism that had been minted before the world had gone nuts. He went along with all the new weird stuff, of course, because the new ideas were so compelling that they were made mandatory. But everyone in the office knew that his heart wasn't in it. Ted was basically counting the days until retirement, and if he had ever lost count and wanted to know the exact number of days he had left, Connor Connorson would have been able to tell him precisely how many there were remaining.

Although Henry lived there with him, Connor owned the house, and he made sure it was the kind of house that contained everything that he had ever coveted, and that it had room to add anything new that he might come to covet in the future. This included a basement full of exercise equipment, which he used religiously, and he had made sure the walls down there were covered with mirrors. Not only did he use all the exercise equipment, he also used all the mirrors, some of them repeatedly.

He had been a fastidious body sculptor since high school, and that part of his destiny had been sealed for him in an unfortunate incident that had occurred one morning during his workout at the school gym. He had been working out for about six months with his workout partner, who was some guy named Jurgen. Jurgen had just that morning introduced the idea of a series of handheld barbell reps that reduced the weight by five pounds each set. You would start at fifty pounds, and go ten reps with it. Then you would rest for a moment and do ten reps with forty-five pounds. Then again at forty pounds. The pain was exquisite, and the payoff considerable. This pattern was kept up until you were down to five pounds in each hand, struggling hard to even make it through ten reps. It presented quite a sight, seeing a couple of big strong guys, quivering and straining to lift something you could hardly even see.

Jurgen had shown Connor how this was done, and he was seated on a nearby bench, urging Connor to put everything he had into it. This is something that Connor was doing, and with a will, when disaster struck. He was down to the five-pound weights, and he was quivering to lift them again, and at that point, doing so unsuccessfully. And at that very moment, the most beautiful girl in the entire high school—named Melinda, not that it matters—walked into the room. Not only so, but she was accompanied by her two best friends, who happened to be the second and third most beautiful girls in the school. So in they all came, the gold, silver and bronze medalists, and when they saw Connor bursting blood vessels in his forehead while trying to get two five-pound weights up to his chest—unsuccessfully—all three of them burst into laughter.

They were not mean girls. They had not come in there to mock the downtrodden or anything like that. But the struggle with the weights was intense, and it did not look as though it *ought* to have been intense. So they really were not to be blamed. You would have laughed also. They all three covered their mouths, and exited the room in an expeditious manner, giggling as they went. Things were compounded when, later that day, the same three girls saw Connor heading into the chemistry lab, and the same thing happened again. The memory of that morning had stuck with them in a particularly vivid way, and so they all burst into laughter again. This episode explained a great deal about Connor's future career path, not to mention his sexual proclivities. *Guys* understood weight lifting.

So it was that the grown Connor Connorson was ambitious. How ambitious was he? He wanted to dunk the moon, and hang on the rim. Nothing distressed him more than the reactionary and evil behavior of the heartland states, and he was determined to get himself into a position to do something about it.

Later that morning, having defeated the router, Connor Connorson walked into the offices of the prosecutor like he owned the place which, for the next three weeks at least, he kind of did. His boss, the aforementioned Ted, had just gotten on his flight to Alaska, off on his annual three-week vacation of almost total disconnect.

Ted was ostensibly hunting moose and bear, based out of a cabin that was somewhere near Timbukthree, or possibly four. And though there had been a time or two when he actually did go out into the countryside with a rifle, most of the time was spent in what was a luxury cabin, in the company of his Alaska mistress, to be distinguished from his Colorado mistress. We will pass by their names because we only brought it up in the first place to explain why Ted Olsen was, as according to his annual habit, almost entirely incommunicado during this sacrosanct vacation time. In fact, we shouldn't say *almost entirely*. We should say *entirely*. It had been five years since anyone back in Colorado had ever heard a peep from him during one of his little getaways.

Connor knew that this trip was upon them, and from a short time after Ace's arrest, he had been counting the hours (there had been thirty-nine of them). The prosecutor's office was so far treating this as a standard destruction of property case, in which Ace was likely to get a stiff fine and probation. But Connor had what he thought were his better angels whispering furiously in his ear, and he knew, knew in his *bones* that this case could be a landmark case. This was destiny. It could provide the foundation stone for a whole new series of cascading rights, the kind of rights that really could usher in the next phase of the revolution. Connor had decided that the charge simply must be murder. There could be no other option.

This was because, when the incident in question had first happened, he had felt the responsibility of destiny settle upon him. He hadn't known what he was going to do about it, but he had known, and immediately, that something *needed* to be done about it. That Tuesday, the day of Destiny's Call, Connor had come back from lunch and found that his secretary, who knew and understood his sense of destiny, had left a news-site printout on his desk, with the breaking story of Asahel Hartwick and Sally Sasani highlighted. Connorson had exploded in an odd mixture of jubilation and rage. This was the case he was born to litigate.

A half hour later, after he had been triumphing in his imagination over all kinds of throwbacks and troglodytes for quite an enjoyable session of daydreaming, he had remembered the duddiness of Ted. In fact, all the younger attorneys there, who were as woke as midmorning, used to call him the Sugar Duddy. Despair had settled upon him then, and that had lasted for forty-five minutes. It was the day after *that* when he remembered the annual Alaska trip, when Ted would be well over the horizon for almost a month. Connor could get a lot done in almost a month. And when Ted came back, if he had played his cards right, there wouldn't be anything Ted could do about it, or do to him. And if on the off-chance his boss showed any disposition to kick, Connor was in possession of information about these annual hunting trips that would probably be of interest to Mrs. Olsen. This had been enough to cause a serene glow to come back to his cheeks, which would probably have been diminished a few watts had he known that since the divorce a few years earlier, there actually wasn't a Mrs. Olsen. Regardless, the plan had been formed in his mind, and Connor felt good about it.

This was a case that had a lot of potential voltage in it, and all Connor had to do was run the wires correctly. But as it happened, while Connor was banking on Ted being gone for three weeks, it actually turned out to be four months on account of a hunting accident. And when Ted finally returned to survey the crater and blast radius, he congratulated himself on having the best-timed hunting accident ever. He looked around, proposed to his Colorado mistress, and promptly retired. But this was somewhat later, and we are getting ahead of ourselves.

And so it was, as Connor walked into the office on Thursday, the day of the great Ted departure, he went straight up to the receptionist. "Did Mr. Olsen make his flight okay?"

"Oh, yes. He texted just as he was boarding." He had been thoughtful enough to do that for the lowly receptionist because she, Cheryl, was the Colorado mistress. But in any case, she knew that he was in the air, and that was all that Connor needed. He was the second-in-command, and he now had control of the office, and he had three weeks in which to maneuver.

So now that the day had arrived, and Ted was safely in the air, Connor seized the reins, settled into his seat on the stagecoach, and picked up the bullwhip. This bullwhip was only metaphorical, but he had handled a real one before, at the Denver Divas Dance the year before, and so he felt fully confident about his daydream bullwhip.

He had the office receptionist schedule an emergency meeting of all the attorneys in the office—there were five of them, not counting Connor—and two hours later, when he walked into the conference room, he was riding high.

And that conference room was a difficult one to ride high in. Like almost all government buildings in Colorado, it was run down. It was tidy, as opposed to being clean, which was a trend that had started shortly after the janitors had successfully unionized some years before. They had been part of a larger government workers union earlier, but that larger union had not paid close enough attention to the hopes, dreams, and aspirations of the janitorial workers of Colorado. They had split from the larger government union just in time, which is to say, they split off right before the pension fund went bust. They had played it pretty shrewdly. They got a brand new pension fund, fully stocked, and were way better off than before. And that is why all the rooms were now tidy, but not clean.

Connor set his note pad down on a sticky spot, noticed it, and then moved it to another sticky spot. None of this dampened his zeal. Nothing that would happen in that meeting was likely to cool his baby jets either, because the entire cadre of younger attorneys were graduates of schools of law that were trying to out-vie each other when it came to that ever-receding standard of wokeness. All of them were as eager as Connor to do battle, and all of them felt the oppressiveness of Ted, which was the oppressiveness of the inadequately woke, one whose radical liberalism was manifestly insincere. That man had just three years until retirement, and he had resolved some time before this that he was going to tick every box he was asked to tick in order to get to that finish line. But the young bucks in the office knew that he didn't *mean* it. They knew that he might even possibly move to one of the heartland states, where he could go back to being the radical one. But here, in the Colorado of the present day, he was about as radical as a cow eating the cabbage.

Connor called the meeting to order, and explained what he intended to do. He did not say that Ted Olsen had told him to do this, and he did not say that Ted Olsen had forbidden it. Connor was the only one with whom Ted had discussed the case at all, and so it was thought best by all parties not to inquire too closely.

The other attorneys looked at him expectantly, like two rows of sea lions on either side of the table waiting for the trainer to throw a fish over the Plexiglas. And as Connor looked at them, he felt a surge of pride welling up in him. This was a crackerjack team. They knew the law, they knew what justice *ought* to be, and as each of them had slept with pretty much all of the others, they knew one another. They were going to craft the future. With their own hands they would craft it. They would build a tower to the heavens. It would be totally great.

"I am going to take the lead on this case," Connor announced, "and I want every available resource that we have dedicated to it. My intention is to charge this . . . this young punk with first-degree murder. He kidnapped Sally Sasani, someone that Steven had plainly identified as his wife, and he . . ."

And here he stumbled and came almost to a full stop. He was going to say "killed her in cold blood," but this seemed a bit strong for an assemblage of metal and plastic, even for such an assemblage who was identified by a citizen as that citizen's wife. The problem was that she didn't have any blood, and it consequently wasn't cold. At the same time, and on the other hand, it seemed lame to say that a young punk had "rendered her inoperable," like he had taken the batteries out of a flashlight. Connor pretended to have something in his throat, and took a sip of water, while his mind raced around inside for a good way to put it. He put his glass of water down, and continued.

" . . . someone that Steven identified as his wife, and he did away with her. In cold blood, he did *away* with her."

The mixed expressions of horror at the dastardly crime, and approval of the course Connor was taking, was a blend that Connor found most gratifying. He cleared his throat and revved his engines again.

"The bedrock of all our liberties is choice—free and untrammeled *choice*. If we don't defend that, then we deserve to lose it all. The one choice that must therefore not be made, that must not be *allowed* to be made, is the choice that challenges or insults the choices of another. What this 'Ace' has done is that he has presumed to invade the life of another, in order to contradict a choice that the other had made. When Mr. Sasani *chose* to see Sally as his wife, that choice is consequently paramount, and must be treated as paramount by all others. When someone presumes to invade the sacred sovereignty of the choices of another, it has to be treated with all the severity that we can muster."

The other members of his team could take a great deal of this. They were eating it out of the carton with a spoon. They looked at him, yearning for more. But Connor had exhausted his supply of deep political science, and besides, it was time for action.

"I know that all of you have full dockets, nobody around here is being lazy. But I want each of you to postpone whatever you can, clear out as much of your schedule as is possible. We need to work together on this one, all together. All hands on deck, in other words."

MONTY LEWIS

Christian Legal Defense (CLD) was an institution with a long and storied history, but the last few decades had been particularly weird for them. They were dedicated primarily to the cause of defending and advancing religious liberty, but they sometimes found themselves taking up cases of conscience in other strange constitutional crevasses. The cases they had argued had ranged from the standard-issue wedding-cake fracas out to the bizarre. The prospect of defending Ace Hartwick was one of the stranger ones, although there had been many oddball cases.

The CLD had been debating the pros and cons of this case at the board level for several days now. Ace had not contacted them, and so there was not a formal request in yet, but they figured—rightly—that it was just a matter of time before they received just such a formal request. Michael Turly, one of their board members, had some Colorado connections, and they thought it was likely that Ace would call the CLD. One of them had even talked to Benson Hartwick about the possibility.

Another of the Colorado connections was Jon Hunt. The CLD was no longer permitted to operate in Colorado openly, but they had developed a number of back channel workarounds. Jon Hunt was one of their assets there, not to mention one of their top lawyers nationally. He had kept his thumb on the pulse of the case from the start, not to mention the fact that he was thoroughly up on Colorado politics. And even though he was not currently serving on the CLD board (though he had served one two-year term previously), he had been roped into the board's discussions about this situation via email and phone.

"I am not sure," he had said. "I just don't know this young man. It might be a perfect case for us. But he might also be one more unstable young gun. And I don't know the family either. But in either case, I am leaning toward offering to help. Even if he has a screw loose, smashing a doll isn't murder, and allowing it to be treated as murder is not something we should allow to pass by us without a challenge. I mean, regardless of the circumstances. But part of the decision should be based on his willingness for us to plead down to what he actually did, which was destruction of property."

The thing that moved the board to make their decision in Ace's direction was an unexpected and providential gift from a previously off-the-radar donor. The CLD was largely evangelical and Protestant, but they had defended various Catholic organizations in the past—adoption agencies, primarily—and as a result of that activity, this particular donor knew all about them. But he knew about it from afar.

Monty Lewis was a *very* wealthy Roman Catholic casino owner from Vegas. And to put it this way is to recognize that the word *very* does not really do justice to the way things were with Monty Lewis and his bank account. There were actually quite a few billionaires from all around the world, the kind who flew everywhere in their own sleek jets that were painted black who, when they were in the presence of Monty Lewis, would shuffle their feet nervously on the carpet. In addition to all the cash, he was kind of a force of nature.

And Monty had watched the unfolding drama in Denver in a high state of disbelief, and had remembered, while fetching a beer from his enormous fridge during a commercial one time, that the Christian Legal Defense had fought (and won) a great battle on behalf of the adoption agency that had placed *him*—when just a mere babe of three months—in his family about five decades before. "I owe those guys everything," he thought to himself. "And the fact that CLD was there for those sweet nuns means the world to me. I am going to call those Bible-johnnies up and lay some cash on them."

When he *did* call them up, he got the executive director on the phone directly, which people with millions and billions of dollars usually know how to do, and he told the executive director that he wanted Ace Hartwick to enjoy the benefits of a platinum-grade defense. He also wanted gold plate all around the edges of the platinum, along with a silver inlay. And he, Monty Lewis, was willing to underwrite the same.

So because of Jon Hunt's recommendation, and because there was really no financial risk to speak of, the board approved legal support for Ace, if he were to request it. Still, for various reasons, most of them having to do with the creepiness of throwing a sex doll into an industrial compacter, it was still a close vote (five to four). After the vote, they quickly agreed to ask Jon Hunt to take the case, which he said he would do. All the costs of the defense would be borne by the CLD, but would have to be run through their back-channel accounts. Jon would serve *pro bono*, and the board would make a donation to one of his favored charities in the heartland states, run through a cryptocurrency account in no way connected to the name Hunt. Entirely legal and above board, except in Colorado.

Once that decision was made, the only thing left was for Ace to indicate in some way that he would be willing to receive the help. Because Jon Hunt was not the kind of person to play coy, he decided that he would just call Ace up, and offer to buy him dinner.

As it happened, he got Ace on the first try, explained that he was a trial defense lawyer and a Christian, and that he thought they might have something to discuss. Would Ace be up for dinner the following night? Ace thanked the Lord under his breath, and said that he would look forward to it. Happy to, and so forth. Ace had been thinking of calling up the CLD himself, but hadn't made up his mind yet, not knowing their legal status in Colorado. His father had told him they weren't operating there anymore.

Jon's idea of a good place to meet was a little hole-in-the-wall Chinese place with the odd misnomer of Gordon's Chinese Best. Gordon O'Malley was the son of lifelong missionaries to Taiwan, which is where he discovered both his talents as a cook *and* his uncanny ability to seek out hole-in-the-wall Taipei eateries that catered to mainland palates. He had served for a decade or more as the equivalent of a Chinese hash slinger, and when he had finally moved back to Colorado (where his parents were originally from, where he had been born, and where his Chinese wife wanted to go), he naturally decided to set up shop on his own. Nothing about his restaurant had an authentic Chinese flavor except for what came out on the plates. The walls were decorated with Western art, in the Remington school, and there were even a few crosscut saws hanging on the walls. The food was Chinese, but the ambiance definitely was not. But the food was enough for a word-of-mouth reputation to get established. Jon had been eating there for many years and had a booth in the back where he liked to entertain his clients.

Ace was five minutes early, which worked out nicely because Jon was five minutes early, too. They met in the parking lot, guessed immediately who the other one was, shook hands, and entered together. Jon headed back to his customary booth, greeted cheerfully on the way by Gordy and his wife Yu Yan.

"The usual?" Gordy called after Jon.

Jon nodded yes, but then added, "and a menu for my novice friend here."

When they were situated in their booth in the back, Jon laid out the basic facts of CLD's offer to Ace. "The two things necessary are for me to interview you about the basic outlines of the case and, speaking frankly, for you to pass that interview. And secondly, it would be necessary for you to request our help. Oh, yes, and a third thing. You need to not mention CLD's role in it at all. Not to anybody."

"Well," Ace said, smiling. "I will do my best to pass the interview. Do you mind telling me what the right answers are?"

Jon laughed, and said, "Well, to tell it straight, the right answers are the honest ones. I can deal with most anything from a client except when they blow sunshine at me."

Ace also laughed. "We are good then. I have no sunshine to blow."

The next half hour was spent by Jon asking Ace questions about his life, upbringing, background, reading habits, and with all of that leading up to *why had he done it?* This was obviously a radical act of sexual insurrection. What inspired it? Who had radicalized Ace? Did he think of himself as having been radicalized? Was it premeditated? The thing that Jon kept coming back to was all the reading.

As it happened, about half of the books Ace referenced were in Jon's contraband library also, and he had made a mental note to get at least three of the unfamiliar titles that Ace mentioned. Jon was liking him more and more, but something about Ace's "readiness to act" still made him a tad nervous. Was this the impetuousness of youth, the kind that a middle-aged Jon was starting to forget about? Or was there something more? Was Ace too hot to handle? Perhaps it was a mix.

As they were talking, they were interrupted twice. The first time was by the food—Ace had simply allowed Jon to order for him, and so he got "the usual" also. It was really good. After his first bite, Ace looked up from his plate of beef with pea pods with wide eyes. Jon said, "I know."

"I have lived twenty minutes from here my whole life," Ace said. "I can't believe I didn't know."

The second interruption was Stephanie. When her father was not home at dinner time, she knew right where to find him, and the restaurant (conveniently) was less than ten minutes from their home. She came by to drop off the keys to their storage shed, which she had borrowed from him earlier in the day in order to retrieve a book she had thoughtlessly allowed to be packed with her high school stuff. It turned out that she was going to be needing it for a class that she was taking now.

Stephanie was the stubborn kind of person who would rather spend forty-five minutes rummaging in a storage shed, which she had just finished doing, than to spend a few dollars on a book that she knew she already owned.

When she appeared by their table, her father introduced her to Ace, who responded courteously. She looked him up and down and said, "The infamous Asahel?" Yes, yes, Ace allowed. He had achieved some level of notoriety of late, which he hoped would go away soon. Stephanie nodded. Good to meet you, she seemed to indicate. She was cool and aloof, but still friendly. Like a sunbeam shining down on the upper slopes of a beautiful glacier.

Her father invited her to sit down by him for a minute. "No," she said, wavering for a moment, and then straightening up. "As much as I would love snitching your pea pods, I really do have to run. I have a class first thing in the morning, and I haven't even touched my assignment yet. So I need to be dutiful."

And so it was that Stephanie disappeared as rapidly as she had shown up in the first place. Ace turned in his seat, and watched her blow through the front door of the restaurant. He turned back to Jon a moment later, who was staring at him.

"The next thing wasn't on my agenda for the evening," Jon said, "but since your eyes are as wide as they were when you first tasted Gordy's pea pods, I would urge you not even to *think* about it. I am a doting father, and do not need someone on trial for murder expressing any interest whatsoever in my lovely daughter."

Ace put up both his hands, palms out. "Not only am I innocent of the charges being leveled against me by the state of

Colorado, I am also innocent of the foul intimations being made by my defense counsel. My stance toward your daughter can be characterized as one of simple admiration. *That* was like seeing the Taj Mahal in person, or the Grand Canyon for the first time, or a beauty from the mysterious east that I saw once while thumbing through *National Geographic*. I was just caught off guard. That's all."

Jon laughed, a little grimly. "Well, get your guard back up. She helps me on certain select cases, and yours will have to be one of them. You will run into her again. And am I to take your reference to my being your defense counsel as your agreement to have me and my secretive backers represent you?" Ace nodded yes. "Great," Jon said. "I have some papers here for you to take, and one for you to sign."

"How old is Stephanie?" Ace asked.

MIRROR PRACTICE

Connor was pacing back and forth in front of his bathroom mirror. "The wife of a citizen must necessarily *be* a citizen. And Steven Sasani moved here to Colorado with Sally as his wife, he introduced her to multiple neighbors as his wife, and coming down to the central point, he introduced her—explicitly and without any ambiguity—to Asahel Hartwick as his wife."

He was refining and honing his arguments and, despite the fog on the mirror from his recent shower, he was making good headway.

"Not only did Asahel *not* contradict Mr. Sasani when he referred to Sally as his wife, he plainly and clearly acquiesced in this identification by agreeing to share a *meal* with the Sasanis. Had there been any true principled objection, it should have surfaced at the very first. It no doubt would have."

Connor paused. If this part of the argument was being laid out when Asahel was on the stand, it would be a good moment to turn and say something like, "Is that not true, Mr. Hartwick?"

He cleared his throat and continued, brushing his hair as he did so. "In addition, on the night of the crime, Asahel agreed to check in on Sally Sasani, to see how *she* was doing. Why would he do something like that, if she were anything like what the defense is claiming—an inert mass of plastic and metal and circuitry?"

Connor was now in his underwear, and he walked down the hall, gesturing to the jury.

"Not only so," he continued freely, knowing that Henry had already left for work, "I think we need to take a careful look at the *timelines* here." Having said this, Connor made a mental note to take a look at the timelines. They had a hard time stamp from the surveillance cameras at the recycling center. They knew exactly when Asahel had arrived. How long a drive was it from the Sasanis to the recycling center? They had an undisputed time for when Steven had asked Asahel to check in on Sally, and that time was firmed up by the time Steven had signed for his package downtown. *Walk it through, Connor, walk it through.* Suddenly he had a stroke of genius: If Asahel had had sex with the doll *before* destroying the evidence, then he had a rape charge to add, not to mention having a really sensational trial.

Not that it wasn't sensational now. That was his work for the day. *Timeline, timeline, timeline.*

Another thought occurred to him. If Asahel had sex with the android, that would provide an additional motive—or perhaps the *only* motive. Perhaps Asahel was posing as a virtue warrior in order to cover up the fact that he was just like everybody else. *Hmmm?*

JON THE MAN

Jon Hunt was a slender man, as slender as a man of his height could be without being skinny. He had been a baseball player during high school, not to mention the first two years of college. That had only ended when a knee injury insisted on it, and yet in the years since that time he had continued to work out, largely because he had a personality that required discipline in every aspect of his life.

He kept a short closely-cropped salt-and-pepper beard that contrasted sharply with his black hair and made him look like an experienced man of the world, which he was. His nose was well-defined, and his eyes were closely set. They were not so close as to seem odd or anything, but they were dark, and if Jon ever suspected any funny business from a witness on the stand, their closeness and color were very effective in boring holes through that witness.

The first skirmish in this trial was not going to be the trial, but a test of strength for the two sides. Ace had received an invitation to address a family values convention in Alabama. He was interested in going, and Jon had encouraged him to formally accept, with the provision that he succeed in getting the court's permission to travel out of state.

Jon had never crossed swords with Connorson before, and he wanted a taste of battle before they got to the real action. A request to travel should fit the bill nicely, he thought.

The courtroom was almost empty. Besides Ace, only the judge, the recorder, the bailiff, and the two attorneys were present.

When the gavel fell, the judge nodded at Jon, and he approached the bench. "Your Honor, my client requests permission to travel to Alabama for three days, in order to address a conference at which he has been invited to speak. We believe the request is most reasonable, and should not interfere in any way with anyone's preparations for trial, or with the trial itself."

Connorson was on his feet almost immediately.

"We believe the defendant presents a definite flight risk."

Jon was ready. "Is that the only concern?"

"Well, it is a significant concern, so I would say that is basically it."

"My client is more than prepared to have the bail amount increased to whatever the court deems appropriate. It is currently set at one million, and we would be willing to have it raised to five."

Connorson wasn't ready for this, and stammered for a moment. "We still do not believe it is in the best interests . . ."

"If there is genuine concern over my client fleeing, then the state could order a couple of state troopers to accompany my client. I have already spoken to him about this, and he is more than willing for something like that."

The prosecutor didn't really care that much about the issue itself because he actually didn't believe that Ace would flee. But he also felt the currents under the surface, and knew that this was a test of wills between him and Jon. He knew it, and also felt the familiar sensation of sinking.

"Your Honor, I do not see why the state of Colorado should spend money to send two troopers to Alabama with this . . . so that he can spread his hate at some conference or other."

Jon replied evenly. "The state of Colorado has not yet demonstrated that young Ace is guilty of any kind of hatred at all. That is one thing. And the other is that I have a kind donor who is willing to reimburse the state of Colorado for any expenses associated with monitoring Ace's trip there and back."

The judge, who was not aware of the undercurrents between Jon and Connor, and who was thinking more than a little bit about lunch already, tapped his gavel. "Permission granted. Mr. Hunt, make the appropriate arrangements about bail, and for the reimbursement payment."

"Yes, Your Honor."

CHAPTER 3

SARA YODER

We must weave another strand into our story. Sara Yoder was a quiet woman who consistently sat in the next to last row of church, and the church in question was one of the stricter orders among the Mennonites, the Old Order Mennonites. She was in her late twenties and worked in her own home as a seamstress. She was industrious and caused no trouble to anyone, except occasionally to herself.

I say that it was among the stricter sects of the Mennonites. The outsiders down the road called them "black bumper" Mennonites. Unlike the Amish, they allowed the use of cars, but also unlike the more liberal Mennonites, they decried the use of chrome to decorate their cars. That kind of bling was just two steps away from the women wearing make-up, and there was no telling where *that* might end up.

The women—and this included Sara—wore their hair up and had a covering for their hair pinned tightly on the backs of their heads. They wore plain dresses below the knee, and completed the outfit with a pair of white tennis shoes. Resistance to the discipline of the community was not unknown, but whenever it appeared, it would do so in understated ways. For example, if a woman was peeved at her husband, or at the elders, she would pull one strand of hair loose and let it hang down over her forehead, a small flag of a small rebellion. But everybody knew all about it.

Sara's mother had died two years before, and her father had followed just a year after that. She had no siblings and no extended family at all. She had been extraordinarily close to her parents, and so the loss to her was enormous—and it was enormous in two ways. First, she missed them both terribly. The vacuum their absence created was difficult for her to manage. The second reason was related. While they were alive, the three had been so important to one another that Sara had never made any other close connections in the community. She was friendly to all, but had no close friends. Her parents had been the same—they had not had close friends either.

The end result of this was that Sara had no one to turn to after the loss of her parents, and this resulted in an ongoing case of the high lonesomes.

Near the end of her father's life—he had been confined to bed for the last three weeks—she had discovered that her family's isolation from the community had not really been an accident or happenstance. About a week before he died, during one of his lucid spells, he had Sara sit down on the chair that was beside the bed, the chair where she would sit when she read psalms to him.

He extended his hand, and Sara took it, marveling at how warm it was, despite the fact that it looked so cold.

"Sara," he said. "I am going to ask you to do something that I was never able to figure out how to do for myself, for all of us. It might be easier for you, being that there is just one of you left. After I am gone, I mean."

"What is that, Papa?" she had said.

"I want you to take the first good opportunity you might have to leave the community. Even when things were at their best, we never really fit here. I don't quite know how all that started, but it did. Your dear mother had the strongest ties here, but even she saw through it. She would agree with what I am asking."

Sara sat quietly. The thought had actually occurred to her—a *number* of times it had occurred to her. She had wondered what was holding her, once her papa passed, not wanting to dishonor her parents, but here, now, her papa was *asking* her to do it.

"Well, Papa," she said. "I must be honest. I *had* thought about it."

"I would be embarrassed for you if you hadn't," he said, and then coughed for a few minutes.

She got him a drink of water, and when he was situated on his pillows again, he said, "I am not telling you when, or how to do it. I think you know why. I don't want to bind your conscience in any way. I want you to feel free to follow your conscience. Just make sure you take your Bible."

Sara nodded quietly, tears filling her eyes. He had died peacefully in his sleep, just about a week later.

She inherited the house, and then spent the next several months getting all the financial affairs in order. She was somewhat startled at how much money her parents had, which she was able to quietly move to a Denver bank, a different bank than the one that everyone in the community used. And after that, she had just waited.

The community was just a couple hours outside Denver, and during market season, they would load up their small fleet of black-bumper flatbed trucks, and take them into town to a farmers market they had been traveling to faithfully for the last twenty years. Sara usually accompanied them and volunteered at various booths. She didn't grow anything for sale herself, but she had always liked coming into town, and the families who had booths always enjoyed her cheerful and capable help.

This particular Saturday, she had made sure that she had packed everything she needed in her backpack, and at the bottom of that pack she had her wallet that had a shiny new credit card in it. She wasn't exactly sure how to use one—her community always used cash—but she felt comfortable that she had one. On top of that she had about one hundred dollars on her.

Once the tables at the market were set up, she disappeared down the street for about half an hour. While gone she went into a drug store and purchased two things. The first was a tube of pale lipstick, almost indistinguishable from lip balm. The second item was a Chicago Cubs baseball cap. She picked it because an aunt on her father's side lived near Chicago. Other than that, she had a dim grasp of what it might mean. She thought it represented a hockey team, although she wasn't quite sure what hockey was.

On the way back to the farmers' market, she stopped in a fast food restaurant, went into the bathroom, and with a trembling hand put the lipstick on. Despite the tremor, she thought she did it all right. It was the first time she had ever done anything like that, and it felt really strange.

After that, she unpinned her black head covering, tossed it and the bobby pins in the trash, and put on the baseball cap. She undid her hair first, put it in a pony tail, and pulled her hair out the back of the cap, took three deep breaths, and shot out of the restaurant. She had intended to buy a drink or something because she had used the restroom, but in her nervous excitement she forgot. She headed back up the hill to the small park where the market was, praying as she went.

She was a set of walking incongruities. Her dress was plain cotton, and she was wearing the same kind of white sneakers that she had worn for years. Apart from the two novelties, she clearly had the Old Order Mennonite look. But the baseball cap made her feel like her head was on fire, and while she had no intention of playing the hussy, the lipstick certainly made her feel like she was *almost* one.

Turning the final corner, she glanced up at the street sign. It read Rubicon. She didn't know what that meant, but it felt like it ought to mean something.

She had not settled which booth she was going to volunteer in, and so she picked one now where she thought the two ladies running it would be most likely to notice. Not the hat, everyone would notice the hat. But the hat was technically still covering her head, and there were no hard and fast rules about the nature of the covering—although a Chicago Cubs hat was certainly violating the spirit of the thing. Rather, she picked the booth where the ladies were most likely to notice the lipstick.

And notice it they did. Mrs. Horst was the first to notice, and right after her exclamation of surprise, Mrs. Stoltzfus joined her. The two women just stood there, an apple in each hand, staring at Sara. Finally, Mrs. Horst spoke.

"Is this a deliberate choice? Not a joke?"

Sara shook her head. "Not a joke. Yes, a deliberate choice."

The two women put their apples down, and walked across the market area to where one of the community's bishops held court over his booth. Sara stood where she was, pensively waiting. After about five minutes, Mr. Ewert walked slowly over. He was a kindly man, and as he approached, Sara could see how distressed he was.

When he came up to her, he asked the same question. "Is this a deliberate choice? Not a whim or a fancy?"

"No, not a whim." She shook her head. "I have been praying about this for a year or more."

"Well, I do not see any sense in drawing this out. If you wanted to contest it, we could have a meeting of the whole congregation . . ."

Sara shook her head again. "I have no wish to contest anything. I am sure you will be quite fair."

"In that case," Mr. Ewert said, and as he spoke she thought she saw something like tears in his eyes. He had always been kind to her. "I have to declare that you are now out of the community, and our people will be instructed to shun you. I am very sorry to have to do this."

Sara was looking steadily at him, and he was looking down at the apples, as though he was considering a purchase.

"I came prepared for this today, and I have the things with me that I need for right now," Sara said. "May I assume that it will be alright to talk to Mr. Stoltzfus about selling my house for me?"

"Yes, that will be all right," Mr. Ewert said. "What about your things there?"

"I will have someone come. Everything that is to go is packed and labeled in the front parlor. I will send someone. Anything else can go with the house."

Mr. Ewert was having some trouble talking, and Sara waited patiently.

"Well," he said, after a moment. "What's done is done. I wish you the best, honestly. When the occasion seems right, I would like to ask you to celebrate with a friend or two, and remember us in your prayers."

With that he turned to go, and Sara noted with surprise that he had left five one hundred dollar bills lying on the table in front of her. She hesitated for a moment, and then gathered them up, and then walked around to the back of the booth where she had left her backpack. After adjusting a few things, and putting it on, she started walking toward the nearest bus stop. It was back down where she had bought the baseball cap.

She had to wait for about ten minutes for her bus to arrive, and she spent that time praying, humming psalms to herself, panicking, and praying again. What she had done did not fully settle in upon her until she took her seat on the bus, a seat on the right that faced straight across to the other side. She put her backpack on her knees, and the full weight of everything descended upon her. She wasn't sobbing, but tears were running steadily down her cheeks, and she was so distracted she didn't bother wiping them away.

As it happened, there was only one other person in the front part of the bus, and she was seated directly across from Sara. It was Stephanie Hunt, looking directly at her.

After a few moments of observing this—and it would have been difficult not to observe it—Stephanie moved impulsively over and sat next to Sara. "Is there anything an intrusive stranger might be able to do?"

Sara shook her head. "I was expecting this. I just wasn't expecting it to be this hard, this heavy."

Stephanie had taken in the odd juxtaposition of the dress and the ball cap, wondered about it, and decided not to ask. Sara didn't appear to mind Stephanie talking to her.

"What stop are you going to?" she asked suddenly.

Sara collected herself, and glanced at the map above the windows. "9th," she said. She had determined earlier that this is where a lot of hotels were, and she knew she needed to get her bearings.

"I can get off there too," Stephanie said. "Can I buy you a coffee? Maybe you just need somebody to listen. I won't try to fix anything, promise."

Sara laughed, through her tears. And then she nodded. "I would like that. Thank you for your kindness," she added. And the bus driver, under his breath, who had been observing all this in his mirror, breathed a sigh of relief and thanked Stephanie also. He hated scenes, but he was tenderhearted, and so he always got dragged into scenes. The reader might be surprised at just how often scenes occur on city buses.

The bus came to a noisy stop—the city not having enough money to maintain their buses properly, and in this particular instance the issue was related to the brakes—and Sara and Stephanie both got off. Stephanie knew that particular plaza well, and pointed to one of her favorite coffee dives.

When they were seated, and had their coffee steaming in front of them—with Sara looking at hers somewhat suspiciously because she had never had any caffeine before in her life—Stephanie asked if she still wanted to talk. They had introduced themselves just after they got off the bus, and had chatted about this and that on their way across the plaza.

"You are very kind," Sara said. "And if you don't mind, I really would like to say out loud what I have been thinking to an actual person . . ." And with that, she started to pour out her story.

After about a half an hour, Stephanie felt as though she was caught up on the basic facts. Sara was going to rent a room in the Sheraton there in the neighborhood for a week or so while she looked for an apartment. She was not at all homeless—as Stephanie had first feared—and seemed quite fine when it came to money concerns. She was even willing to consider buying a condominium, after what a condominium was had been explained to her.

Where she was lacking was in the realm of day-to-day transactions. She was terrified of having to use her credit card, and she was also quite unsure about shopping for clothes. She knew that her plain dress and ball cap would have to go—although she was intending to save the cap as a souvenir.

And that was how Stephanie wound up spending the next couple of hours walking Sara through the basics. First she took her to an ATM, and taught her the mysteries there. After that, they went to a couple of clothing stores, one of them being Stephanie's favorite, and Stephanie helped Sara choose her look. That was a bit harder because Sara knew what she *didn't* want to look like, and little else. The third thing they did was purchase a phone for her, and Stephanie made a point of entering her own information into it. And last, almost on a whim, Stephanie steered her into an employment service, and as it happened Sara came in at just the right moment, because she landed a job as a receptionist who just needed to answer the phone. Which she thought she could do while she got adjusted.

CHAPTER 4

NARNIAN SNOW DANCE

NARNIA DOWN SOUTH

Ace looked carefully at Jon, and then asked, "Have you been in any of the free states in the last fifteen years or so?"

Jon shook his head. "No, not really, not since the troubles began. Whenever I go there, it's just to fly in for trial appearances, and then fly out again. I know some of their airports and some courtrooms, but that's about it. "

"It was the weirdest thing being out there. You know how here in Colorado I am the out-of-control radical one? The militant normal? But when I was in Alabama for that conference, for the first time in many years, I felt surrounded by normal people, hundreds of them. Completely surrounded by the kind of people you only read about in books. And I was the one who was still half a bubble off. They were all very nice to me, and they had me there to address their conference because of the stand we are taking here, but inside my head I felt like I had popped out into the middle of the Narnian snow dance."

"You've read Narnia?"

Ace grinned. "Yes. I found a set in a box up in the attic a couple years ago. I forget what I was looking for. My dad must have stored them up there after they were banned. I was kind of surprised at his little act of defiance in that. Why didn't he pulp them as required? I don't know. Why were they banned, anyway? I was just a little kid when that happened."

"That was the work of our old friends, the Colorado Human Rights Commission. The way Lewis treated the Calormenes was racist and hurtful."

"But there aren't any Calormenes. Did the CHRC get a stern letter from the Calormene embassy?"

Jon smiled ruefully. "Believe it or not, there was actually a case . . . I didn't follow it carefully because I was on the other side in those days. I was among the bad guys, pursuing my own bubbles. But as I recall, the whole thing hinged on a passing mention, in *The Horse and His Boy*, of the fact that Tashbaan, that great Calormene city, had minarets in it. Right near the beginning of chapter 4—I looked it up after I was converted. A minaret is a prayer tower attached to a mosque, and once you had that key to break the code, it became plain and obvious that the Calormenes were a place-holder for Muslims. A hate crime out there in plain sight. And while they were wicked to ban such wonderful books, it has to be admitted that on the question of fact . . . they had a point."

"Got it," Ace said. "Just more craziness, in other words."

"Just more craziness," Jon agreed.

"Anyway, back to my point." Ace scratched his head. "Here in Colorado I feel like a rampaging radical. Talking with people there in Alabama, even though everyone was nice enough not to point it out aloud, I felt like a liberal squish that everybody was being nice to for some reason."

"Yeah, well, feelings are deceptive," Jon said.

"So you say. But I really need to tell you about it sometime." Ace said.

"Why not now? Now is sometime."

HACKERS

So Ace told Jon the full story of the Alabama trip, and about five minutes into it, Jon called Stephanie in to join them. And after the complete story was told, with all notes compared, and all interrupting questions—mostl-y from Stephanie—were answered, the tale was something like this.

Ace had given his talk the evening before in an over-crowded auditorium, standing room only. Jon had helped him write an introductory paragraph that disclaimed any reference to the details of his case, but which acknowledged openly that the issues involved in his case were relevant to a wide range of issues that were "confronting our generation."

And the talk had gone very well. Ace was a natural speaker, though with no training in it, and despite the size of the room, which was enormous, his personality projected to the back walls, and had even bounced off in some places.

His theme had been sexual energy in culture. The central idea had occurred to him after his arrest, during his first night in jail, when he was trying to remember and reflect on something he had read in Chesterton once. His idea was a distinction between disciplined cultures, repressed cultures, and dissolute cultures. There is a tendency, Ace had said, for repressed cultures and dissolute cultures to play off each other, each one reacting to the excesses of the other.

"But there is a third way," Ace had said, as he had built toward his conclusion. "Disciplined cultures use sexual energy the same way a giant earth-moving machine uses hydraulic fluid. All of it is channeled and focused—when it stays inside the system, there are very few things one of those machines can't lift."

He had gotten a standing ovation, and was surrounded by a cheerful and chattering throng afterward, with Officer Neil standing right behind him, arms crossed, and looking very serious. The people wanting to shake Ace's hand had formed a line, and the third person in that line had been Thomas.

"Thomas Murray," he had said as he shook Ace's hand firmly. He then earnestly asked how long he was going to be in town.

Ace turned around and looked at Officer Neil behind him. "Our flight isn't until late afternoon tomorrow, right?"

"Right," Officer Neil had said. "Six fifteen, actually." There were a lot fewer flights to Denver now, for some reason.

Ace had liked Thomas right off, and so he turned back around and said, "We are free tomorrow morning, any time after breakfast."

Thomas grinned widely. "Great. You have got to see my research. Your talk tonight touched the thing with a needle. *Rem acu tetigisti.* But I don't want you to think I am a snob. I am not a Latin scholar—I learned that one from Wodehouse."

Thomas was about ten years older than Ace, but it was obvious that they were close enough in age to become friends, which they began working on almost right away.

"So why don't I pick the two of you up late morning, take you to lunch, and then we can go by my office to show you what we're doing. Then I will be happy to donate some informal Uber-services to get you both to the airport in plenty of time. Sound good?"

And so it was that the three men came into the foyer of Thomas's office. Thomas turned to Officer Neil, and asked, "Would you have any problem if Ace and I had a visit back there in my office?"

Officer Neil shrugged. "No difference to me. I am here on a flight risk mission, not on a surveillance mission. Just let me take a gander at your office to make sure there are no inappropriate paths of *eeeegress.*" He grinned at his own mastery of bureaucratic argot. He was hoping for a desk job in the near future, and had been practicing. Officer Neil knew exactly what his marching orders were, and what they were not. He had not been all that dismayed when his companion Officer Mark had flown the coop, because he knew that it had been no part of his duties to keep an eye on Officer Mark. If Officer Mark wanted to defect to the heartland states, who was Officer Neil to stop him?

So, having shrugged, Officer Neil walked into Thomas's office, which was a medium-sized affair crowded with books—books on every conceivable flat shelf, and small towers of books on the floor by the shelves. When he had *assssscertained* that there were no windows or doors, he went back out to the waiting area and waved them both in. "Suit yourselves. You can say anything you want in there unless it is a disappearing spell that results in Ace being gone, and me with a lame story to tell." He then sat down in one of the chairs by the door, and picked up an old magazine.

Ace laughed. "We wouldn't want you to end up like those guards in Acts when Peter got away and Herod got mad." Officer Neil just looked at Ace blankly. Bible knowledge was not a thing in Colorado.

And so it was that as Officer Neil was settling in with his magazine, Thomas gestured for Ace to go ahead of him into the office. Thomas went around to his desk chair and moved his monitor around to where Ace could see it easily.

"So here's the problem, Ace." Thomas tapped the screen of his tablet with a pencil. "Whenever you see wholesale titillation and razzle-dazzle, you can be assured the real game is somewhere else. And that's what we have with these sex androids. Not to mention that whole industry."

"What do you mean?" Ace said.

"There are the proles, of course, going along with all the bribes, getting their kicks, using the porn and the dolls like Huxley's soma was going to run out tomorrow. But when it comes to going along with the bribes, there is not as much of that as you might think, and more about that later. The people at the top of this thing are hunting bigger game. All of it is in Lewis's *Abolition of Man*. Bless me, what do they teach them in these schools?"

Ace picked up his phone to make a note of the book.

"Never mind that," Thomas said. "You'll never find a copy in Colorado. I can grab one for you before you go."

"I can't believe how you can just go and pick up a book like that. I also have a hard time believing how not being able to do so still seems normal to me."

Thomas laughed. "Speaking of subversive books, I have another recommendation for you that I just finished reading. It was published just last year, and is all about the Troubles—I think you would find it fascinating. I'll pick it up for you at the bookstore on the way to the airport. That, and *Abolition*. We'll have to tear the covers off before you head back home. I am sure the Border Patrol would be more than a little interested in you showing up with a copy."

"What's the title?" Ace asked. "And what exactly happened back then? We don't get a lot of information about it, and what we do get is pretty obviously lopsided. Has that propagandy feel, if you know what I mean. It reads like early Soviet agricultural art would read if it were a book, you know?"

"It is called *A Theological History of the Troubles of 2024*. It is by a couple of guys—brothers—last name of Garver. I knew a lot of the stuff in there already, but some of it was really surprising. And the big picture is really surprising."

Ace nodded, interested. "What's the takeaway?"

"They argue that there were three main currents in the heartland that led to the Troubles. Each one of these currents had their antithesis in the deep assumptions of the blue states. One of the currents was theological, the second was quasi-theological, and the third involved oil and natural gas. But these guys tied all three up into quite a neat little theological bundle."

Ace laughed out loud at that. "Okay," he said.

Thomas continued. "So there were three men behind all of it, each one of them oozing his own kind of charisma, in his own kind of way. The first was a preacher who came out of nowhere. He was the New Testament guy at little nothing seminary in the Midwest. Iowa, I think. It was like the Spirit of the Lord coming down upon one of the minor prophets, and he started filling up stadiums. He was one of those Reformed fellows, but it was hot gospel anyhow. His name was John Henry, and there was a divine sense of humor thing in that because he was a steel-driving preacher. The second guy, the quasi-theological one, and speaking of stadiums and rallies, started an anti-contraception movement. He was a Catholic guy from Louisiana, Tony DiAngelo, but he was living in east Texas when it all started. He had a fifteen-minute spiel about demographic winter, scary enough to curl your hair, and then he would give an invitation for couples to come down to the front of the stage and throw their birth control gizmos into the bonfire. There was no gospel in it—it was just a three cheers for babies kind of thing. But for some reason that caught fire, too."

"And oil and natural gas?" Ace was deep in story grip.

"No natural gas rallies, sorry to say. But it had been about two years prior to all this when the technologies for extracting the goods became really sophisticated. Not only so, but the technologies for finding oil and gas reserves became even more sophisticated than that. As a result of those developments, people started joking that they needed somebody to develop a gadget that could discover a place that didn't have any natural gas reserves."

"I don't see the possible connection," Ace said.

"This last guy, Allen Jansen, was originally from up in Alberta, until the Canadian government chased him down to North Dakota. He was the CEO of the third largest oil company in the field then, and as a result of his visionary thinking and visionary back-room-dealing, he was soon the CEO of the largest oil company in the history of mankind. I think his oil company might be alluded to in Nebuchadnezzar's dream of the big statue."

"So what did he do?"

"Two things. First, he saw what was happening with the first two movements, and cut some shrewd deals with the governors of all the states running down the middle of the country regarding pipelines down to the Gulf, and the willingness of those governors to tell the Federal government of that time to take a hike if they tried to stop the pipelines from being constructed. So the states started telling the Feds to pound sand. But not too hard, they said, lest you find oil."

"That makes sense," Ace said.

"But the second thing was a total curveball. Jansen arranged for all these governments to not hassle him if he openly advertised some pretty eccentric—for that time—hiring requirements. They are all pretty standard now though. He would give bonuses to married men who had at least three children under the age of ten, and he would give additional bonuses for his employees for staying married, and also for additional children. And the base pay was such that the wives and mothers could stay home."

"Really!" Ace said.

"Right. In their book the Garvers speculate that these three men—Henry, DiAngelo, and Jansen—met together on more than one occasion. They admit they can't prove that part absolutely, but their speculations seem really reasonable to me. They were all certainly in the same cities at the same time on at least four occasions."

"What was the result?"

"In retrospect, everything should have been entirely predictable. The estrangement between the blue states and ours became almost total, and in addition, our states grew really wealthy. And that is what the conditions were like when the great Roe Reversal decision came down. And here we are."

Ace nodded. "So that was it, huh?"

"Well, mostly it. The Roe Reversal happened in a time when the thinking of the general population had been radically altered. And the downstream ramifications of the double-R decision took about five years to unfold. Oh, and there was one more thing that happened after that, but I think it was just sort of the cherry on top."

"What was that?" Ace asked.

"I am afraid I am going to load you up with books . . . hope you have room in your suitcase."

Ace laughed out loud. "I am in your debt, and would be happy to take any books you might have. And I would make room in my suitcase if necessary."

Thomas got up and started rummaging in one of his cluttered bookcases. "I actually have an extra copy of this one. The cherry on top was the utter collapse of Darwinism, at least in our heartland states, and in most of eastern Europe. The universities in the blue states are still hanging on, not to mention Germany. But they are very much playing defense now."

"I knew there was a controversy out here, but during my freshman year in college we all had to take a mandatory Darwin course as part of the core curriculum. No graduation without passing it. One of my instructors talked about Darwin the way Pope Urban used to talk about the Holy Land."

"Right," Thomas said. "The trouble for Darwinism had been building for decades—first with the creationist movement, supplemented later by a movement called Intelligent Design. Riding alongside that whole parade were various freethinkers, who weren't creationists or ID people, but who were just critics. We can just call them hecklers. They were mostly atheists, but didn't mind punching holes in what they regarded as a sham and embarrassment to science. And on top of that there were a host of regular scientists just doing normal science, but with some of them periodically turning up anomalies that just didn't fit with anything."

"Like what?"

"Well, the thing that ripped it was the discovery of another T-Rex skeleton in the Black Hills. This one had so much soft tissue that it was more of a carcass than fossilized remains. There had been soft tissue found in dinosaur bones here and there going back years. One of the people involved in the discovery filmed it with his phone, posted it online, and ten million views later, it was kind of hard to deny that the entire Darwinian timeline had to be scrapped. Those that were ready to scrap it did so. Those that were not ready to circled the wagons, preparing to fight off the coming fundamentalist wave."

Ace looked up at Thomas. "You see all these things as connected?"

"Yeah. Everything's connected, always connected. Economic suicide is accompanied by demographic suicide. Sexual license helps to keep everybody distracted. That is related to intellectual suicide, and without God, there is no reason not to be suicidal."

Ace raised a hand. "I could listen to this kind of stuff all day. But you were going to show me some research. Or tell me about it?"

Thomas laughed, and turned to his computer. "What our team has done is this. We hacked—don't worry, on the governor's orders—into the data banks of the top three sex doll manufacturers. Our governor here is running for president of what's left of these United States, but don't tell the governor of Wyoming. The word in the back corridors of our state government is that if California leaves the Union, he's in. And this project of ours is his big splash entry. But it is going to be a big splash whether he jumps in or not.

"As we anticipated, those manufacturers are trying to become big sex data. Just like the old tech giants—remember when Google was big?—used to log every key stroke, every movement of the cursor, every web page visited. In the same way, these perverts are keeping track of all their customers' sexual actions—how many times, how long . . ."

"What for?" Ace asked.

"Why they want that info is one thing. Why we wanted it, or how we can use it rather, is quite a different thing. They want control. They want to use sex to steer everybody to go right where they are told to go, and to sit there quietly. All their customers have a short-horizon lust. These rulers, these elites, have a long-horizon lust—*libido dominandi*. They want to rule the world, pure and simple, even if it is a smoking ruin by the time they get to rule it. And with exhaustive sexual information, they think they have found the rudder."

"I think I get it," Ace said. "But maybe not."

Thomas leaned back in his chair, and quoted something from memory. "'Nature herself begins to throw away the anachronism. When she has thrown it away, then real civilization becomes possible. You would understand if you were peasants. Who would try to work with stallions and bulls? No, no; we want geldings and oxen. There will never be peace and order and discipline so long as there is sex. When man has thrown it away, then he will become finally governable.'

"That's Filostrato," Thomas continued, "one of the bad guys in Lewis's *That Hideous Strength,* a companion volume to *Abolition.* The one thing that Lewis didn't fully develop is how the masters will make all the geldings and oxen somehow believe that they are still really stallions and bulls. And that is what the hyper-sexualization of blue state culture has been—a feint. From their perspective, a genius move, actually."

"I see." Ace looked at the graph on the tablet again. "And what is your team after in this?" he said.

"Let me tell you a story," Tom began, "about my grandmother. It may seem like I am changing the subject, but I am not. It is kind of a family legend. This was way back in the days before the Troubles, when my grandma was young and just getting started on her family. They eventually had nine kids, but they only had four at this time, and she was big pregnant."

Ace sat back in his chair, picturing the scenario.

"Now, before the Troubles of '24, different kinds of folks were all jumbled up together, way more mixed than now, and if you had a passel of kids, you could expect comments about it at restaurants, grocery stores, wherever."

"I can imagine."

"Well, my grandma was standing on a street corner one time, waiting for the crossing light, and her four kids were standing there, all obedient like, and there were about three men standing there too, and one other lady. Lots of times these comments would come from the women, or so I am told. Well, like I said, they were standing there, all patient, waiting for the light to change, and the woman turned to my grandma—who is the sweetest thing, incidentally—and offered what passed for a standard witticism on this subject. She said, 'Don't you know what causes all this?' And she gestured with disdain, passing her hand over the kids' heads. My mom was one of them, and she remembers it."

Ace grinned, waiting.

"And so my grandma smiled her brightest and most cheerful smile at the lady, and with her old-school Alabama accent, the kind you could spread on crackers, she said, 'Why, yes, we do. And it looks like I'm getting a lot more of it than you are.' At that, all three of the men standing there laughed out loud, the woman turned the same color as furious, and crossed against the traffic. If she had had petticoats, they would have been flouncing."

Ace laughed. "Great story. And it is pertinent how?"

"Well, it turns out my grandma's riposte was not only funny, but also massively, globally, universally true."

Ace shook his head. "I must be thick," he said, "because I am not getting it."

"Here is the deal. Sex multiplies when it is restricted. This is why I thought your talk last night was so fantastic. When sex is everywhere, when everything is sexualized, what happens is that actual sex starts to evaporate, like water on a parking lot. When you drive through the blue states, you are confronted with it everywhere—billboards, ads on gas pumps, porn in gas stations, mandatory sex ed in all those grades, and all the pride marches. Lots and lots and lots of talk. Have you been to a mall on your visit here?"

"Yes. I forgot to pack enough underwear and the troopers had to take me. That's where Officer Mark jumped ship, actually. So yes, I have been to one of your malls. And it was very nice," Ace added politely.

"And did you notice anything about the people there?"

Ace thought for a minute. It had been very different, but he hadn't really had any time to think about it—which he now did. After a minute it came to him. "Strollers!" he exclaimed.

"Right," Thomas said. "Strollers everywhere. Babies. And babies, I am willing to inform you if you didn't know before, come from actual instances of actual sexual intercourse."

"Okay," Ace said. "Tell me more. Even though I knew that."

"After the Troubles, a number of dramatic changes occurred in our states. They didn't seem like a big deal at the time, but they rapidly turned into a big deal. Porn was outlawed, and became very difficult to obtain. It was no longer available at motels, for example."

"Yeah," Ace said. "It is pretty noticeable."

"Once women rediscovered what they are for, it was not long after that that men discovered what *they* are for. And what they are for is protection and provision. Once the protection of women was back in place, the provision exploded."

"You put it that way," Ace interrupted, "but back home in Colorado I could find plenty of people who would say that 'discovering what they are for' is simply code for 'putting women in their place.' They would describe it as rolling back all the advancements of feminism."

"Advancements, eh?" Thomas said. "There's another way to look at it, man. They mean that 'putting women in their place' is a shorthand expression to justify oppression. Women actually belong up here, but you put them down there, that sort of thing. The problem is that the only thing really accomplished by your vaunted feminism was that women were uprooted and made miserable, and the men were uprooted too, and made even more miserable."

"Go on," Ace said.

"There is another way to take the phrase 'putting women in their place.' Something, or in this case someone, that is out of place is displaced. Or lost. Being 'put in your place' assumes some kind of oppressive power from above. But 'finding your place' has entirely different connotations. Tell me, did the women pushing all those strollers seem unhappy or oppressed to you?"

"No. There was a lot of contentment, laughter, satisfaction. It seemed like a very happy place. And I don't think it was the sale prices in the stores."

"Okay. So then ask me about my research."

"I was wondering when you were going to get to that. Or if you ever would . . ."

"Thanks for asking. Well, we spent about six months getting into their systems. Once we cracked the big corporation, Dollz, the other two came quickly. And we discovered that all of them were tracking absolutely everything. And we got it all."

"To do what?"

"The report we developed comes in at about 495 pages. There is an advance copy right here," Thomas said, pointing to a large volume on his desk. "The bottom line is that all this Kinkytown stuff really is kinky. It really is bad. It is also comparatively rare."

"Rare? What do you mean? Those companies are huge."

"So are the companies that manufacture exercise bikes and rowing machines. They are huge, too. That just means that their products sell. It doesn't mean that they are used all that much."

"Okay, I'll bite. How little are they used?"

"Well, in all the blue states, there are approximately 1.4 million owners of the advanced android dolls—the kind that your Sally Sasani was."

"All right. . ."

"Guess, on average, how many times each one has been used."

Ace shrugged. "From the way you are setting this up, I would guess a low number, but I really don't know what a low number would be."

"Three. The average owner of one of those things has had sex with it three times. There are a handful of outliers, on the mentally diseased end of things I am guessing, who use their dolls a lot more than that. But the whole thing is really perverted and, more to the point, really sad and pathetic. Lame."

Ace sat still for a moment, stunned.

"So the big takeaway is . . .?"

"That the repressed states are liberated, and getting a lot of it, and the liberated states are repressed, and hardly getting any."

Ace scratched his forehead. "This is unbelievable."

"I'll give you another factoid, even more unbelievable. More perverted, more lonesome, and even more sad."

"Yikes."

"Have you heard about the brothels that use robo-animals? No? Lucky guy. There are a couple in Oregon, and about six in California. These animals are manufactured by these same big companies. We got that information too. About sixty-five percent of the clients at those brothel-barns pay their fee, go off with their rented critter, and come back later, not having done anything. They wanted to be seen as perverted and as bleeding cutting edge, but they don't actually do anything. The kink is in their soul, not in their lusts."

"Gosh," Ace said.

CHAPTER 5

THOUGH FATHER AND MOTHER FORSAKE ME

BENSON AND ROBERTA

Ace was in his bedroom, and leaning back in his desk chair, which he had turned around to face the bed, and his feet were on the bed. He was reading—not that it matters a great deal to our narrative—*Institutes of Elenctic Theology* by a chap of yesteryear named Turretin. He was entering into yet another round of what the Reformed affirm and the Socinians deny when a light tapping came through his door.

"Come in!" Ace called, and because he knew it had to be one or more of his parents, he stood up. And sure enough, his father Benson came in, with his mother close behind him. Her face was inexpressive, but he could tell she was worried.

Benson cleared his throat, the way he usually did when he was about to be important. Roberta stood behind him, slightly to the left, and though she was not moving at all, there were—somehow—some clear signs of restiveness.

"Son . . ." Benson started.

Ace looked up with a clear expression that indicated that he knew what was coming, which he actually did.

Benson hesitated, but thought for a minute and continued. "You know how your mother and I have always sought to seize any moment that God might give us, in order to turn it to a redemptive and evangelistic purpose."

Roberta didn't roll her eyes when Benson said "your mother and I." She just stood there, as silent as Lot's wife a couple years after the explosion. But she managed to roll her eyes without really doing anything.

Ace nodded, and waited for his father to continue.

"Our central concern in all of this was not the, um, *fact* that you decided to, um, dispatch Sally the way you did. I do understand youth and impetuosity, and given your premises, I do understand what followed."

Roberta stood silent, dangerously silent. Ace glanced at her for a moment, distracted. He had never seen her like that before, and didn't know what was happening. But his father's voice drew him back.

"The great problem, and the reason why we feel we must step away from you for the time being, distancing ourselves from your intransigence, is your refusal to seize what could be a powerful redemptive moment and a stirring witness to the unbelievers."

Ace looked up sharply. "You mean by apologizing . . ."

His father nodded, almost pleading. "It would humanize you to your opposition. It would show that Christians are not above correction themselves. *When you point a finger . . .*"

"*Three pointing back at yourself* . . . I know." Ace sighed, but not audibly. He sighed somewhere down inside.

"Refusing to apologize when virtually the whole world is demanding it is the same thing as saying that you will never admit you were wrong about anything. And *that* runs clean contrary to everything we believe about the gospel."

Ace was silent for a moment, saying nothing.

His father waited, and then asked, softly enough. "Well?"

"Dad, the world is demanding that I apologize for *one* thing, the action of destroying that Sasani doll. I have not apologized for that because I do not think I was wrong about *that*. It does not follow that I somehow believe I am never wrong about anything."

Benson just stared at him, and so Ace tried to pick up the thread again.

"Dad, I always believe I'm right. But I don't believe I'm always right."

"*What?*" his father exclaimed. "More of your little word games? At a time like this, *word* games?" With that he glanced at Ace's copy of Turretin, now resting on the bed.

"Dad, I am not claiming that I have always been right about everything. I *know* I have not been. I know myself to be a big fat sinner, and I could give examples if you want. But I believe what I did was right, given the circumstances. To apologize here, just for the sake of making peace, or for getting myself out of a bad jam, or even to create an opportunity to witness, would be like taking a pig to Moses so that he could sacrifice it. How could the God of truth be pleased with the unclean sacrifice of a lie?"

His father shook his head. "And it strikes me that you would rather cling to your opinions than to do something that might speak to the lost."

Ace decided on just one more try. "Dad, is that *your* opinion? And are you clinging to it?"

"Your theological word games won't work on me, Asahel."

The two simply stood for a moment, looking at each other across an almost infinite chasm.

After another moment, Ace cleared his throat. "Okay, Dad. No more of the meta-stuff. Can I ask you a very practical question?"

"Well, yes. If it is pertinent. If it is about what we are discussing . . ."

"Dad, how many *actual* non-Christians have expressed this concern to you? As compared to nervous Christians anticipating what the non-Christians *might* be thinking?"

"I haven't had this come up in a witnessing encounter, if that's what you mean."

Ace nodded. "Yes, that's exactly what I mean. And how many Christians have spoken to you about their concerns about what random non-Christians *might* bring up? But which none of them actually do?"

"So now you think we are making things up, is that right?"

Ace waved his hands in front of him, like he was shooing off a couple of yellow jackets. "No, no! I don't think you are just making things up. But I do believe you are so concerned to not be offensive or off-putting to nonbelievers that you always run everything by your internal censors. And they can be much stricter than the actual unbelievers are. The meshes on your filters are pretty tight. That's all."

"Ace, I have been doing evangelistic work for decades, and I think I have a pretty good grasp of what average non-Christians are thinking and saying . . ."

Ace held up his hand, not in surrender, and not in mock surrender, but in a gesture that appeared to mean that he thought further discussion would probably be yelling at the wind. "Dad," he said, "I am sure this is difficult enough for you and Mom as it is, and so let's not argue any more about it. I am content for both of you to follow your conscience in this."

He looked at his mother, and cocked an eyebrow. She was still standing there impassively. He thought he had seen her flinch when he had said the word *both*, and it was clear to him that something was going to happen there at some point, but it was also clear that it wasn't going to be happening just this minute.

Then he looked back at his father. "So what are you going to do?"

Benson was clearly discomfited by the question, and cleared his throat nervously. "Ace, we love you dearly. We will pray for you constantly. The one thing we won't be is by your side so long as you continue being so intractable. If you ever see this clear . . . just a phone call away, and I would help to get you back on track in any way I could. You have so much potential . . ." And he trailed off.

But in the history of the kingdom, Ace thought to himself, *how many men had thrown away "undeniable potential" for the kingdom by playing it safe? By sticking close to the shore? By burying a talent in a napkin on account of the hard master?*

Keep talking to yourself that way, sport.

Why didn't the parable show us the men who invested ten talents, and lost them all? Or five talents, which were thrown, through a series of reckless investments, into the deep blue sea?

Ace barely managed to pull himself back into the conversation. He was not sure what his mind was doing to him. His mind was trailing off in one direction, but his words stayed on point. At least there was that.

"When would you like me to move out?" he asked.

At this, both parents looked startled, his mother more than his father, and she looked pleadingly at Benson. But he, though surprised also, seemed determined to ride it through. "Um, we hadn't settled on a time," he said. "But as soon as you can practically manage it."

Ace had known that this moment was coming for a while, and he was entirely prepared for it, which is to say, he *thought* he was entirely prepared for it. He had long since identified the inconsistencies with which his father's thoughts were riddled, and even had names for some of the more common ones. He knew the patterns of their conversations very well. Depending on the topic, he knew how each one of them would go. Their conversations worked their way down well-worn grooves. Each conversation was unique, and yet they were somehow all the same one. And the place where they would all end was a roadblock of cautions about intellectualism.

Benson was not an unintelligent man, but he *was* a simple man. Ace was much quicker, more widely read, and Benson had been aware of that gap for about five years now. Most of the time he was simply proud of it, the way normal fathers would be, but whenever they came into conflict—usually around this one issue—Ace's quickness almost always exasperated him. He found himself being competitive, and he didn't know what to do with it. Whenever he began his cautions about intellectualism, he knew how lame it sounded. He didn't like it, but didn't know what else to do, or say.

After their conversations, Ace would be unsettled too, but for different reasons. He would work through the arguments again in his mind, and could not see any alternatives to the way he had gone. And he was constantly mystified by the things his father would say and then go and do. The arguments were watertight, and his father's thinking was not watertight.

And yet, now, when his father turned and walked out the door, his mother following, it was as though a cold steel sledgehammer hit him in the solar plexus. And it was like John Henry was swinging the sledge. An irrational desire to *be* irrational went over his head like a wave. He wanted nothing more than to jump up, run out into the hallway and call them back. The feeling was unspeakably strong, and he had no idea why he didn't do it. He just sat there.

He knew his father did not have a coherent approach to anything. He knew the answers to any reasonable questions he might ask would not be forthcoming. A feeling similar to the one that he had fought standing in the hallway of the Sasani home, outside their bedroom, fell on him. It was like a net that had been suspended from the ceiling, and then dropped on him. He knew he had no moves.

If he just surrendered, all would be well. If he continued to struggle, there would be nothing but . . . well, nothing but *struggle*. Struggle in every direction. A world of struggle.

He sat down on the bed, and remained there, virtually paralyzed, for what seemed like hours. An urgent need to visit the bathroom finally dislodged him, and after that he made his way down to the kitchen for a drink. After that he went back upstairs to the chair where he had been before, sat down again, and the feeling descended on him again. And so he sat some more.

And the feeling was one that required—that demanded— that he seek his father out, and acquiesce completely. And Ace knew also, down in his bones he knew, that the thing was impossible. He felt like he had to surrender, and he knew that surrender was impossible. And he also had a fleeting thought that not surrendering while feeling the way he currently felt was yet *another* impossibility.

He knew it was a spell. He was in a blue funk. It was just a thing. It wouldn't last. It couldn't last. But it did last, and he continued to just sit there.

His phone buzzed. He glanced at it. It was Stephanie. He picked up, dully, and said "Hey" perfunctorily.

"Listen," she said. "My dad has a file of papers he wanted you to look over, acquaint yourself with. He asked me to get them to you. If you are free tomorrow, we could meet at Cafe Coffee to make the transfer. That's about halfway between us, right?"

"Sure," Ace said.

"You sound pretty down," she said. "Did something bad happen?"

"Well, not cosmic bad," he said. "But no fun, at least for me. My folks are detaching themselves from my approach to cultural engagement. I will need to find a new place to stay."

"Oh! I'm sorry," she said. "Let me . . ." Then she stopped abruptly. "Let me check on something," she ended lamely.

"Alright," he said, not paying much attention. "What time should we meet?"

"Ten?" she said. "Ten thirty? You pick."

Ace said that it didn't matter, thought to himself that nothing mattered, picked ten thirty, said good-bye, and hung up the phone. And yet, after talking with Stephanie, he felt better. He had no reason for feeling better, but he did.

COFFEE HOUSE JEANS

The next morning Ace got up slowly, not at all his usual ebullient self. He didn't feel the same way he had felt the night before, except in his gut. He felt normal in every respect, with the exception of his large intestine. He felt like his intestine had somehow gained thirty pounds. But he thought he should be able to function normally without looking dejected. He *was* dejected though, or at least his intestine was.

Ace was at Cafe Coffee for about ten minutes before Stephanie arrived. Though it was not his usual spot, it wasn't entirely an unusual spot either, so he was somewhat familiar with his surroundings. He had a minute to pick out a table where they could talk, and then he went over and ordered a coffee for each of them.

The place was fairly crowded, and so it was that the order arrived just about a minute before Stephanie did. He waved, and she walked over to his table, and looked down at the steaming coffee that was waiting there for her. Ace had risen when she arrived, and was standing by her chair.

"How thoughtful," she said. "How sweet. How presumptuous."

Ace smiled, somewhat grimly. "No, just thoughtful. The coffees are both small and I figured I could drink both of them if I guessed wrong. In the grip of a gambler's spirit, I was just placing a bet. If I lost the bet, I would be happy to go get whatever you might actually prefer." He started to move toward the counter.

Stephanie sniffed at it. "No, no, you guessed close enough. I can overlook your thoughtfulness this time."

Ace came around the table and pulled out her chair for her.

"Are you trying to make a scene?" she said. "Who does *that* anymore? I think I saw it in a movie once—you know, one of those movies you can stream from the good side of the bad side of town? One of those dark web movies?"

"Not trying to make trouble . . . folks don't do that anymore, sure. But they are also demented on a whole range of issues. So who cares what *they* do or don't do?"

They were both sitting down by this time, and both of them were hunched over their coffee. Neither one spoke for a minute. After that minute, Stephanie reached down into her bag and pulled out a folder, the folder that was the reason she was meeting with Ace in the first place. Her father had asked her to deliver a set of materials that he wanted Ace to review before the next hearing, and which he didn't want to transfer digitally. She slowly moved the folder across the table, and Ace magnanimously thanked her.

After another minute or so, with things being pretty quiet there with the Stephanie/Ace party, one of the baristas walked by their table, and Ace's eyes followed her for a couple of seconds, his hand first going up and then, when she didn't stop, lamely going down again. It was an ineffectual move when it came to catching the attention of the barista, but it nevertheless turned out to be a very effective conversation starter.

"And that's *another* thing," Stephanie said abruptly. "I want to tell you something. May I tell you something? I am asking, and I suppose this is where you should say something like 'go right ahead.'"

"Okay then," Ace replied. "Go *right* ahead." And he grinned again, but there was a certain grimness that remained in his smile. He already knew what she was going to bring up.

Stephanie had apparently come to the coffee shop prepared to vent. Though she felt sorry for him after what his folks had done, she still thought he needed to fix . . . to fix *something*. As part of her background reading on the case, she had worked through a small pile of newspaper articles and opinion pieces on the subject of Ace's contumacious attitude. And though she disagreed with all of them, sometimes violently, she still didn't know Ace, and the general tone of all the articles had affected her perception of the young man across from her. She was entirely of her father's opinion that Ace ought not to be on trial for *murder*, but she had somehow come to the view that his self-righteousness was not to be endured quietly.

But before recording their conversation, another thing must really be mentioned. With regard to the exchange that followed, an outsider might be baffled at how frankly Ace and Stephanie were able to speak to each other, and this might take a brief word of explanation. Stephanie was a product of the government school system, and Ace had gone through a Christian school. But that Christian school—as the price of staying open for business—had agreed to all the demands of Colorado Human Rights Commission, which included allowing officials from the state to conduct all the sex ed courses from third grade on. And the result of this compromise was that both Ace and Stephanie had received exactly the same education on the subject of human sexual customs, conduct, and conversation.

And though Ace had eventually reacted in what the state of Colorado considered a highly reactionary way, as evidenced by what had happened in the Sasani doll situation, there was one area where Ace and Stephanie had responded to all the indoctrination in exactly the same way. That was the almost complete freedom that both felt in talking to other people about sexual matters. Previous generations would have felt the "too much information" threshold pass sometime before Stephanie and Ace would ever have felt that way.

"So here you are, Mr. *Christian*, in the throes of a national controversy over crushing that fellow's artificial wife, the gaudiest sex scandal *ever*, one that wants to become a murder scandal if somebody lets it, and you go out in public in order to leer at that barista's rear end. And in a crowded room too."

"Well, let's state the facts accurately. I wasn't leering. I merely glanced at her. I simply wanted to get her attention to find out if they put my cinnamon roll on the wrong train."

"Look, girls *know* when they are being checked out. And they know when other girls are getting checked out."

"I dare say they do, at least much of the time. But they don't know this infallibly, and they don't always know *why* a guy is looking. Sometimes it is old-fashioned lust. Sometimes it is artistic appreciation. Sometimes it is exactly what the young lady thinks it is. Or it could just be that he paid for a cinnamon roll that has somehow failed to materialize. And last, sometimes it is to wonder why that girl's friends let her go out in public like that."

"Oh, and so now you are saying that *your* glance was the disapproving glance of a Mrs. Grundy?"

Ace smiled again. "Oh, I didn't say that."

Stephanie gestured impatiently, almost knocked her cup over, and sat back exasperated.

Ace leaned forward. "Look, are we still at that same part of the conversation? The part where we all say 'go right ahead' and speak freely?"

Stephanie looked up. "I suppose so. Sauce for the goose."

"May I have your permission to make an observation? Even though it is kind of obvious? May I point out what everybody should have seen, but somehow hasn't?" There was a dangerous glint in his eye.

Stephanie looked worried for a second, but then shook it off. "Okay. Say on."

"How many women in here are wearing jeans?"

Stephanie thought she had seen a woman in a skirt near the door, but she wasn't sure. "Over ninety percent, I suppose."

"Okay, how many mom jeans? And how many tight jeans?"

Stephanie glanced around the room. There were an awful lot of tight jeans. And no mom jeans. "Quite a few tight jeans," she said.

"So would it be safe to say that there isn't a woman in here, at least not one that I can see, including that barista, who got dressed this morning thinking something like *you know, I really don't want men looking at my tush with any kind of fond appreciation today, so I think I will wear my roomy pair?*"

Stephanie smiled in spite of herself. "I think we can consider that scenario unlikely."

"Meaning?"

"Meaning no woman here thought that."

"Okay. We are closing in on our quarry."

Stephanie laughed at him. "Did you read a book of strategy sometime that said the best defense is a good offense?"

Ace laughed with her. "Well, I think that happens to be true. But that is not why I am saying any of this. I have had to work through this issue a few hundred times. Now that girl that kicked off our discussion, the one who didn't bring me my cinnamon roll . . ."

"Well, strictly speaking, they all didn't."

"Point granted. I mean the cinnamon-roll-less girl who walked by the table here. Because I am not blind, I do know that if she had put a quarter in her hip pocket, I would have been able to tell if it was heads or tails. So much is public information. This is because we live in a time when the men are gawkers and the women are exhibitionists."

"Why would our time be unique in that? That would seem to be the way of all flesh."

"No, there is one thing more, and this is the thing that reveals our peculiar societal pathologies. Men have always liked looking, and women have always liked being admired. That, as you say, is the way of all flesh. The thing that is so screwed up about *our* time is that women have gotten to the point where they can display themselves in a most shameless fashion, desperately competing with the porn ladies and the sexbots, all while reserving to themselves the inscrutable right to be mortally offended if some man they don't like takes them up on their open invitation, the invitation that is being extended to everyone in the general public who has a working pair of eyes."

"You are quite eloquent on this subject," Stephanie said. "You almost have me in tears. Poor little buddy. All these shapely women sashaying past the Pure One."

"Not asking for your pity or compassion. And most certainly *not* your understanding, which I clearly don't have. But I work hard at not being a pig, and would give myself—depending on the day—a B minus. Sometimes a bit better."

Stephanie was mildly annoyed with him still, and a bit more annoyed with herself for being annoyed. What came out next was perhaps ill-advised.

"So then, are *my* jeans too tight?"

Ace smiled the grimmest smile of all. "When I saw it was you coming in, I made a point of not looking."

Stephanie pressed the point, which perhaps she shouldn't have. "And *why* did you make a point of not looking?"

"Because the night I met you, at the restaurant, your jeans were too tight. Since this is a delicate subject, I will only say that your tailgate *derriere* is just the kind I approve of. But I only know that because you showed it to me."

Despite her efforts to not react to the implied rebuke, Stephanie colored noticeably. "Maybe you are doing so well—if B minus can be called doing well—because of low testosterone. Maybe it is not godliness coupled with self-discipline at all."

For the first time in their conversation, a jibe went home, and the pointed end of it went a lot deeper than Stephanie had intended. Ace flushed slightly, and the tips of his ears got hot. He sat up straight in his chair and said, somewhat stiffly, "That's as may be. Perhaps you may want to check with the young woman I eventually marry. If I choose wisely, she won't tell you anything about it. But she and I will know."

The next thirty seconds at their table were truly awkward, and walked slowly by, trying to act like ninety seconds. Neither of them said anything. Suddenly Ace laughed out loud. "Please forgive me," he said, rubbing his face with his hands. "I reacted. I shouldn't react like that. In my defense, I don't usually. But please forgive me."

Stephanie sat for a moment. After his conversion, her father had started to do something similar—abrupt apologies, out of the blue. *That* took some getting used to, but was far better than the way it had been previously. In any case it broke the ice for Stephanie's apology.

"No," she said. "Please forgive *me*. I really need to watch my tongue far better than I do. What I said was out of line and over the line. And I really shouldn't have brought up my jeans. Sorry about that, too."

Ace nodded, and the next silence was not nearly as awkward as the previous one had been. After a minute, she added, "And it was particularly bad for me to do all that on the morning after what your parents did. I *am* sorry. And that reminds me, my father said to tell you that we have a vacant basement apartment you can stay in. Do you have a lot of stuff?"

"I have a lot of books, but I don't have to move them. I just need to pack a suitcase, and load up the books I am currently reading. Please thank your father. I would love to."

"You can come over any time," she said.

"Thank you."

By this point, Ace was becoming aware of the fact that they had been flirting, and he was about five minutes ahead of Stephanie in the realization. He yelled at himself deep inside to knock it off. *Don't be stupid.*

"I'm a virgin," Stephanie said suddenly. "Apropos of nothing in particular. I don't know why I felt I needed to tell you that though. It must have seemed like sharing time."

Ace said, "I see." He looked up. "Does that have anything to do with your dad coming to Christ when you were in high school?"

Stephanie nodded. "You know I am not a Christian . . . but let's be honest . . . my father's changes do have me thinking about it. But I didn't want you to think I was an out-and-out heathen . . ."

"Despite being deep into libertarianism . . ."

"Right," she said. "Dad told you about that? Maybe that's why I said something about . . . about being a virgin. My libertarianism . . . especially after I got to college . . . look—the libertarian men can be roughly clustered into two groups. There are the party commandos who are largely interested in women and pot and with no one telling them what to do, and then there are all the economics majors who were Murray Rothbard nerds. I had no interest in being the five hundredth woman for any of the first group, and even less interested in being the first woman for any of the second."

"Well, I quite understand. Doesn't quite rise to Sermon on the Mount levels, but still it should be considered a good thing." He grinned, and then paused for a moment. "Since you apparently want a heart-to-heart talk, I am *not* a virgin."

Her eyebrows shot up. "Have you told my dad?"

"Your dad?" he said. "Why would I tell your dad something like that? Besides whatever it was that possessed me to tell *you*."

"Don't be a naive goof," she replied. "You surely must know that the prosecutor and his friends in that hyena-pack media are on the hunt for *that* lucky girl, whoever she was, not my business. And if they find her, you can bet that I will learn far more about all of that stuff than any of us wanted to know, because I will have read about it on the internet news aggregation site of my choice. Did you really think that their investigators would be uninterested in any details of your sexual history?"

"Well, I am a lot of things, but naive isn't one of them. One of the reasons it took me ten minutes to decide whether to take that Sally doll thing to the recycling center was the knowledge that if I was caught, as I thought I likely would be, they would go through my history with all of the muck rakes west of the Mississippi."

"*One* of the reasons? Ten minutes?"

Ace shook his head. "I'll probably tell you more about it some time. And I will tell your dad about it. I wasn't trying to hide anything from him. I just didn't think that it had any *legal* relevance."

On her way home, Stephanie found herself hitting the steering wheel repeatedly. "Stupid, stupid, *stupid*!" Why had she just blurted out to Ace that she was a virgin? She was even more upset with herself because she knew, she plainly knew, that she had done this because she had wanted him to know.

SARA ARRIVES

During her first week in the city, Sara had a couple of crying episodes, but they were rare, and becoming rarer. And in between those episodes, she was enjoying herself immensely. She spent most of her time looking for an apartment, which she found on the third day. It was a very nice apartment, located within easy walking distance of all the necessities that she thought she might need. There was a grocery shop about two blocks away, a pharmacy on the same block, and on the other side of her apartment building was a bus stop on the main line. *This will certainly do*, she thought to herself.

She reported for work the following Monday as a temporary receptionist at a law firm, and it was only a ten-minute bus ride away from her apartment. That job lasted for three weeks—the regular receptionist was recovering from foot surgery—and she found herself really enjoying it. She had never worked with anything electronic before, like the phone system in this office, but she was a quick study, and it did not appear to anyone there that she was on a learning curve that had more or less started in the Bronze Age. It just looked to them that she was unfamiliar with *this* kind of phone system, and they all just assumed that she was proficient with that *other* kind of phone system.

She had a ready smile, and looked for all the world like a cute city girl, born and bred. Stephanie had been a huge help in picking out her clothes, and showing her how to apply her new make-up. Over the weekend, Stephanie had called her up to help her go get her hair done. It remained long, but not like before. Now it was *done*. Now her hair was on purpose.

Sara spent her three weeks at the law office brightening up everyone's lives, and when she had to leave, the office staff actually threw a going-away party. In part this was because they were going to miss Sara a lot, but it was also because the regular receptionist was usually pretty surly, and they were all pretty confident that the foot surgery was not going to diminish that tendency.

And so it was that when the receptionist at the prosecutor's office decided to take a much-needed vacation, she notified Connor Connorson the night before that vacation would start, and he cussed a bit. The receptionist's ability to act like this was a function of Colorado's Byzantine labor laws, coupled with the fact that she was sleeping with the man who was currently off on his Alaskan safari. With regard to the labor laws, these have to be understood as routinely siding with whoever had a yen to rip off somebody else. Connor was in full support of such laws, but this did not keep him from swearing for about five minutes at the gods of inconvenience. He had a trial to prepare for, and did not have time to go find a receptionist. He also did not have time to consider the link between his political ideals and this particular inconvenience. But even if he had had the time, that particular train of thought was unlikely.

In exasperation, he sat down at his computer, typed "temp agency" in the search bar, and called the first number that popped up. It happened to be the number of Sara's employer, a cheerful sort named Tami, and she was picking up the phone just as Sara walked in.

Connor asked if they had anybody there who had worked as a receptionist in a law office, and just as he asked this, Tami saw Sara walk through the door. Her eyebrows went up, and Sara's eyebrows went up, and Tami pulled the phone away from her mouth. "Where were you just working the last few weeks?" she mouthed.

"Greerson and Sons," Sara answered. "Law office."

"Law office!" Tami chortled, and returned to the call. "I have someone here who can start right away."

Sara got the address, went back to her apartment for a few things, and then hopped the bus. What with one thing and another, she made it to the prosecutor's office in just under forty-five minutes.

CHAPTER 6

MOVING CHESS PIECES

CAVERNOUS

Jon leaned back in his chair. "So, Stephanie told me that your past fling with—you said her name was Camila?—was one of the reasons you hesitated before taking the sexbot to the recycling center."

Ace nodded. "Yeah, that's right. I knew that if I was arrested, which was likely, and if they dug *that* up, or if she came forward, there would be a ruckus about it."

"And yet you didn't tell me about it?"

"Like I told Stephanie . . . I didn't think it could have possibly had any *legal* relevance. I wasn't trying to sandbag you. And it was embarrassing. Somehow I thought it was not a big deal to the *case*, however embarrassing it might be to me personally . . ."

Jon sat for a moment, whistling through his teeth. "Well, technically, you are right. It doesn't have any legal relevance. You got that part right. What *does* have legal relevance is that shocked look on your attorney's face when someone on the other side floats something across the courtroom that he never even heard of. Attorneys like me hate being embarrassed by things that the other guy knows that he should have known. That's probably the biggest thing. But that didn't happen, and I know now."

"So do I," Ace said. "My apologies. Honest."

Jon sat quietly for a minute. "So . . .?"

Ace looked at the ceiling. "So I suppose you are wondering about the meaning of my phrasing in saying 'one of the reasons' . . .?"

"Right. Is there anything else tucked down inside that phrase that could conceivably come up in the courtroom, blowing my eyebrows off, and thus embarrassing me? I don't look nearly as distinguished or formidable without my eyebrows."

"Okay. Possibly. And in my defense—for not telling you this part before—is that I now know more about what is going on than I did when we first talked. So here it is. If I testify, and if the prosecutor asks me point blank about it, yes, possibly. I need to ask your advice about what I should say, actually."

"So then," Jon said, "I do need to know about it."

Ace exhaled slowly. "If he makes a big deal out of the timeline, noting that I must have stood there for about ten minutes before going back to my house to get the t-shirt for the doll, and he presses me for all of the reasons for my hesitation, I could say something that would surprise you. That is, if I do the 'whole truth' and 'nothing but the truth' bit."

Jon leaned forward suddenly. "We will *talk* about this, and we will agree beforehand whether or not you would be under any obligation at all to respond. But I want to hear what you were thinking first . . . which was . . . what?"

"You know the doll was provocatively undressed, and placed, and when I came into the doorway, the thing said, 'Asahel is a *sexy* name . . .' I knew that I was being set up, invited, summoned, seduced . . . I would need to have been an idiot not to see that. But all that was just what Steven Sasani was doing. He had to have programmed her to say that, for example. But something *else* was going on in there."

"And what was that?"

"This first thing was Sasani's idea of temptation, which was just a couple notches above a nuisance. If I wanted a sex doll, who in Colorado doesn't have access to a sex doll? But behind that, and quite distinct from it, was a thoroughly *satanic* temptation, and it felt like thousands of pounds of something, crushing me, suffocating me. It was like being under five hundred soaked mattresses. And it wasn't just abstract pressure—there was a different kind of pressure there, pressure with a personality. And grandiose promises were being made."

Jon nodded, solemnly. "And so you are saying that there were two different temptations, going on simultaneously? Two distinct temptations to do the same thing?"

"Right. There was mild curiosity, and a touch of lust, on the sex doll Sasani side. Easily resistible. But behind that, and with a very different quality, was . . . some kind of a cavernous lust. I knew that if I did this thing, it wouldn't simply be a sexual sin—like what I had done with Camila. I was being enticed to come over to the other side, completely, irrevocably. It was in brief an invitation to damnation, and the horrifying thing about it was that it was enthralling. I have never experienced anything like it before. And hope never to again."

"*Wanting* to be damned? Pitching your temptations that way would seem to me to be a niche market."

"Of course it doesn't make sense. If sin made sense it wouldn't be sin, as I read somewhere. But there was an element of sense in it. There was grandeur, there was high bribery, and there was the exhilaration of massive amounts of spiritual adrenaline. Robert Johnson at the crossroads, Faust and his bargain. Gold, and glory, and lots of girls. And *then* the damnation. But I knew that to choose one was to choose them all, and that was part of the attraction. A big part. And that had me wavering for a good ten minutes."

"So you were in this thick fog of wanting to be damned. What broke the spell for you? I suppose that something had to have done it . . ."

"It was my phone. I have it programmed to chime the hours of prayer at me. Like a set of church bells in your pocket. It went off, and so did the devil. And then, right afterward, so did I. To get Sally a decent t-shirt. As soon as I was out the front door, my head cleared completely."

SARA AT THE DESK

Sara found her stride at the prosecutor's office fairly easily. By the second day, she knew everything that was expected of her—which wasn't much, as she was a temp receptionist—and she set about surpassing all the expectations they might have for her.

By the second day, she knew that the office was a tangled web of unregenerate envy and striving, and by the third day, she knew that the place was evil.

She had been preoccupied for the previous month or so, getting herself situated in a new life, and so it was that the whole Asahel affair had largely sailed past her unnoticed. But now that she was working, and had most of her apartment together, and didn't take an hour getting her make-up on straight, she had started to piece the story together. Back in the community, nothing was more irrelevant than the politics of "the English," and all their stirrings, and doings, and frothings were just what the kings of the earth were accustomed to do.

But now she was starting to take an interest in politics, in spite of herself. It would be hard for her to miss that she was in an office that was engaged in prosecuting one Asahel Hartwick, and he was being prosecuted for . . . *murder?* For crushing a sex doll? She had taken a hard double-take when she first learned that. She had also taken a hard double-take when she had first looked up what a sex doll was.

When that was coupled with the levels of profanity around the office, combined with the glowering and unhappy faces, she soon reached the conclusion that these were not her people, and that the regular receptionist could not return soon enough. Whoever the people were out there who were opposing these people in here, in this office, *those* people were her people.

She had already reached that decision, which came easily enough, but—as often happens—she then had to act on that decision with a suddenness that quite startled her.

CHAPTER 7

#

GOVERNOR FELIX

The governor of California was beside himself, and his fury was of the sort that usually resulted in what his mentor back in the Berkeley days used to call "direct action."

His name was Emmanuel Felix, and he was half way through his second term. He was truly a strange mix—he was canny when it came to his personal options and the main chance, and he was a superb politician, and this was welded onto—in quite an uneasy seam—the fact that he was an economic nincompoop.

Even under the best of circumstances, this is hard to get away with, but Felix was a truly odd combination, with juxtapositions everywhere. Not only was he personally shrewd with his own money, and clueless with regard to finances at whatever transition point turns it from "money" to "economics," but he was also an ugly man. But this ugliness—of the plain kind, not the grotesque freak show kind—was combined with uncanny amounts of personal charisma. He could talk virtually anybody into virtually anything, and this was a function of that charisma sloshing out of him whenever he made any sudden movements whatever.

His ugliness was of the strong chin kind, not the weak chin kind. Whatever he was doing, whatever he was saying, whatever he was up to, he would fill up whatever room he came into. His hair would have been lanky had he been foolish enough to grow it out, and his beard would have moved him over to the grotesque column had he taken it into his head to do something like that. But even if he had done that, his charisma well would not have run dry.

Here was the man who had successfully navigated the positioning of California in its bid to be the first state to secede from the Union since South Carolina's unfortunate and incomplete attempt two centuries earlier. The Supreme Court had set the stage for such maneuvering by means of a footnote in a border dispute case that had arisen a few years before between North Dakota and Montana. The footnote allowed, in a throwaway line, that secession *could* legitimately be considered a constitutional option. But this was only the case if, for example, the people of the state concerned had registered their approval of that secession in two successive referenda.

That initial dispute had been over an oil reserve that had been discovered and which was almost entirely underneath Montana, but with the ideal places for drilling into it located in North Dakota. Most of the chocolate shake was underneath Montana, but the straw was in North Dakota, and Montana wanted some of the revenue. The case itself was settled without too much commotion, but Governor Felix was close buddies with one of the justices, and was the kind of close buddy who happened to have some dirt on his friend, meaning that they had done some things together in college that would be distressing to the average viewer of the evening news. That is, they would not be distressing to Governor Felix, who was out of the closet and proud of it, but it would be most distressing to the justice concerned—a Justice Smeltworthy, for those interested—who was purported to be one of the conservative justices, or what had passed for a conservative justice during the silly season that was his confirmation process. Whatever the case, he was *not* out and proud, which is what made the photos more than a little awkward. I refer of course to some college-era photos that Felix had in his possession.

Felix had taken Smeltworthy out to the most expensive lunch in the Washington area that he could find—in order to soften the blow with that chicken dish the restaurant was famous for—and over lunch he had arranged for Smeltworthy to insert that footnote. Nobody noted it at the time because it was a footnote, it was Smeltworthy what done it, and nobody appealed to it for about six years.

Governor Felix was tired of being a lowly governor, and wanted something he could be president of. He wanted to govern an entity that could declare war on somebody. The presidency of the United States was excluded to him because he had been born in Austria, and it was not really possible to deny that. He was a naturalized U.S. citizen, which wasn't possible to deny either. There had even been a news story on the Felix family becoming citizens, which meant there was even film footage of him becoming an American. Besides, becoming the American president would involve catering to all the rubes and cornpones in the fly-over section of the country, and Felix didn't think he was up to that. His skin twitched just thinking about it.

His ambition was enormous, and was swollen up in inverse ratio to his knowledge of how a loaf of bread finds its way to a grocery store shelf. Like a master quarterback, he could read the field wonderfully when it came to his own perks and privileges, having—over the course of a lifetime in public service—squirreled away millions in numerous accounts. He knew how to add and subtract.

But, to underline it again, when it came to money on the loose, money in the pockets of others, and particularly when it came to money that corporations had mysteriously obtained, or the smaller reserves of the upper middle-class taxpayer, he hadn't a clue. He thought of public money as coming from a limitless aquifer of funds deep beneath their feet. Those who opposed him were obstinate and stiff-necked people who inexplicably did not want to pay a modest amount to install a new well and pump.

Felix was not a religious man, but he had a deep and abiding religious faith—not that he would light votive candles or anything—in the state. And this should have been obvious to anyone watching: it was why he had the serene notion that the state would never run out of funds. How could it? Gods never run low.

Governor Felix was aware of the prosperity of the red states—he had visited there enough, and their prosperity was kind of hard to miss—but he invariably thought that what they were doing was "cheating" or "refusing to pay their fair share." He had been a young man when the mass exodus of businesses and businessmen from California had begun, and this too was interpreted as radically self-centered behavior on their part. The ventures that remained in California kept going bust for some reason, and this was invariably attributed to "bad luck." His ignorance of how this kept happening to the same kind of people was sincere, although it was also culpable. He *should* have known better. He had gotten through college. He had also had a driver's license for decades.

There were parts of his state that were teetering on the brink of Third World conditions, but where Governor Felix lived there was no sign of *that* kind of thing. When various enterprises failed, that enterprise usually being a government-business "partnership," he was always informed of the disaster via a report with plenty of graphs and pie charts, and he never went out to the field to see anything for himself. Whatever he could see with his own *eyes* was necessarily opulent, and glistened in the sun.

He believed—with a heart that was wholly surrendered he believed—in the sexual revolution. He was an enthusiastic participant and knew that the new order of humankind could not be expected to arrive so long as there were bitter cling-ers. The institution of marriage really had to go, untrammeled access to abortion was a must, free pornography was a basic human right—all of this was woven into the fabric of his heart and mind.

And this was why he had responded to the news of Ace's behavior over in Colorado with such a cold fury. He had been on the phone with the governor of Colorado numerous times, from the very first day the news broke, and he had formed the idea of direct action when he was first informed that it was to be a simple "destruction of property" case. He calmed down somewhat after he heard that it had been upgraded to a murder charge, but the idea of direct action remained, kind of floating in the back of his mind.

So as the general public saw it, Ace's trial looked like a reg-ular trial. And Felix had assurances from the governor of Col-orado that there was going to be a guilty verdict regardless. But Felix was still nervous. He had some intelligence operatives in Colorado, and they assured him that Connorson's vanity had already lapped his competence about ten times. And Felix was such a true believer in the sexual revolution that he had a fur-nace of hatred in his gut set apart for Ace and people like him. He would not be satisfied with some kind of technical victory, with an obviously fixed "guilty" verdict trickling in. He wanted Ace's end to be *spectacular*. So when the clown show that was the prosecution began to show some signs of unraveling to back-channel observers, Felix being chief among them, and clown after clown tumbled out of that little car, the possibility of direct action floated back to the front of his mind. Once the notion coalesced behind his forehead, it only took a few moments to harden. And once it had hardened, it was just a few moments more before he was on the phone to his director of security.

The director of security was actually something more than his director of security. As the United States had been going through its slow-motion unraveling, a number of the governmental functions that had previously been carried by the feds had been quietly, gradually, picked up by the states. And different aspects of these governmental functions had been assumed by different states, depending on local politics and interests.

In California, the governor had accumulated something of a private army. He knew that when the inevitable food riots came, he could not count on federal help. And so he had quietly and efficiently built up a significant number of troops, operating ostensibly under the aegis of the National Guard. And he had made sure that this force contained various special forces teams, trained and ready for forays into any neighboring states as occasion demanded. The occasion of Ace-in-Colorado seemed to him to be one such situation. He knew in his bones that Colorado was going to bobble it, and he also knew—from the electric reception that Ace had gotten in Alabama—why on earth had Colorado allowed something like *that*?—and from the way the trial and PR circus in Colorado appeared to be going—that the end result could easily be that the progressive movement everywhere was going to be made a laughingstock.

This director of security was the governor's right hand man, and he was in charge of all the armed forces in California. After future independence, and after Felix was *El Presidente*, this man—his name was Ryker—would be the commandant of all the armed forces. He was not a career politician like Felix was, but he fully understood everything once Felix explained it to him.

In this case, Ryker understood why Ace had to go, and he told the governor that he had just the unit for an operation like that. Any particular time frame? The sooner the better? Ryker thought he might lead that unit himself. Got it. Bye.

That evening Ryker drove thoughtfully out to the base—he wasn't about to deliver these orders using electronics. The drive was about forty-five minutes, and since most of it was in the desert, he thought he could use the time to unwind a bit. Besides, an old girlfriend lived just on the other side of the base. Maybe this would be a good time to catch up.

A PROVIDENTIAL POTHOLE

Just as the wheels of Pharaoh's chariots started to come off when the Lord undertook for Israel, so also the right front wheel of Ryker's car went into a pothole when the Lord undertook for Ace Hartwick.

Ace and Stephanie came out of the print shop where they had dropped off some prints to be made into foam core posters—Jon was the kind of attorney who liked to use visuals with a jury. Stephanie went out the door that Ace was holding for her, glared at him briefly, and started back toward the right, heading to the lot where their car was parked. Ace trotted for a minute, caught up with her on her right, walked a couple of paces, and then moved briskly over to her left.

Stephanie glanced at him. "So *that* seemed intentional. What was that about?"

Ace seemed slightly embarrassed, coughed slightly, and said, "It was in a book I read—an old book, admittedly—where the author said that a gentleman always walks between the curb and the lady he is with."

Stephanie stopped and stared at him. Ace took another step, stopped, and turned back around. "What?" he said.

"Who was this author?" she demanded. "Was it Roland of York, or someone else from the fourteenth century?"

Ace shrugged. "A little thing, but little things are big things. If you take my meaning."

"No, I don't. Move over," she said. "I'm going to walk there."

"No," Ace said.

Stephanie stared some more, and then lowered her gaze. "Not worth fighting about. But I can honestly say that there are times when I can't *believe* you."

Their little spat over, or at least with the verbal part of it over, they walked for another half a block, and were about to turn right again to head for the parking lot. A car engine racing caught Ace's ear, and he looked back over his left shoulder, and saw a hybrid Jeep Cherokee speeding up, about twenty feet behind them. As it came, Ace saw an arm extending from the front seat on the passenger's side, with an unmistakable pistol shape in the hand. He caught a vague glimpse of a ski mask inside, and he instinctively braced himself.

Everything in the next second seemed to happen all at once. Stephanie had not turned to see the car and was simply walking as before. The Cherokee pulled alongside, and the arm was fully extended. At that moment, the driver—who would hear about it later from Ryker—hit a pothole with his right front tire. Now this was the kind of pothole that Denver had become famous for, and given the fact that it was the kind you could fit a five-gallon bucket in, the remarkable thing was that Ryker got his shot off at all, and even in the general direction of the young couple.

The bullet whirred past them and shattered the brick facing of the store behind them. A number of startled pedestrians were looking at the car, and several were trying to get the license plate number. Not that it would have done them any good if they got it, because the plates were entirely bogus. But they were being good citizens anyway.

Ace stepped away from Stephanie, and they both looked at each other, eyes wide open. Before they had a chance to say anything, some of the nearby pedestrians rushed up to see if they were okay. They were, and so after a few moments everyone started to drift back to their routines. All the excitement was plainly over. When they were gone, Stephanie said, "Don't you think we should report this to the cops?" Ace grimaced. "I have no doubt that whoever is behind this is well outside the reach of the local cops. And the local cops are probably not out of *their* reach. But I think your dad would tell us that we need to report it. It could be used against us if we didn't report it, right?"

"Right," Stephanie said.

Ace shook his head. "The only real botheration is that talking to the cops will be a good two hours down a rat hole. But let's get it over with."

RESPECT PORN

The following day, Jon heard the front door open and close, and waited for a moment while she hung her coat up.

"Stephanie!" Her father called to her from his study, when he saw her flit by his doorway on her way to her room.

"Minute!" she called back.

It was actually two or three minutes before she appeared in his doorway again, with an apple in her hand that she had fetched from the kitchen. "Sorry I couldn't stop earlier. I was afraid I would die of starvation. I thought I might languish on the way."

Her father gestured to the wingback chair he kept there for visitors. "Hey, bright eyes. Do you have a moment for a serious question? Or two?"

"This is about Ace, isn't it?"

Her father nodded. "Yes, about Asahel."

Stephanie sat down in the chair, put the apple untouched on the side table by her, and put both her hands on her knees.

"From the fact that you sat down, I gather that you don't mind me asking?"

Stephanie shook her head. "No, I don't mind you asking. I really appreciate it, actually."

"So my question is simple, really. Do you have feelings for him?"

Stephanie covered her face with her hands, just for a moment, and then lowered them. She looked straight back at her father. "It would be far more accurate to say that I have feelings *because* of Ace. My emotional weather right now is in a state of absolute churn."

Her father looked at her sympathetically.

"Look, Stephanie, since your mother left, and because of the reasons she had for leaving—many of them pointed, barbed, and compelling, if we are being honest—I have not felt that I have had much moral capital when it came to giving you advice about relationships. Fortunately, you seemed to have a pretty good instinct for avoiding the toads, Lionel excepted, and so I haven't felt that you really needed my input. I didn't feel like I was leaving you unprotected, in other words. But I would be willing to listen now, if you would like, and I would be willing to give you my thoughts, if you wanted them."

"I would love it if you would listen to me," Stephanie said. "And I would be really grateful for anything you have to say."

And so at this her father just waited while she composed her thoughts.

"There are two things I can't get right side up," she began. "Ace makes me feel things I have never ever felt about any boy, whether in high school, or now in college. And after what he did in that assassination attempt, I have felt like one of those damsels in those dark-web respect-porn videos."

Her father's eyebrows shot up. "Wait . . . what?! *What* is a respect-porn video?"

Stephanie laughed. "Oh, you haven't heard about those? They are two to three minute video vignettes where a defenseless female of some sort is rescued from some terrible danger by a dashing hero. I have heard that when they first started coming out, there was sex in them, like regular porn. But they were a big hit, and the producers or whatever figured out early on that they were not a big hit because of the sex. Now they are just rescued maiden fantasies, five to ten minutes each. I have only seen a couple of them. A classmate in freshman year—and boy, was *she* a piece of work—showed them to me. They are really corny, but I couldn't watch more than two. But that was because they really messed me up. They use *all* the illegal stereotypes, and a few of the remaining legal ones. They are all over the dark web."

Her father sat back in his chair. "I keep saying things like 'now I have heard of everything,' and I really need to stop saying that. It is *never* true. Anyway . . . you were saying something . . . else?"

"Yes. I felt just like one of those women in the videos, and while I really thanked him for what he did—he knows I am grateful—I just barely restrained myself from saying *my hero,* and squeezing his biceps. And the more I think about it, the more I realize that I have absolutely no categories to understand someone like him."

Her father waited, silently, knowing that she was not done.

"There is some kind of profound conflict going on. I know that. And I know all the propaganda from the Colorado Human Rights joke *is* propaganda, and that it could not bear five minutes of serious analysis, and yet it turns out that I have been entirely shaped by it anyway. I respect Ace like no other guy I have ever met, and as soon as I start to think down those lines, like I am actually looking up to him, I start accusing myself of being a silly little female. I start *acting* like a silly little female, at least on the inside."

Her father waited again.

"He messes me up worse than those two videos did."

Jon leaned forward. "We haven't had a real chance to talk since the shooting. What did Ace do, exactly?"

"Well, we were walking down the sidewalk, on Second, near those tattoo parlors, and I heard a gunshot from a passing car. At the same moment, I heard an angry *whizzz* go by our heads, like a half-pound bumblebee that figured out how to go a thousand miles per hour. The bricks just to the right of us, on the store front, shattered. Without any hesitation, without missing a beat, Ace picked me up by the waist, pushed me flat against that wall, and then stood in front of me, his back to me and his arms splayed out. I was completely covered, completely protected. He just stood that way until the car with the shooter in it tore through a red light, and around the corner."

"Uh huh," her father said. "I get it. He certainly is a fine young man." Jon's esteem for Ace, already high, had gone quite a bit higher. "What was the second thing? You mentioned earlier there were two things."

"Well, as you well know, Ace is a Christian, and I am not. And he is the kind of Christian who would never have anything to do with someone who isn't. He doesn't wear it lightly, in other words."

"So I think I see what the problem is there, but you tell me what you think it is."

Stephanie replied, "I decided, back in high school, that I wanted nothing more than to be intellectually honest. I made that decision after two semesters with Mr. Satler in sociology—he affected me like looking at the winos downtown could make someone want to be really careful with alcohol. But I realized that meant being honest with *myself* in the first instance. If you can't tell yourself the truth, then anything you say to all the others will necessarily be spin."

"Go on."

"So I realize that there is no possible logical connection between whatever possible feelings I might have for Ace, on the one hand, and whether or not Jesus rose from the dead, on the other."

"I do take your point," her father said.

"If I ever were to become a Christian, which I *was* thinking about before Ace, honest, it can't be good to attempt something like that with tainted motives. And my motives right now are tainted all the way through, top to bottom, front to back. Jesus didn't rise from the dead because Ace has dimples when he smiles."

"Well," her father said, "this second issue is actually an easier one for me to speak to . . . because I went through the same thing exactly."

Stephanie's eyebrows shot up. *"Really?"*

"Almost exactly, I should say. When your mother left me, and ran off with a *woman* to boot, she was aiming at my pride. And, I have to say, she had a pretty big target, kinda fat and out there, and it would have been pretty difficult for her to miss. I was miserable, humiliated, embarrassed, angry, the lot. That lasted for about two months—you probably remember it."

"I remember it very well. I was really worried about you."

"But Jesus didn't rise from the dead because my male vanity was insulted. Those things are not *logically* connected."

"Right. Exactly. So what happened?"

"I came to the realization that they *were* logically connected."

"And that's the kind of thing I just don't see."

"Our individual motives didn't exist two thousand years ago when Jesus rose, and so His resurrection is in no way dependent on them. But our individual motives for everything we do *are* interconnected with everything else we do, and that means they are connected to our reasons for refusing to repent. When the gospel is preached, the invitation given is to *repent and believe*. The circumstances we are in don't have anything to do with the resurrection in history. But they do have something to do with our motives for repenting, or not repenting, as the case may be. They do affect our willingness for the resurrection to have been a real historical event."

Her father paused for a moment. Stephanie was looking at the floor. "Go on," she said.

"So all along it was my smug male vanity that had been preventing me from wanting God in my life. That was the wall. *That* was the barrier. In my conceits, I wanted to be the ultimate self-made man. Like a puffy-faced two-year-old, I was all about 'me do it.' That was my idol, and although your mom didn't intend the results that came about through her actions, that was the idol she successfully knocked down."

"And so what is *my* idol then?"

"I suspect—although I don't know—I suspect that this is where your second issue maps onto your first issue. You are in a frightful churn because Ace makes you feel like you want to submit to him, fully, completely. That collides with your desire to be fierce, independent, and autonomous."

"That's the same idol as yours . . ."

"Well, yes. You are your father's daughter. Sorry about the baggage you got from me."

Stephanie blushed, but still pursued the point. "So how does this relate to the issue of Jesus?"

"If Jesus rose from the dead, being fierce and independent is not quite the virtue you thought it was—at least not in the same way. Ace makes you feel like you want to throw down your shield and surrender. You now know what that emotion feels like. But once your shield is down, no telling what might happen. That same shield is what you have been using to keep Christ away also."

She stood up, and picked up her apple. "Do you remember how you used to call me your little spitfire?"

Her father smiled. "I most certainly do. I hope you realize that there were occasionally *reasons* for doing so . . ."

Stephanie laughed. "Oh, I know that part. I really appreciate you being willing to say things like this. And I *will* think about it. Promise. But at the same time, I hope you realize that what you are saying makes me *want* to spit fire. And throw things. I would have thrown this apple if I weren't so hungry."

Her father smiled. "'Night, doll babe."

CHAPTER 8

THE THICK PLOTTENS

STEPHANIE MAKES TWO SPLASHES

A battered Toyota pulled into the spacious, pot-holed, and faded parking lot located on the north side of the courthouse, in between that courthouse and the community center. The community center had rooms big enough for the kind of press conference that was intended to happen, as well as rooms small enough for the weekly meetings, also held there, meetings dedicated to the empowerment of deaf alcoholics.

The asphalt had originally been black, jet black, but since it had been put down quite a number of years before this, back when those responsible for parking lots had monies available for things like asphalt, the color was now decidedly gray. A very non-jet gray. The little islands around the light poles were full of cheat grass, and there were even pockets of grass pushing up through the potholes.

Left alone for another century, the parking lot would be completely reclaimed by nature. Except for the light poles.

After parking it, a slimeball attorney got out of his Toyota cautiously, and then opened the back door on the driver's side, and rummaged for a moment before pulling out his briefcase. We perhaps do not know him well enough yet to consider him as a slimeball, but from the first moment he enters our story, he is doing so in a manner calculated to fit that description.

The slimeball attorney did not have a name to match. His name was dignified enough, and probably a little bit too digni-fied, and the business cards he had his name embossed on were a little bit more dignified than *that*. His business cards looked like the invitation to a coming out party for a Houston debutante in the early 1950s. And since we are talking about it so much, that attorney's name was Dwight Glastonbury III, Esq., and he was the one who had called this "most important" press conference for ten am that day, and had done this on the previous day—and so here he was now.

He had let the press know that what he was going to an-nounce concerned Asahel Hartwick's *past*, and that they would be gravely disappointed if they were to miss it. There were some things about his behavior in the *past* that would interest them very much indeed. Young Ace was by no means the holy joe that he was purporting to be.

As it happened, Glastonbury was representing a young wom-an named Isadora Meadows, a young lady who had attended the same Christian high school that Ace had attended. Their times had overlapped by exactly one year—Ace's senior year, and her junior year. After the controversy broke, and after it began to look like Ace might have some public support, even in the blue states, she had contacted Glastonbury, having gotten his number off a billboard. He wasn't an ambulance chaser because the ambulances would just drive by the billboard. He didn't need to *chase* anything. The billboard was stationary.

Isadora had told Glastonbury a lurid tale of lies, sex, abuse, and terror. Ace was a predator, a dangerous man, one whose toxic masculinity just seeped out of him and puddled on the floor. He had groomed her at first, dazzling her with promises of fame and glory, which she had believed because he was a lofty senior. And then he had lured her to a secret lair of his, she couldn't remember where exactly, and had threatened her, raped her, threatened her family repeatedly, and he then had topped it all off by fat-shaming her.

Glastonbury had believed all of this, quite naturally, and scheduled the news conference at a community center right across from the courthouse, and had timed it so that the reporters covering Ace's trial could just pop in across the parking lot in order to listen to Glastonbury read Isadora's statement accusing Ace of numerous dark deeds, and concluding with an eloquent peroration, urging us never to let go of that hard-won lesson, which was the absolute necessity of "believing all women." The plan was to have Isadora sit quietly at a table in the front, while Glastonbury's legal assistant, a buxom nullity named Soledad, sat beside her in order to hand her tissues at regular intervals. The morning after he had hired this particular assistant, while he was shaving, he had told himself that he liked his paralegals to have a pair of legals, "if you know what I mean." Dwight Glastonbury III, Esq.

did know what he had meant by that, and had winked at himself in the mirror. He had that kind of mind, and he flattered himself that he exuded a great deal of *sang-Freud.*

The room was populated with hard plastic stacking chairs with steel frames, the kind that interlocked the chairs on the sides. The plastic was a not unpleasant gray hue, but that was kind of hard to see because every chair was filled. If you were fortunate to have a seat, you could see the back of the chair in front of you, and could ascertain the not unpleasant color that way.

If you looked down between your feet, you would have seen thirty-year-old linoleum tiles, held together by the wax that had been applied over the course of that entire time, and buffed repeatedly so that the strange mixture of wax and dirt gave the floor an eerie organic patina.

But the people who were gathered there did not appear to notice their surroundings. They were there for the occasion. They were there for the *event.* They were there because they were acutely interested in the applied sociology of personal de-struction, and they had every expectation that they would see something like that unfold in real time.

So the room was packed, all seats taken. Additional reporters were standing up and down the aisles, and cameras were set up all along the back. The pack reminded Stephanie, who had just managed to squeeze in the side door, of a crowded dog pound, with numerous mongrels quivering with excitement, waiting for the county official to throw some meat over the fence.

Across the room she noticed Lionel, standing in the far aisle. After a moment of wondering what *he* might be doing here, she resolved the mystery fairly quickly. He was no doubt there to show some sort of Christian solidarity with violated women everywhere, feeling, as he did, that Christians needed to be the first to acknowledge their complicity in the oppressions that we see all around us on a daily basis. An involuntary shudder started at Stephanie's ankles, and raced to her neck and head. *Gaakkk*, she thought to herself. *Double gaakkk*, she added, in case she had missed it the first time.

Glancing at the cameras in the back of the room, she made her way down the right side of the room, and stopped after she got into a zone that she guessed could be easily covered by the cameras. She had come because her father had mentioned in passing that a reporter friend of his had given him a heads up about Glastonbury's teasing of the story to the press, and how it was likely to be particularly fruity. Jon didn't ask her to come, and he didn't ask her not to. She had just decided on her own that she shouldn't stay away.

While she was standing there, back to the wall, waiting for Glastonbury to get his show on the road, her eyes accidentally met Lionel's, and he nodded at her approvingly. *Good to see you here*, he vibed at her. *Let him think that for a few minutes. After that time*, she thought, *he will cease thinking that, and he will think it no more*. The thought filled her with some measure of satisfaction.

The next ten minutes staggered around the room a few times, and then sat down abruptly, drunk. After that, five more minutes crawled around for a while on its hands and knees, looking for the door. Stephanie kept looking at her wristwatch. What *was* the hold up?

A little bit of microphone feedback suddenly broke through the chatter in the room, and the whole place quieted down immediately. A sound tech scurried off, trying to get away from the front of the room as fast as possible. Glastonbury, followed by Soledad, followed by Isadora Meadows, came through the door in one corner of the front, and the two women assumed their places at the table, while Glastonbury took his place behind the brown lectern, a rickety piece that was apparently held together by the veneer.

"Citizens of Colorado," he began portentously, "I want to thank you for being here today. I am grateful that you have chosen to lend an ear to one of the countless marginalized voices that unhappily make up such a large portion of our population.

"As a matter of law, custom, and justice, I want to affirm here today what we all know to be a foundational truth, one fortunately now incorporated into the Constitution of the great state of Colorado, and that would be the foundational truth that in order to genuinely come alongside the victim, we must *always* believe the woman."

Stephanie had been pretty sure he was going to say that, or something very much like it, and she was mostly prepared for what she would be likely to do *if* he said that, but was not absolutely sure, until that very moment, that she was in fact going to do it. But a moment later, she realized that she was doing it. She was shouting at a very startled room full of reporters.

"Why did you molest *me*, then, *Dwight*?" She put as much English spin on her Dwight as she could. If Dwight were a ping-pong ball, he would have hit the table and then bounced sideways.

The entire room stopped, as though it had collectively walked into a wall. And suddenly, off to her left, Stephanie saw virtually every camera in the back of the room swivel toward her. She waited until they were all positioned on her, decided in her heart to make it extra zesty, and shouted again.

"So why did you molest and rape *me*, then, Mr. Righteous?"

Glastonbury, who did not have anything like this in his notes, went a pasty, chalky gray, and looked down at his notes anyway. Then he recovered himself, at least partly, and looked up with a deep panic in his eyes. He said, "No, no. I never did anything of the kind . . ."

"What happened to believe all women, *Dwight*?" Stephanie yelled. She had found out that she really liked saying *Dwight*.

"Doesn't the Colorado Constitution say that you must believe all women? Dwight? Didn't you just refer to that?"

The Dwight in question stood there flummoxed, not knowing what to say or do. His press conference, his moment of triumph, was turning into something else entirely. Stephanie saw some of the cameras turning back and forth, getting some reaction shots from him, and so she decided to give them all as much of a show as she could.

"When I was fifteen, remember? Do you remember that, Dwight? In the bushes at your parents' home?"

Virtually the entire room was whispering frantically to one another now, but Glastonbury still had a microphone. He yelled into it. "No, don't believe her . . ."

"*Her*?" Stephanie looked truly angry now. "Her? Did you just assign a pronoun to me? Isn't that illegal, too?"

"This is just ridiculous. Just ridiculous." Glastonbury some-how knew that if he did not regain control, as in right this minute, he would never ever regain control. "Preposterous," he shouted, with veins sticking out on his forehead.

Soledad just sat there, one fist full of tissues, and Isadora sat beside her, not having received any of them yet.

And then Stephanie said her final piece, and did so in a mo-ment that must frankly be acknowledged by all to have been in-spired by the muse of all press-conference heckling. She shouted out, "Let me prove it. Let me pick one of the reporters here, from one of the reputable stations, and let him search Dwight's phone. I can tell him right where the files and photos are. Pho-tographic *evidence*, Dwight!"

At this, Glastonbury broke, and bolted from the room. Of course there would be no photographic evidence on his phone of any kind of wrongdoing with Stephanie—since they had never set eyes on each other before that morning. But, as Stephanie had guessed, there was plenty of other stuff on his phone, stuff that would be illegal even in Colorado as it had now become. We might even go so far as to say that he had stuff on his phone that would have been illegal in Belshazzar's Babylon. So, as I say, he bolted from the room. The two women up front followed him confusedly.

In the meantime, a garbled account of what had just hap-pened inside the room had made it out into the main hallway, which was by this point almost as crowded as the room was.

That hallway was crowded with red hot enemies of Ace Hartwick, mostly from the sex-doll aficionado community.

They had come to cheer on anybody who was going to bring any kind of comeuppance to Ace. This community, if you want to call it a community, had grown quite large in the Denver area over the last ten years. The first major step had been the decision to allow EBT cards to be used at the brothels—whether sex doll brothels or bio-brothels. And then when the condition of being an involuntary celibate, or incel for short, had been made an official disability by the state of Colorado, the numbers began to accelerate. The most recent milestone was the issuance of state-certified dolls as a way of dealing with PTSD.

At any rate, all these people had been pretty upset at Ace's recycling of one of their plastic pets. They had started with outrage at the time of Ace's arrest, and their emotions had done nothing but grow hotter as the weeks progressed. They were now approaching volcanic. There were not a few reporters in their number, and so the word of this press conference, and its anti-Ace nature, had spread swiftly. That is why the hallway was filled with hostiles.

And now it appeared that some radical right-winger had sabotaged the press conference. Rumors flew up and down the hallway, and morphed at very high speeds. Someone near the door started yelling and pounding on it, and the others in the hallway took up a chant. And then a number of them surged into the room, a room that had already been packed before.

By this point, Stephanie had made her way halfway across the room, hoping to escape through the door on the far side, a door emptying out into an arterial hallway. To her dismay, on the way over to her destination, she ran into Lionel, who was still clucking and tutting, and being officiously concerned. He didn't say anything about what Stephanie had done, but indicated to her that perhaps they had better make haste. Stephanie had no desire to be with him at all, but he was between her and the door she had been heading for. She looked around for another way. Maybe there was a different door.

But before Lionel had a chance to turn, one of the aggrieved members of the hallway contingent had forced his way to within shouting distance of Stephanie. "What did you mean by that, you little bio-slut!" he roared, trying to shoulder his way closer.

"Not what *you* wanted apparently," she said, and stuck out her tongue. With that, the man howled, and lunged, punching Stephanie in the right eye. She had never been punched before, and staggered a step or two. It took a second for her to collect herself, but when she pulled herself up to her full height again, she watched as Lionel's eyes got very wide. She blinked once, and when she opened her eyes again, he had managed to disappear. He was clean gone—he must have dropped to his hands and knees in order to scurry off that way. She couldn't quite figure out how he did it. But he was *gone*.

In the meantime, the man who had hit her was winding up again, still yelling. But suddenly, without any warning, *he* disappeared. He dropped to the floor, hitting his chin on a chair on the way down. Someone behind him had pulled out both his legs from beneath him, and that someone was now stepping over his prostrate body. The individual concerned was wearing sunglasses and a blond wig, looking like nothing on earth, and he leaned over to Stephanie and said, "It's me, Ace. Would you mind following a plan I have concocted since the outbreak of these, um, proceedings that you initiated?"

Stephanie could hardly speak for joy and for the pain in her eye. "A plan from somebody, anybody, would be just about perfect right about now."

Ace said, "When I turn around put both hands on my shoulders, and put your head down, between my shoulder blades. Don't let anybody else see who you are."

He then turned his back to her, and she followed his instructions perfectly. He then put both his arms up, like he was in a blocking drill in football practice, and he started to make for the far door. If you had been privileged to look down on that scrum from the ceiling, and if the jostling spectators and reporters had for some reason reminded you of an Arctic ice floe, then Ace would have been the ice breaker ship, with Stephanie being towed behind.

Once they got to the door, the hallway outside was crowded, but not jammed. They were able to get out to the parking lot without incident, although they could still see scuffling through the front doors of the community center.

"Thank you," Stephanie said. "Thank you. *That* was dicey."

Ace looked at her directly for the first time, and said, "*Yikes.* We need to get something for that eye. Where's your car? Can you drive? Can you see out of it?"

"I came on the bus," she said.

"Perfect," he said. "I'll drive you home. Come on," he said. He took her hand and began to trot toward where he was parked. Part of his urgency was because he saw a part of the crowd starting to spill out onto the front steps, and some of them were looking around with a higher level of interest than he liked to see.

When they reached the parking lot, he heard a few shouts erupting from behind them. Fortunately, the exits to the parking lot were away from the buildings, so he didn't have to drive any closer to the crowd that was fomenting in front of the community center.

When they got to the Hunts' house, Jon was out. Ace fished a pack of frozen peas out of their freezer, wrapped it up in a dish cloth, and had her sit in the shade of their front porch, holding it on her eye. He sat with her there for about a half an hour.

He wanted to ask her why she had blown up the press conference on his behalf, but decided to wait until later. She thanked him multiple times for not being Lionel, and he thanked her more than a few times for risking herself like that in order to derail the news.

"So tell me about Isadora," she said.

"I went over this last night with your dad. He was kind of hot about it at first, but calmed down when I explained that my contact with her was limited to passing her in the hallway at school, if that, as I am just guessing about that. I have no idea who she might be, or what might be driving her. Nothing to it, and nothing remotely connected to anything like that. But you knew that, apparently, popping the aspirations of Dwight Glastonbury as you did."

"Well, I surmised as much. But mostly I just *hate* trials by photo op. So I decided to hold a different kind of trial. A *reductio* trial, to see how they like it."

Ace laughed at that, and they sat quietly for a few moments, not speaking at all. Ace eventually got up, deciding to leave before it got awkward. "Bye," he said. "I have to pick up some books at the library. I will be back later."

"Seeya," she replied.

It was about fifteen minutes after Ace had gone that Lionel drove up to the Hunts' house, with three of his friends he had picked up on the way. He appeared to be the kind of man in whom the tag *self-awareness* had almost no place to attach itself. If self-deception were a form of spelunking, he came across like the kind of person who would have been lost in Carlsbad Caverns for more than a few years now. And yet, Lionel—even Lionel—suspected that Stephanie might be upset with him. He had decided he ought to come over to Stephanie's house immediately in order to smooth things over.

And this is how it came about that Stephanie Hunt managed to become a media sensation, twice in one day, and with each episode largely independent of the other one. For some people it didn't really count because they didn't figure out that it was the same girl until a day or two later. But most knew immediately that it was Stephanie, all right.

The first incident was, obviously, the disruption of the press conference, a disruption which had been entirely successful. Only one outlet even mentioned what the press conference was supposed to be about in the first place. All the stories were about the heckler who accused Dwight Glastonbury, and about Mr. Glastonbury's ignominious flight. And let our record reflect that Stephanie was quite insistent that what she did there should *not* be considered a false accusation, but rather an instance of her testing a hypothesis: Did Dwight really mean what he said about believing all women? "My hypothesis was that he did not mean it, a hypothesis which was subsequently confirmed. Science," she said.

But the second media sensation was what happened next, there on the Hunts' front lawn, while she was resting on the front porch, holding the frozen peas to her blackened eye. Lionel hopped out of the car and jauntily approached Stephanie. His friends followed behind, a bit more warily, having a bit more self-awareness than Lionel appeared to have.

"Stephanie! Glad you made it out!"

And when Lionel said that, Stephanie stood up, almost throwing the frozen peas. But instead she exploded at him verbally.

"You need to get out of here right *now*."

He spread his hands out toward her, palms up, like an earnest television evangelist. That was the first gesture caught on video by Lionel's friend Arkin, who had for some mysterious reason decided to film the happy reunion, and who then kept filming when it got interesting in other ways, ways unrelated to happy reunions.

"Stephanie, I . . ."

She raised a warning finger. "If you don't leave, and pronto, I am going to say some pretty *mean* things. And I would rather not have to."

He tried a second time. "Stephanie, I really am glad you are safe. I came to see . . ."

She erupted again. "Lionel, you ran *away*. The punching started and you just disappeared, leaving me there. You can't come back now, glad to see me safe. You don't have the *right* to be glad I'm safe." She lowered the frozen peas, so that he could see her black eye.

He didn't say anything, but stood there in the same gesture of pleading.

Stephanie leaned forward intently, and with a really fierce look on her face. Her good eye was fiery, and we may guess that the other one was fiery also, if we could only have seen it.

"Lionel, if I say what I am thinking, it will be really mean, and really, *really* crass, and then my father will think—even if he doesn't say it—that I ought to apologize for talking that way. But that would mean apologizing to *you*, and I frankly don't think that I would be up to a task like that. I am doing everything I can to warn you about your need to make yourself scarce . . ." And despite the fierce look in her eye, Stephanie was still speaking in relatively measured tones. She had to work to do it, and the effort was apparent, but she was doing it.

Lionel tried once more, and it was frankly ill-advised.

Stephanie lost her temper, completely and totally, and shouted at him. "Lionel, I already *have* a pussy. What made you think I was in need of another one?"

And that was the moment when Arkin thought he should perhaps be done with his amateur film project. He hurriedly put his phone away. But that was also the moment when another friend of Lionel's named Gaston—but not really a great friend when you consider what he decided to do next—thought that he was going to need to borrow Arkin's phone as soon as he got a chance, and get that nifty little exchange out onto the internet, where some more people could see and enjoy it. He accomplished this from the back seat on the drive home—all he needed to do was tell Arkin that his battery was low, and he needed to borrow a phone to text his mom that he wouldn't be home for dinner. Instead he emailed the video to his own account, and uploaded it a few moments later.

And that was how it came about that "Stephanie Lets Lionel Know" had 4.6 million views a couple of days later.

And from the thousands of comments online under the video, it would seem that most viewers were particularly taken with the expression on Lionel's face right when the video ended. "Like a gobsmacked codfish," read one. There were also more than a few comments in which Stephanie was asked out by the commenter, and promised a good time.

It was clear by the next day that Stephanie was going to be an online sensation, coming at the public from two distinct directions, and so decided she needed to have another heart-to-heart conversation with her father, the second one in just a matter of a few days. She liked talking with her father at this level, a *lot*, but was really embarrassed by how she had vented at Lionel.

She was pleased with how the press conference had gone, black eye excepted, but was humiliated by her loss of control, and by her language, and by the fact that somebody had filmed it, and all her conflicting emotions didn't help. She was soaring over how she had helped Ace, and she was simultaneously crawling along the floor because she couldn't get the vision of Lionel's last, slow-fade expression out of her head. He was a royal dweeb, but he didn't deserve the international drubbing he was currently getting. She had only read a handful of the comments below the video before she had flushed red and had to shut her laptop. It was right after she closed it that she impulsively decided to go see if her father was home and in his study. He was, and so she went in, sat down, and buried her face in her hands.

"Please talk to me," she said.

* * *

Exactly one day after the million-view mark was passed, this same incident was why Stephanie was interviewed by two pudgy lesbians representing the Colorado Human Rights Commission. Their names were Nina and Ryann, and they were currently an item. They would blow up as an item a couple of months after this, but that doesn't really enter into our story. It is, as far as we are concerned, neither here nor there.

On this visit, they were particularly interested in determining whether what Stephanie had said to Lionel constituted "hate speech," or was in any way intended by her to imply that it could ever be appropriate to use a reference to "female genitalia" as an "insignia of abuse."

"Well, yes," Stephanie said. "I lost my temper, but not my control. I warned him that I was going to be mean, and he just wouldn't listen. So I just told him in terms I thought he might understand."

"Yes. But *what* you told him, or what you clearly implied, was that he was the p-word. And it seemed clear to all of us on the committee—there were six of us there—that you were using it in a derogatory manner. That word is *highly* offensive."

Stephanie's eyes got wide. "But the Colorado Human Rights Commission is the *sponsor* of the annual Proud Pussy march. With the hats and everything."

"That's different," the stouter one said. "That's a *pride* event. Pride events are fully protected under the law. Slut pride would be another example. But if you call someone a slut insultingly, pardon my language, and if there is any indication that you believe the person receiving that appellation should *not* take pride in the fact of being identified that way, then the people of Colorado have every right to be gravely concerned. The same with the p-word. And, as it turns out, the people of Colorado *are* gravely concerned."

Stephanie sat quietly for a moment, just as her father had instructed her to. He had prepped her thoroughly for this inter-view. Then she said, "What would you like me to do?"

The two women glanced at each other. "Our normal prac-tice—since we regard the center of our work as primarily *educa-tional*—is to issue a warning, and attach a hundred demerits to your file. We did open a file on you, and if something like this were to happen again, which we trust it won't, you would receive a hundred and fifty demerits for a second offense. That would bring you to two hundred and fifty, which is the threshold for mandatory sensitivity training. But if you decided to take that training now, voluntarily, it would entirely erase your current demerits. But we would leave that up to you. If you think you would like to do that, you can just call our offices to register for the course. Here's our card."

"Are you going to ask me about what happened at the press conference?"

"No, no. I believe another agency will be taking care of that. You should hear from them within a day or so. I think that episode was assigned to the Colorado Bureau for the Maintenance of Free Speech. Their concerns are entirely different. But if you get any demerits from them—and it is not our place to say whether that will or will not happen—they will go into the same file. Very efficient, and a result of the reforms the people of Colorado instituted two years ago."

"Well, I think that's it, at least for now," the other case worker—Nina—said. With that, both Nina and Ryann struggled for a moment as they stood up from the couch, which was kind of a production. They stood at the summit for a moment, panting, and then gathered up their notes and laptops from the jet black coffee table, and started their departure.

One of the ladies, and this time it was Ryann, turned around at the door. "Your black eye is honestly pretty garish. Should I have a domestic violence counselor contact you? You live here alone with your father, correct?"

Stephanie shook her head *no, thank you, not needed*. "I was actually clocked by one of the sex doll rioters at the press conference." *One of your people*, she thought.

But did not say that out loud, along with quite a number of other things she did not say. Her father had been quite firm about that. "I think you have accomplished quite enough in that vein," he had said.

Nina and Ryann sat in the car outside for about fifteen minutes before pulling out of the driveway. They were having an argument, one that was three-quarters professional disagreement and one-quarter lovers' tiff.

"I have half a mind," Nina said, "to put fifty demerits in her father's file."

"Does her father even *have* a file?" Ryann said sarcastically.

"I will bet you ten dollars he does," Nina replied. She whipped her lap top out, and pulled her admin page up. There were a few chilly moments in the car while she waited. "Yup," she said eventually. "Here it is."

"What for?" Ryann asked, interested in spite of herself.

"He has one hundred and fifty demerits here. His wife left him for another woman some years ago. That's one hundred demerits when a woman files for divorce, and if she joins the sisterhood, it is another automatic fifty."

"What was the case? Was there even a case?"

"No, it was after that Abuse Reform Act, remember that? When a woman finds a man guilty enough to leave him, the state of Colorado decided to simply stand by her, and open a file regardless. He probably doesn't even know he has a file open. And I have a good mind to put another fifty demerits in it."

"He would have to be notified then, though, right? I mean, if demerits were entered for cause?"

"Yes, that's the downside. I would rather a dangerous character like that have a hundred and fifty demerits he didn't know about than two hundred that he did. He is an attorney, remember, an activist on the other side. If he knows about it, he might be able to pull off some funny business."

"What would the fifty demerits be for? That's what I don't see." Ryann turned and looked out the window, a little hurt.

"For giving that poor girl that black eye. Didn't you see that thing?"

"She said some guy at the press conference gave it to her."

Nina's voice caught a little. "In cases like this, you can't go on that. I had an abusive father growing up—he would get angry all the time. I got three black eyes from him. That's what made me go into this line of work . . . and one of those black eyes I had . . . it was just like Stephanie's. Almost *identical*. Goes to show."

"Maybe her boyfriend gave it to her," Ryann said. In the Nina and Ryann world, whenever a woman got a black eye, it was certainly domestic abuse. That part would go without saying. That would not be a bone of contention between them. But Ryann was a few feet closer to the truth of the matter than Nina, in that she acknowledged the possibility of more than one possible actor. And that is why Nina replied in the way she did.

"Don't come telling me about it. You don't know what it's like. Three black eyes I got. And I got them from my *father*. She lives in the same house with her *father*. Do I have to draw you a picture?"

"Nina, she said that he didn't do it."

"Classic. Textbook. Entirely predictable. I'm surprised they didn't cover this in that school you graduated from."

They sat there for another minute, and then Ryann said, "I apologize, Nina. You are ahead of me in so many ways. I was just a little hurt because you did most of the talking to Stephanie. And you had promised me that I could talk more. Are we good? I am truly sorry."

Nina grunted in a way that could be taken either way, and then said. "Fire her up, and let's go. Time to get out of here."

And so it was that the two women drove off, back to their natural habitat, a deep thicket of double standards. No language was off-limits, no matter how crass, so long as it was uttered in the celebration of vice; and no language that indicated any level of disapproval of vice, no matter how mild, could be tolerated for a moment. All of it was lumped under the catch-all word *hate*. And you, dear reader, simply because you have entertained questions in your mind about this, have been awarded fifty demerits.

CHAPTER 9

ISADORA REQUESTS A DO-OVER

The first thing that Isadora Meadows did the following day was sack her attorney. She arranged to do this, *in* person, *at* his law office, because she wanted to see the expression on his face. As it turned out, Glastonbury's look was similar to how he had looked when he was first getting input from Stephanie at the press conference. It was starting to appear to him, and rightly, that his one chance at fame and glory was gone with the whistling wind.

When she was done outlining his fatheaded defects, she slammed his office door on the way out for emphasis, cracking the window, and then she slammed the door to the reception area as she headed down the hall and toward the elevators.

On the previous day, Isadora had been fully and completely expecting to be in the limelight, at long last, and she knew, deep in her soul, that she had every right to occupy that limelight. It was her long-denied birthright, and she had been genuinely invested in the moment. She invested all her emotional resources in it beforehand. She had even practiced the night before with the tissues. She had known of her claim and title to this fame since junior high school, and yet somehow it kept eluding her.

And so, even though she had long experience with letdowns, this particular letdown was severe. It was far worse than usual. It had seemed so in the bag. At first, years before, she had thought that her destined glory would come to her through reciting her rewritten woke poetic versions of blues lyrics at local establishments with open mic nights, versions that recognized that many of the tragic stories in which "the-woman-done-her-man-wrong" were stories that had another side entirely. But the audiences kept not showing up, or leaving early, which of necessity interfered with their enthusiastic reception of her art, and eventually interfered with the desire of most of the local establishments to host any more open mic nights. After she had graduated from high school, she had ventured into the related world of poetry slams, but that proved unsatisfactory as well. That tiny world was filled with other poets who wanted people to listen to *their* stuff, as though such a thing were even possible. They were the kind of poets, and the kind of people, who spoke when her desire was for them to listen. She also had a small group of friends who would complain to one another bitterly, all of them also being destined for greatness. But it turned out that neither was such grumbling fellowship the appointed path to the elite zone. And several times along the way, as something of a Hail Mary pass, she had also experimented with what she was now trying with Ace, but they had both come up a bust.

Before she had moved to Colorado, she had accused her PE teacher of a singular misdeed, back in Kansas, but that one had come a cropper. She was young, and somewhat new at it, and had forgotten that if her PE teacher had an alibi for the time she alleged he was groping her, the whole case would of necessity fall apart—particularly in states where such cases were still investigated on the merits. And the time she had written on the police report happened to be the same time when her teacher, one Mr. Watkins, was singing the lead role in *The Music Man* in front of an enthusiastic and highly entertained audience. As Mr. Watkins was therefore able to produce about three hundred people, give or take, who knew that he couldn't have done it, she had been forced to retreat into a confused jumble of "may have been mistaken" sorts of noises.

The second time had been in Utah, where she had moved with her mom after the divorce, and that had been an initial success. Afterward, her math teacher, who was flunking her for inexplicable reasons that *he* said had to do with her quiz scores, was placed on administrative leave for three days. Her charges there had been more general and vague, in ways that would not allow her to be pinned down by specific questions, and so she was able to cause quite an initial stir.

But that one came apart during the police interview with her. She generally knew how to blow sunshine at her teachers, except for math teachers, but she did not know how to blow sunshine at cops. Or Utah cops at any rate. She might have done quite well in Illinois or Connecticut. The Utah cops would ask her questions, and then, thirty minutes later, they would ask her the same question, only slightly different, and they noticed when the answers were more than slightly different, and then they would ask her about *that*.

Teachers never asked you the same question in the course of the same test and if they had, they wouldn't have expected you to answer it the same way.

Poor Isadora was cunning, after her fashion, but not exactly quick on her feet, and so by the time the police were done interviewing her, they had about six flat contradictions in their notebooks. She retreated into the thicket of confused retractions, qualifications, and blame-shifting, and managed, on account of her age, to not get charged with anything.

But this! This situation was a gift out of the sky. Ace was universally hated by all the important people in Colorado, and so she knew she would have a sympathetic audience to play to, sympathetic from beginning to end. She knew that the media would not be awkward or tedious. And she had been in the same high school with Ace for a full year, which should almost be taken as a *sign*.

And then . . . Dwight had *choked* in his moment of truth, looking for all the world like someone had bounced a large rock off his forehead. And he was undone by a girl, and not only that, by a girl who obviously thought she was cute. But not as cute as Isadora, she muttered. *I can tell you that.*

And Isadora *was* cute too, or had been once. The piercings and Halloween hair were now something of a distraction, and deep inside her soul Isadora had diligently been taking her ugly pills for at least ten years, and that was finally starting to show on the surface as well. They were slow-acting, time-release ugly pills, but they were nevertheless very effective. But there were the remains of cute about her still, depending on the lighting.

However, Isadora was nothing if not industrious, and after her exit from Dwight's office—and now that he is disappearing from our story we will make free to call him Dwight—she strode purposefully to the nearest bus stop. She needed to get downtown, where the Survivors' Resource Center was. The governor had just established it within the last six months, and the chances were good that they would still see the opportunity in this as well. She had almost gone with them at the first, but had let that ambulance chaser Dwight get his foot in her door. She was pretty sure they would be glad to see her. Her cause was still good; the case was still hot; Ace was still the hated one.

She hoped the counselor she had first talked to, the one before Dwight had gotten to her, was in that day. She had been *so* supportive. Thelma had been her name. Was that right? Was it Thelma?

She remembered the way to her office, and sure enough, there it was, on a small brown bureaucrat's tag by the door—Thelma Lewis. Isadora took several deep breaths, hoped she was in and that she was in a good mood besides being in, and tapped on the glass.

"Come in!" The voice within sounded a bit eager. The center was still new, and had not yet caught on with the public, and so the staff, while well paid, was largely at loose ends with not much to do.

Isadora walked in, trying to look meek and confident at the same time, and was partially successfully in this. And Thelma, to her great relief, appeared fully prepared to forget all, forgive all, and embrace her as a wandering sheep back into the fold. Isadora decided at that moment that she would return to the sisterhood, fully woke, and that she was going to burn all her boats.

"Thelma," she said, "I want to begin with a confession. The last time we spoke you warned me about the patriarchy, and how pervasive and insidious it was. You said it gets into *everything*, and how it even gets into the resistance against the patriarchy. When Dwight came to visit me, he spoke so convincingly, and he sounded so woke that I . . . I *believed* him. Even though he was so evidently male. And how male he is was then established to the whole world by that blockhead performance at the news conference."

Thelma was nodding sympathetically, and said, "Yes, and I will wager that the contents of his phone that he was so eager to keep out of the hands of others would reveal additional male layers."

From this Isadora concluded that she was approaching this whole thing along the right lines. She stopped for a moment, and then resumed.

"So did you see it? I mean the news conference, or clips of it?"

Thelma nodded again. "Yes, I knew as soon as I saw it that I would see you here again. I could tell how disappointed you were in your attorney. And so I watched it several times through."

"And that Stephanie person . . . silly little muffin!" Isadora almost spat.

"Now, sister," Thelma said. "Never underestimate your enemies. Dwight was, as you put it so elegantly, a blockhead. But this Stephanie—I watched her particularly. A reactionary, no doubt, but she was no blockhead. We could use talent like that on our side, I can tell you that."

Isadora looked up sharply. "What do you mean?"

"She read the room perfectly. And she took the measure of your Dwight perfectly. I watched her size up the audience, and I think she understood Dwight, and all of his Dwightness, *and* the contents of his phone, within about two seconds. It was quite a remarkable performance."

This kind of dispassionate analysis of an enemy was a new concept for Isadora, and so she sat still for a moment. Apparently hating someone did not include a requirement that you hold them for a dunce.

"What about Asahel Hartwick?" she said after a while.

"Well, he's another one," Thelma said. "You may not know his attorney, Jon Hunt, is Stephanie's father. We need to be very careful here. I speak to you this way because we have a real need to get down to some strategic analysis if we are going to pursue this. Of course, it wouldn't do to talk this way in the hallways, or in the cafeteria. In public, we *do* want to hold to the line that reactionaries are stupid. It is an important public doctrine. But it would be really stupid of *us* to believe that in private. What motivates the masses would be disastrous for us to accept."

This was another new concept for Isadora, who up to this point would need to be considered as numbered among those masses. "What do you suggest?"

Thelma tapped the side of her coffee cup with a mechanical pencil. "Well, there are two options. One is to file a civil suit, which is the direction that Dwight was trying to go. The second option is for me to call the prosecutor . . . Connorson, I think it is . . . and talk to him about rolling your story into the case for the prosecution."

"But the advantage of a civil suit is that damages at some level would likely be awarded . . ."

Thelma held up a finger. "That is probably true. But if you join in this criminal trial, testifying to the character of this Asahel, and if you play it in such a way as to become a star—I do have connections that can make sure that happens—then there will almost certainly be a book deal coming out the other side of it. And then you will have the financial advantage regardless of what happens with the verdict. Less risk, the same payoff. Or perhaps more."

"You really think it is possible that Asahel might get off?"

Thelma shook her head again. "Almost certainly not. I know some people in the governor's office, and the trial is going to go down a path that has been well greased and well prepared. Of course they have to make it *look* like a regular trial. I don't think there will be any surprises *that* way. I simply mentioned the possibility out of an excess of caution."

"Okay," Isadora said. "What do we do then?"

"Well, you have to decide which way you would like to go. I recommend that you let me talk to Connorson, but it is your decision. I am happy to work with you either way."

Thelma sat quietly, waiting for Isadora to respond. It seemed clear to her that talking to Connorson was the way to go, and what she hadn't told Isadora (yet) was the fact that her husband, Mia, was the acquisitions editor for the biggest publisher in Colorado. That could wait. The details of the contract could wait. And the surprises that Isadora would experience when she finally understood the contract could also wait.

Isadora looked around the little office, not noticing how dreary it was. Thelma was being supportive, and that was all that mattered to Isadora. It did not occur to her that this was precisely how Dwight had reeled her in. He had laid the empathetic sentiments on with a trowel, about three inches thick. She had responded to that, just as she was responding to it now.

She looked at Thelma, and said, "Let's do it your way. Let's go with the criminal case."

LIONEL JOINS THE WRONG TEAM

Lionel stepped into the prosecutor's office uncertainly. He looked over to the left and saw Sara Yoder at her station, gathered that she was the receptionist—although because of recent advances in egalitarian office layout and furniture arrangement, this was hard to tell—and made his way over to her.

"Good morning," he said.

"Good morning," she replied. "How may I help you?"

"I wanted to see the prosecutor, if that were possible. If not, I would like to make an appointment to see him, as soon as possible."

"I see," Sara said, standing up. "Will he know what it is regarding?"

"No, I don't believe so," Lionel said. *What is a girl like that doing working in a place like this?* "If he is at all available, I am asking for fifteen minutes."

"I will check," Sara said. She made her way over to Connor's office, while Lionel's gaze followed her carelessly. He stood up, jingled the change in his pockets absentmindedly, and then sat down again.

Sara, in the meantime, was having trouble communicating with Connor. She said that there was a gentleman there to see him, if possible. She said that she had recognized him from a video, which she had, but was having trouble describing the video to Connor. "You know," she said, half-whispering, afraid that Lionel might hear her, even though he was way across the office, "the man who got told off by the daughter of that attorney you are up against?" Sara had already decided that she would not let anyone in this vile office know that she knew anybody related to any of this.

Connor laughed out loud. "Pussy man? Of *course* I will see him. I wonder what could possibly bring him here? Show him in." In addition to his other traits, Connorson was an insatiable gossip. He thought that whatever Lionel had to come to see him about, it would be good for a story or two.

But Lionel, whatever else he appeared to be—vain and conceited and effeminate would about cover it—was not stupid. He was there for purposes of his own, and revenge would have been a reasonable guess, and he had done enough research on Connorson to bait the hook well.

"I gather," he began, "that you have seen the video?"

"*The* video?" Connorson replied. "Yes, yes, I have seen it."

"I will not insult your intelligence by trying to pretend that my motives in this are white and pure, like snow in the high country. I do think that . . . that female needs to be taken down a few notches. And I think that I have something in my possession that might help to accomplish that. In your hands, I mean."

"You have my interest," Connorson said.

"You may have inferred from the video that she and I were acquainted prior to that time?"

"Yes, I did. Boyfriend/girlfriend?"

"Nothing as fixed as that. I took her out for coffee two or three times. I might have called them dates, she might not have."

"So this is all very interesting . . ."

"I am a cybertechnician, and not a shabby one either. On one of our dates, her phone started fritzing out, and she started to put it back in her purse in exasperation. 'Let me see that,' I said. 'That's my job.' She handed it over, and I had it fixed for her before our coffee got to the table."

Connor nodded again. "You still have my interest, but . . ."

"The short form is that while I was working on her phone, I was able to swipe her pass code. I have since done some checking, and I believe that I can get into her computer at home, and, depending on how generous you are feeling, I *might* be able to crack into her father's computer. There are no doubt some things there that you might find . . . fascinating."

Connor sat up straight. Now this was something he could deal with.

"I just walked in off the street, and I am not asking you to simply trust me. I know that you know that I am Lionel, the man she told off, but you don't know much else. Here."

And with that, Lionel handed across a slip of paper with a web address on it. "This should establish my *bona fides*. And no, I don't mind giving you that URL because it goes to a website of my own design, and the address changes three or four times a day, at random intervals. When I get into someone's *stuff*, shall we say, I have a way of housing everything of theirs all there. I already have hers, and am very confident of getting her father's content within a day or two."

Connor noticed that Lionel had not once said Stephanie's name. "Go ahead," Lionel said. "Type it in. I will give you the password—that changes all the time also."

Connorson swiveled in his chair, typed in the address, and entered the password. "Click on *projects* in the upper right," Lionel said. Connorson did, and sat back amazed. Right before him, ranked in apparent order of importance, he saw four or five profiles of Stephanie, tiled from left to right. Then underneath that was her bank account, and beneath that, a list of files that she had been working on recently.

Connor turned back around. "I am sold," he said. "What is the price?"

"I don't want to be greedy, but I do believe in motivation. I would like two hundred thousand dollars total, when all is said and done. I would like the prosecutor's office to put up twenty-five percent of it now, with the remainder to be paid out of the assets of the Hunt estate after you are done with them. And

I would like Ste . . . and I would like her to know that I got that amount of money from them, and thank you kindly."

Connor fully understood the resentment that Lionel was dealing with, but that did not make his feeling of disgust disappear. It fact, it accentuated the sensation. But what he said was, "Deal."

Lionel stood up, smiling with satisfaction. "I think I can be back here with some intel for your case and have it compiled within a couple of days. Sound good?"

"Perfect," Connorson said.

And with that Lionel exited, nodding briefly to Sara on his way out. He allowed himself a chuckle once he was in the elevator. None of what he had shown to Connor had come from Stephanie's computer. Lionel had spent the previous two days creating all of it himself.

A DEEPER WAY

Thelma's approach to things kind of startled Isadora. She had always had her eyes on the main chance, of course, and she was fully prepared to lie in order to get there. But she had been brought up in a way that meant she knew she was lying when she did. But the way Thelma was talking, it seemed that she fully believed the details that the two of them were concocting together.

It took about forty-five minutes before she worked up the nerve to ask Thelma about it. She needn't have worried because Thelma took the question right in stride. "Oh, dearie," she said. "I forgot that you hadn't had any training in this."

"Training in what?" Isadora asked.

"Not that it is any fault of yours," Thelma said. "The discipline really is new, and I only picked it up two years ago when I went back to the university for my master's. That was right before I got this position with the new institute."

Isadora shook her head. "But *what* discipline?"

"Epistemological Identity, or EI, as we call it. People have been instinctively appealing to it for decades—whenever someone says that something is *true for you, but not for me*, an appeal is being made to the foundational tenet of this discipline. But the discipline did not come into its own as a stand-alone field of study until the pioneering work of Dr. Germaine Tufts. Her groundbreaking work *Identity and Knowledge* set things on the right path. At least for her."

"Wasn't that the woman who was tried for trying to drown three of her kids in a lake or something?"

"Yes, yes. That was *their* story. But it was actually her acquittal that first made her realize the significance of the defense she first stumbled upon at that trial. Since that time, the field has exploded, at least in the sensible states. Some of our law schools have even begun to offer a course or two in it."

"I am afraid I don't get the reason why this is helpful," Isadora said.

"The world we are up against," Thelma said, "is a world constructed by liars who have arranged everything for their own benefit. The patriarchy is out in the open in the red states, but it still operates here in the blue ones, as you saw with our friend Dwight. It is actually more insidious here because of the pretense of friendship. And when I say this world is constructed by them, I don't just mean the big picture. I mean *every detail* of our lives, as we perceive them. These lies are propagated by the patriarchy, and they always seem plausible, even to us. The only way to fight their narrative is to invent a contrary story. And even if it is not what people used to call the truth, it is always a lot closer to it than what *they* are spinning."

"But what does that mean?" Isadora said.

"It means," Thelma replied, "that when you make something up, you are not 'concocting' anything. You are a member of an oppressed class—a woman, a survivor, and someone who has been fat-shamed, not to mention those other things you told me, like about how your poetry was mocked by various haters—and this intersectional reality means that whatever you say is the truth, *by definition*."

"That's powerful," Isadora said.

"It is the full meaning of liberation," Thelma replied.

SARA MAKES HERSELF USEFUL, AND LIONEL SURPRISES

Connor Connorson dropped a file on Sara's desk as he was heading out for lunch. "This is for Detective Morrison, who should come by in the next half hour or so. Tell him that I will have the file on his older case by tomorrow. This is the new info on that Hartwick case."

With that he promptly disappeared out the door, as had the other denizens of the prosecutor's office. Sara was sitting there at the receptionist's desk all alone, and without any qualms of conscience, she flipped open the file. Resting on the top was a memo describing Morrison's duties over the weekend, which apparently consisted of tailing one Stephanie Hunt. Sara's eyes got big at that.

She had recognized Stephanie in the news reports from the meltdown of Dwight's news conference, and after that, she had heard about the video with Lionel. She had looked that up a few evenings later when she had a chance. But all her experience with Stephanie directly had been as a recipient of nothing but unparalleled kindness. And she had already decided that if life outside her Mennonite community was going to be like life in this prosecutor's office, it might be a good idea to make plans to return to the old paths. In fact, about the only thing that kept her from doing that was her experience of Stephanie's kindness. In her previous life, she had never seen anything so foul or profane as what went on daily in these offices. But neither had she ever encountered anything so gracious as the way Stephanie had been to her. And here *these* people were putting a detective on retainer to tail her friend!

And with that, she pulled the memo for Morrison off the top of the file, typed up a near-duplicate, practiced Connorson's scrawled excuse for a signature at the bottom a couple of times, duplicated that, and shredded the old memo. What this meant is that Morrison would be sitting at a different house, a few miles away from where the Hunts actually lived, waiting to tail somebody else. And he would sit there for quite a while because nobody of Stephanie's description would come out. *Ha*, Sara said to herself.

But unbeknownst to Sara, and in a sort of divine sense of humor thing, there *was* a young girl who lived at the false address, and who (at fifty feet) looked a lot like Stephanie—which was certainly to be considered a plus for her. Sara had picked a false address at random, although she went the extra mile by making sure that such an address did in fact exist. Thus it came about that Detective Morrison spent his weekend driving to a pet shop, a hair and nail salon, a deli, an afternoon cinema, a mall, a restaurant for dinner, and then a nightclub. The following day was a bit slower, but much the same. Morrison came back with the dullest of reports and a large invoice the following Monday, and told Connorson that he was fairly certain that Stephanie was not a key player. How could she be?

As a small bit of misdirection, Sara's first time venture was a spectacular success, and nobody involved in that part of the business ever found out that it even *was* misdirection.

Sara spent the rest of her day in the afterglow of a deed well done. Her conscience approved entirely. In addition to the fact that she didn't really know how many laws she was breaking she had the thrill or sensation that accompanies being very naughty, thanks to her Old Order upbringing. After all, she knew she had to be breaking *some* laws. It was a most agreeable combination.

Almost as if it were a reward, it was that evening that the first real excitement of her life happened. She gathered up her things at five p.m., and a glance out the windows showed that dusk was well advanced. Her bus stop was on the other side of the parking garage, and as the wind looked cold, she decided to risk cutting through the garage. She had been warned against that by one of the women attorneys, but having been brought up among pacifists, she still had a great deal to learn about the kinds of things mankind is capable of. And besides, the wind looked cold.

She took the elevator down to the second level, and then cut across the garage, where she was going to take the stairs down the next level to the bus stop, which was right *there*. If the garage had been a safe place to be, it would have been the most reasonable route to take, all the time, every evening. But the human condition is fraught with difficulties, and she should have gone out into the wind.

As she approached the stairwell, she suddenly started and jumped back a step. A voice came from behind the pillar next to the stairwell, and said, "Well, what do we have *here*?"

Sara stood motionless, fumbling in her purse. Stephanie had given her a small can of pepper spray, and she was trying hard to find it. It had to be in there, but her hand was somehow coming up with nothing.

Two figures stepped out from behind the pillar, and then a third from the pillar on the other side of the stairwell.

"What's your name, honey?" The man spoke for a second time, and Sara said nothing. They were not racing toward her—or she might have risked running—but they were walking, slowly, deliberately. Her mouth went dry, drier than she believed possible. "Leave me alone," she said.

"But why should we leave you alone? You are beautiful, and we are so *lonely*. And you look lonely, too."

Sara took another step backward. She thought she had found the pepper spray, and was trying to flip the top off of it with her thumb, and without looking like she was doing anything at all.

"What do you have there in your purse, sugar?" the man said.

Suddenly another voice spoke, off to Sara's right. Someone had walked down from the elevators the other way. Sara's heart leapt with joy, and then she turned and saw that it was that perfectly awful Lionel man. Her heart sank lower than the place where it had been before. That was the man in Stephanie's video, and the man she had seen visiting with Connorson earlier that day. He must have stayed up in the office longer than she had assumed. But why Lionel?

But the voice was not speaking the way Sara thought a Lionel would speak.

"Time for you gents to move along," he said.

At that, all three men laughed together, and Sara heard the ominous *scchhick* of three switchblades coming out. She didn't know what that sound meant, but assumed correctly that it had to be bad. A second later, she saw the light glinting off three blades. Everything after that point happened so fast that she had trouble getting it all in the right order later. The man nearest Lionel sprang at him, his right arm swinging up in a vicious blow. Sara stifled a scream and shut her eyes. What she heard was a sharp but deep *crack!* followed by the kind of high-pitched scream that she had thought about emitting herself, but had somehow choked back. She opened her eyes, and Lionel's assailant was writhing on the parking garage floor, holding his arm, which was sticking out at a grotesque angle.

One of his friends, the one who had first spoken to Sara, swore savagely, and he jumped at Lionel. The third one, the one standing at the rear, was clearly having second thoughts already.

The second attacker came at Lionel the same way—their gang apparently had standard moves—and this time Sara watched in fascinated horror.

Lionel's hands were a blur, and in a moment his second attacker was on the floor next to the first one, his arm looking very much like his companion's. Lionel looked up at the third man, not even breathing hard, and said, "I want you to get these men out of here, and you have about ninety seconds to do it. Any longer than that, and you will have to make it out of here with three broken arms after we are gone."

With that he beckoned Sara to come and stand by him, which she did. The panicked third man had put his knife away, and picked up the other two knives as well. With some trouble, he got the first assailant to his feet, and he just stood there, shaking, leaning precariously to the left. With a little more trouble, he got their leader to his feet, and they began to stagger toward the stairwell.

"A little faster, please," Lionel said, producing a gun.

Sara stared at all this, struck for the first time in her life by the impotence of pacifism, by the horror of crime, and by the glory of rescuers. The three men walked faster, and disappeared down the stairwell.

"Let us give them five minutes to make themselves abundantly scarce," Lionel said. "The hospital emergency room is just two blocks away. That should give them enough time to invent a story."

By this point, Sara was simply staring at Lionel, without speaking. He looked back at her inquisitively.

"Well," she said. "I must thank you. With all my heart, I thank you. If you had not come along, I would have been in a terrible spot. *Thank* you."

"You are most welcome," he said. "Glad to be of service. But I didn't happen to come along. I followed you because I needed to speak with you."

"You *followed* me?"

"Yes. I had a question for you, and if these recent events have not altered our relationship too much, I think I still do."

Sara's eyes widened. "Well, your question will have to wait, because I have a set of questions for you. And perhaps they will all blend into the same question. Who knows you're like this?"

Lionel laughed, and it was the deep confident laugh of a man who has just broken a couple of thuggish arms, and considers it all in the path of an evening's responsibilities.

"So may I ask you to sit down for a minute and have a coffee with me? There is a shop right near your bus stop. It will delay you for a short time, but I trust it will not wreck your evening. And you may ask me any questions you want. And I do believe you are correct—they may wind up all being the same questions."

"All right," Sara said.

"And if anybody from work sees us there and asks you about it, you can just say that I noticed you working there as a receptionist and asked you out."

Sara looked at him sharply. "And that would be true. You *did* ask me out."

CHAPTER 10

MOTHERS

CAMILA

A couple of years after Jon's conversion, after he decided to start working with the CLD, he realized that he needed an assistant he could *really* trust. That was Stephanie's senior year in high school, so she arranged to do an internship with her father during her final spring semester. The experiment had been a spectacular success, and ever since that time Jon would (off and on) hire her as a part-timer, in order to use her help on particularly sensitive cases. His regular legal assistant was fully capable of managing the office, along with the movement and filing of papers and briefs, but there were times when Jon couldn't really afford to have his regular help present during some interviews or discussions. It would be a risk for him, certainly, and a *high* risk for Marcia, for that was the name of his legal assistant, if Jon were ever caught working hand in glove with a disreputable out-of-state operation like the Christian Legal Defense.

This problem became even more acute after the CLD was formally branded a hate group and banned from operating directly in Colorado at all. This meant that anything to do with his connections to the CLD had to be kept out of the official documents. And because Ace's case was of paramount interest to the CLD, Jon decided he had to bring Stephanie into all the discussions.

That is, he decided to bring her into the discussions—as his legal help only—after he had cleared it with Ace.

Ace, for his part, was more than happy to have her present in the room, in that she was anything but an eyesore, but Jon was on to him, and so remained suspicious about Ace's motives for wanting her in the room. But suspect motives or not, Jon needed Stephanie there.

And so it came to pass that the three of them sat down late one afternoon to work through whether or not they needed to nail down the status of this woman from Ace's past. After long discussion between Jon and Ace, with Stephanie looking on quietly, taking notes, it was finally decided that it was probably necessary to check on her. Ace had been with her about five years before this. She had been the younger sister of one of the maids in the house next door to the Hartwicks' and had been at least three years older than Ace.

"That was a time when I was extremely frustrated with my father," Ace told Jon, with a glance at Stephanie. "Not defending myself, just explaining. There was a point in there when I wasn't at all sure I even believed in God—at least that is what I was telling myself. If believing in God meant being like my father, I most emphatically did not *want* to believe in God. She had been hired on as extra help for some social event in the neighbor's back yard. I think I met her while helping them carry chairs to the back, or something like that. We were flirty for a bit, and then later in the evening, after the party was going hot, and her work with the set-up was on the sidelines, she came back around and found me in order to offer herself. It was a one-time deal, that was it."

Jon's eyebrows went a little bit up. "That was it? That was all?"

"Right. I never saw her again. But the two weeks following that were an emotional hell for me. It really shook me up because I felt like such a royal hypocrite. I was president of the youth group at church, had been a camp counselor, all that stuff. And my chief complaint with my father had been with his manifest hypocrisies—and I realized that I was not actually rejecting him by that kind of rebellion, but rather was on the road to *becoming* him. I also had a nightmare about a week afterward that about scared my jammers right off me. I would tell you more about *that* dream except I wouldn't want you thinking I was a charismatic. During that time was when I became a serious Christian and, truth be told, all of that was *why* I became a serious Christian."

Jon nodded. "So fix the chronology for me. The temper incident at your Christian school, that time when you were almost expelled. When was that located with regard to this?"

"That happened about six months earlier. In fact those were the two bookends on my little bookshelf of rebellion. The incident in the cafeteria was the start of it, and right after this immorality was when I repented."

Stephanie had been quiet during the whole conversation, partly because she wasn't part of the *official* official team, being neither lawyer nor client, and partly because she was totally peeved with this predatory female, whoever *she* was. But eventually she sat up straight, cleared her throat, and said, "Being mindful of my place, which has no official capacity at all in this beyond that of note taking, may I ask a couple of questions?"

Jon looked at her indulgently, as he usually did, and nodded.

"She came on to you, is that right?"

"Right. Nothing ambiguous about it. She said something like *let's just go do it,* something like that."

Stephanie seethed inside, being not quite sure why, but she managed to get to her next question. "And you were fifteen? And she was at least eighteen? So if there was a crime involved . . ."

Her father said that was right. "This was not a legal situation at all, and to the extent it might be one, it would be a legal situation for *her.* Our problem is entirely one of PR. As much as everyone wants to pretend that our legal system turns on the evidence as presented and the text of the law, that stopped being true quite a long time ago. This is going to be a trial in the glare of multiple spotlights, yelling spectators, and subterranean tectonic pressures. And this particular story, were it to come out, would be treated as a heavy spoonful of bacon grease for the fire. Our young Cotton Mather here has taken his stand for Morality and Purity out in the public square, and that was when some intrepid reporters managed to find some trashy porn under his bed. It has no legal import, although it may have legal *consequences*."

Stephanie glared at her father affectionately, and then turned back to Ace. "One last question. So where, if we might ask, was this affair of the heart . . . um . . . conducted? Anything particularly scandalous about that?"

"No, nothing that I can think of. There is a thick hedge back behind our house and the neighbor's."

Stephanie was about to say *how romantic*, but stopped herself. Why was she being so jealous? This was years ago. This was a strategy meeting, not a moment to stand by her man. And he wasn't her man. Not yet anyway. Stephanie stopped herself, and made it more emphatic by swearing at herself inside her head. She still didn't believe in his God, and mental swearing made her feel a little better.

And so after a bit more discussion, it still seemed right that they should try to ascertain what kind of player this woman would be likely to be, were she ever to become a player.

There were obvious risks in it. On the one hand, the reprobates and bad guys on the other side didn't even know that there was such a person, and, even if they assumed that there might be one (or more), they didn't have a clue as to who she or they might be. So the risk in checking on her was that they might lead them right to her. *They* might put this ball in play.

On the other hand, Jon hated surprises. "More than anything, I *hate* surprises. I would rather lead them to her and not be surprised in court with something about it than to play it safe and have her turn out to be some lying vamp that they spring on me. 'The prosecution calls Ms. Marlene Dietrich,' they will say, and she will walk across the courtroom in slow motion. And I will look down at the notes to see what I have prepared for this contingency, and will realize that I have nothing prepared for this contingency. There will be cold sweat on my forehead. I *hate* it when that happens . . ."

Stephanie said, "Father, you are doing it again. How many times has Marlene Dietrich been sprung on you. I mean, really?"

"In my nightmares, numerous times. My job as an attorney is to not let my nightmares come to life."

And Ace said, "And her name was Garcia. Camila Garcia. Nothing Germanic about her."

Because Ace still remembered her name, tracking her down had been pretty straightforward and simple. She still lived in the Denver area, was now married and had a couple of kids. They were able to pull up a picture of her online, and Ace confirmed they had the right Camila. The one surprise for all of them was that her husband was a pastor of an Assemblies of God church on the north side. With *that* discovered, it was rapidly decided that Stephanie could easily attend services the next Sunday, mingle with some of the people there, and come back with a preliminary report. As far as she could tell, was there anything to be worried about from that quarter of Ace's past? They might not learn anything at all, or they might learn a great deal.

The one argument against doing it in this way was Stephanie's current celebrity status. Even if she were not followed there, she would likely be recognized there, and if somebody then called the wrong people about that, there they would all be. But in the end they still decided to just go for it. Jon hated courtroom surprises a *lot*.

"Fine," she said to them. "*I'll* be the one who goes to church. Maybe you two arranged this so I'll be converted. But I am warning you both that if *that* happens, I won't stop with half measures. I'll come back speaking in tongues, too. That'll show both of you Presbyterians."

And so it was, just a few days later, that Stephanie pulled into a rundown church parking lot ten minutes before their services were scheduled to start and got out of the car fully preparing herself to *really* dislike Camila. The church had (obviously) once been new, and had not been a first-rate place even then, but even though it was now run down, the entire place was tidy and clean. The grass strip between the parking lot and the highway was mowed and trimmed. There was no litter anywhere, and for that part of Denver, this was saying something.

Several times during the previous night, and once on the drive over, Stephanie had gotten to the point of hating Camila. But as it happened, as much as she was looking forward to it, she was given no real actual opportunity to dislike Camila at all. Right after she stepped into the auditorium/sanctuary, she was greeted warmly by . . . Camila.

"Welcome, welcome," Camila said. "Have you visited us before . . .? You seem familiar somehow . . ."

Suddenly Camila's hand shot to her mouth, and her eyes got very wide. "Oh!" she said. "You're the girl in that Lionel video. Oh, your poor *eye* . . ."

She abruptly pulled Stephanie a few more steps away from the aisle, leaned over and said, "When my husband showed me that video, I must have laughed for half an hour." And with her hand on Stephanie's arm, she started to laugh again.

But at just that point the worship band started up, and Camila leaned forward, and said, "*Please* don't run off after the service. I am so glad to meet you. We have a fellowship dinner right afterward in the basement, and you would be most welcome to stay with us. We would *love* to have you. And I would also love for you to meet my husband, and to visit for a moment. There is something I do need to tell you. Now that I know who you are."

As Stephanie made her way to a seat somewhere in the middle of the church, she was muttering to herself in disgust. "Some secret agent I turned out to be." She sat down, still muttering.

She had never been to a church that was anything like this before, and so she thought that she had no expectations. But then, during the course of the service, when her expectations were consistently surprised, she decided that she actually *did* have some expectations. They kept bumping into what was actually happening.

The music wasn't half as bad as she had been expecting, and the sermon was twice as good as she had been expecting. Not that she was an expert on sermons or anything, but it was not a holy roller sermon at all. The hour and fifteen minutes flew by, and before she knew it, Camila's hand was on her arm again.

"Will you stay?" she asked.

Stephanie nodded, and Camila smiled. It was an impossible-not-to-love smile. "Follow me," she said.

"You're a guest, and so you go through the line first. I brought you, so I will accompany you. We don't want you to be lonesome. And then we will sit in the corner over there so I can tell you something important. Peter said he would take care of the kids so I could talk to you."

As they were settling in at their table, Peter and the children came by so that he could meet Stephanie. She complimented the sermon, and he thanked her. Then he turned to the kids and said, "Come on, littles." As they were leaving, he turned back and said, "We are admirers of your, um, work."

When the two women were situated at a long table, back in the corner, Camila's brown eyes turned serious. "I am so grateful you came," she said. "And I thank God that I met you before the service so I had a moment to think about it. All this is *providential*."

Stephanie just waited. It appeared that all the information she had been sent to assemble from various bits and pieces was going to be delivered to her in one, medium-sized, twenty-pound package. And so she just waited.

Camila took a deep breath, and started in. "I am going to speak discreetly so that my words can be interpreted in many different ways, but by you, only one way. I trust you will understand."

Stephanie nodded, fascinated.

"I know that you are the daughter of the attorney representing that fine young man. I want you to know that I met him, that young man, once, and that it was a year before I was saved. After I was saved, and when my husband first proposed to me, I told him everything about it. He knows that I am talking with you now and he approves of everything I am going to tell you."

Stephanie nodded again.

"The devil is an accuser, and he loves to accuse. We have rebuked him and intend to have nothing to do with him. The controversy your boyfriend is now in is all about Jesus—and you should be very proud to have a boyfriend like that, incidentally. But this is not about sex, or murder, or any of that stupid stuff. It is all about Jesus. And so you tell your daddy that we have been praying for him already, and we will continue to pray for him."

Stephanie had flushed red when Camila called Ace her boyfriend, but it still didn't seem worth correcting. And on top of that, she didn't want to correct it. And when she realized *that*, she flushed again. She was finding herself being pleased in unexpected places. She was pleased that *Camila* thought he was her boyfriend.

"And on top of all that, you also tell your daddy that you were privileged to meet with the quietest Pentecostals in the history of the world. Nobody here is going to say anything to *anybody*. Silent as one of those tombs in the middle of one of those Egyptian pyramids. As quiet as *that*."

Camila appeared to be done, so Stephanie thanked her, and the two women sat quietly for a moment. Then Stephanie spoke. "So all that's what I actually came to find out. But while I am here, would you mind telling me how you were 'saved'?" Camila smiled again, and her smile was still incandescent.

"Mind? I never get tired of it. I have to stop myself from telling it to the cashiers at the grocery store, not always successfully.

I had started using drugs, all kinds, when I was sixteen, and by the time of my conversion I was as strung out as it is possible for a girl in my weight class to get. After a bad stretch of a really awful couple of months, I was walking down to the freeway to throw myself off a tall overpass. I had stopped to use the restroom at a convenience store on the way there—first things first, right?—and as I was leaving the store I heard somebody say, 'Look at the bulletin board.' I looked around and there was nobody there. And because the bulletin board was in the back of the store, back by the soda fountain, I turned to leave again. The voice came again, 'Look at the bulletin board,' and I still couldn't see who was speaking. So I swore out loud, the s-word—I don't talk like that anymore—but I wanted to hide from whoever might be listening the fact that something spiritual was happening to me. And something *was* happening. It was uncanny, and I knew that *Jesus* was back there by the soda fountain, and so I didn't want anybody thinking that I going back there to meet *Him*. But when I got there, there was no Jesus, and the bulletin board was completely empty, with the exception of one notice, with those tear-off phone numbers at the bottom. You know those? There was only one phone number left, and the notice simply said, 'Want Freedom from Drugs? Call Here.' So I tore the number off and called, while still on my way to the overpass. The number was for *this* church—we have a very fruitful drug rehab program—and my husband, who wasn't supposed to be here, for some reason picked up the phone. It was way after hours. He admitted me to the program, right there on the phone, and sent one of the rehab volunteer ladies to pick me up. I was saved by the second meeting, and the morning after that, while I was brushing my teeth, I realized that all of my gunk was *gone*. It was all gone, gone, gone, and I was over the moon."

Stephanie didn't know what to say, and so she just said thank you. A moment later she added, "Well, I should be on my way. Thank you for everything."

As they got up, she realized that the basement had largely emptied out. There was only one woman sitting at the doorway by the stairs, and as they approached her, Camila said, "Hello, Victoria," preparing to introduce her. The woman looked up, nodded at Camila, and then looked over at Stephanie. "Hello, Stephanie," she said.

Stephanie stopped, startled, and stared for a moment. "Mother!" she said.

VICTORIA

Stephanie looked at Camila for just a moment, and then sat down next to her mother, Victoria Hunt, stunned and quiet. Her mother took her hand, and they just sat together for a few moments.

When Stephanie spoke, it was to Camila. "How do you know my mom?"

"It makes sense she's your mother," Camila said. "You're both so pretty. Victoria has been in our rehab program here for the last eight months. People with regular jobs have a special track where they come in for daily meetings in the evening. She's doing fantastic."

Victoria and Camila looked at each other, and both nodded. Camila said, "I'll be upstairs when you're done. I'd like to say good bye to you, Stephanie."

Stephanie nodded in agreement, and Camila went up the stairs.

The first thing that happened was that Victoria held up her hand in a kind of resolute "I have to do this now" kind of way. "Now Stephanie, there is something that I just must say at the very beginning of everything. May I?"

Stephanie nodded.

"When I left your father, I was simply angry, bitter, frustrated, resentful, and more angry. I was simply doing *anything* I could think of that would hurt him. I know now how much it must have hurt you also. Please forgive me. It was all just an overflow of bitterness. That is why I chose to run off with that . . . that woman. But after about three months I came to the conclusion that overweight butch lesbians are overrated, and so we 'broke up,' if you want to call it that. Because she had been my therapist, and was so good with words, it took some time for the reality to dawn on me. But it *did* dawn on me, and we broke up. Within a few weeks of that I started using drugs to deal with my wreck of a life, and that worked about as well as you might expect it to. It started with prescription drugs, and downward into the other stuff. What was left of my self-respect, and there wasn't much, rapidly went down into the basement too. In short, I left Jon out of anger, but after a few months, I stayed away from you, and Jon, out of nothing but shame. Please forgive me for all of that."

Stephanie nodded, tears welling up in her eyes.

"I thought about you every day, honestly I did. But I did not want you to see what I had become. I wasn't even a hot mess any more, having cooled way off. Everything was just *lame*. I kept resolving to pull it together, and then to come and see you, but there was *always* something."

"How did you wind up here?"

"Well, I am working as a realtor now, and I met Camila because they were looking to sell their house. Her husband asked her to set everything up, and so she came by to see me first. We were sitting in my office, quite private, and after we did all the paperwork related to the house, she just asked me about my drug use straight up. At the time I thought she must be psychic, but she told me later that from her background she could see all the signs of a strung-out woman straight off."

"So what did you do?"

"Well, God must have been working me over beforehand, at least as I see it now, because I was as ready for a change as it gets. I broke down in tears, and when she had me pray the words of a prayer she had in her purse, I just followed along, as relieved as anything."

The two women, mother and daughter, sat for another half an hour or so, just visiting. Finally, Stephanie said, "Well, I do have to get back." They exchanged phone numbers, and Stephanie said, "I am going to be texting you every day. May I?"

"Please," Victoria said.

Stephanie then went upstairs. Camila was sitting on a couch in a reception area for the church offices, watching her children playing on the floor. Stephanie came in, gave Camila a hug, and said she had to go. "But it was *really* good to meet you. Thank you for everything."

On the drive home, Stephanie kept pulling the longest strand of her hair, and tucking it into the corner of her mouth. It just barely reached. It was starting to seem to her like this Jesus thing was everywhere. First in her dad, then in Ace, then in Camila, and now with her mom. It was really good to see her mom again. And how could she complain if her mother was a Jesus freak? She wasn't with that awful woman anymore, and she wasn't on drugs. She had seemed really nice now, really pleasant, the way Stephanie had tried to remember her from her junior high years. And on top of everything else, Stephanie started to recognize how much she had been stuffing down inside ever since her mother had left. She had *really* needed her, and had not allowed herself to think or act like she really needed her. But now a retroactively fulfilled longing welled up inside her, and her eyes filled up with tears again. For a moment she thought she might have to pull over because she couldn't see very well. And apparently Jesus was part of that package.

As she pulled into her neighborhood, to the recognition of absolutely no one, she drove past a girl who looked a lot like her, heading in the other direction, tailed by a detective with the name of Morrison. All three of them were oblivious, and nobody was ever the wiser.

PATRICIA

The final thread in our account started to become visible when Stephanie was really struck, for some reason, by a line in the concluding paragraph of a column that Ace had written for the *Boise Statesman*. It made her think that he must have been reading Chesterton right before he wrote it. The line was this: "There is no way to treat things (like sex androids) as though they are bio-women without this resulting in the treatment of bio-women as though they are things."

As she put down her tablet to think, her mind drifted off to something that she and her father had briefly discussed early on. But when their first search turned up empty, they hadn't ever gotten back to it. Yet. Steven Sasani had been married before, back in Arkansas. And as far as the state of Arkansas was concerned, he was *still* married, to one Patricia Sasani, age forty-eight. But with that fact verified, they were unable to uncover any trace of her.

But when she read Ace's observation, the cynical part of her mind and heart (which was not an insignificant part of Stephanie Hunt) began to race. Why would this former spouse have to be back in Arkansas? Why not *here*? With that, once that random thought had occurred to her, she determined that nothing would be lost if she drove by the Sasani residence that evening after dinner. If she saw anything odd, or even kind of odd, she would mention her hunch to her father. It was just a drive-by look-see.

The reason it became more than just a drive-by began to unfold as she drove by the front of the house, and not too slowly. As she did, she saw Steven Sasani pull out of driveway and drive off in the opposite direction. She guessed it was he from the fact that he was pulling out of that driveway, but as he drove under a street light, the light flashed across his face. It was certainly Steven Sasani. So he was safely gone. And in a car.

She turned down the next street, and then turned left again into the alley that ran back behind the Sasani house. And when she pulled her car over, she stopped and got out. Since Sasani was clean gone, she thought she could afford a peek. She walked slowly toward the back fence, gravel crunching under her feet. She stopped at the fence, and after a few moments began to walk along it, looking intently at the back of the house. Then she stopped abruptly. Down at ground level, behind a bush, was a basement window, with one of those stainless steel wells around it. And coming through that window was a pale yellow light. As she looked at it, she saw—or at least thought she saw—a shadow flicker across it.

She was an impulsive girl, and so Stephanie did not even think about it. She had not seen a gate anywhere, so after she looked around for a dog and didn't see one, at least initially, she vaulted the fence quickly, and made her way across the back lawn cautiously. She wasn't particularly afraid of dogs, but she didn't particularly want to be bitten by one either. Neither did she want a bunch of noise, and barking was noise.

When she got to the window, she saw that the steel well was big enough for her to fit in, and so she knelt down in it gingerly. There was a thin curtain over the window, but she could no longer see any motion, if there had been any.

Preparing herself to jump out of the steel well and run for it if necessary, she tapped on the window. Nothing happened, but was there movement in the room? Stephanie waited about thirty seconds, and she tapped again. This time, after a moment, it looked as though the curtains rustled, just slightly. She tapped a third time, just one tap. The curtains pulled apart, and an eye, a woman's eye, looked out.

"Are you all right?" Stephanie asked. "Do you need help?"

The woman pulled the curtains apart, shook her head, and cupped her ear. Behind her, Stephanie could see a threadbare room, a simple bed, a table beside it, and one television in the corner.

"Are you all right?" Stephanie asked again, this time mouthing the words in an exaggerated way. She didn't know if that would help, but it was worth a try. The woman shook her head again, and pointed at the upper left corner of the window, and then, deliberately, and the upper right corner. The window was designed to fold out, but on the outside of the two upper corners a small steel plate was screwed over the jam and the window frame. Stephanie pulled out her phone, flipped on the light and looked closely at each one. There were four screws in each, Phillip's head. She looked back at the woman, held up one finger as much as to say *just a minute*, and vaulted out of the window bay.

She ran back across the yard toward her car, thanking her stars for her father's insistence that she always keep a rudimentary tool kit in her trunk. "You never know," he would always say. And *that* turned out to be right. You never did.

She got the trunk open, rummaged for a minute, grabbed the screwdriver, felt the tip in the dark to make sure, and ran back toward the house. She had a little trouble with one of the screws, but getting the plates off went rapidly. When she was done, she signaled to the woman inside, who had been watching intently, and the woman reached up and turned the latch. Stephanie jumped out of the well again, and the window creaked open, and jolted to a stop at about a forty-five-degree angle. Stephanie knelt down and spoke to the woman.

"Hi," she said. "I'm Stephanie."

"Oh, I know you," the woman said. "You're the girl who let Lionel know. I am Trish Sasani."

"Would I be right in assuming that you would like to get out?"

"You don't know how much of an answer to prayer that would be."

Stephanie looked at the woman, who was of a medium build, and then at the opening of the partially opened window. She thought that would be a struggle. She glanced down at the window chains, and rejoiced to see that they were set with small Phillip's head screws also. She set to work on them immediately. The last screw stripped out, and so Stephanie just stood up, and jumped down into the well, landed on the window frame, and smashed it into the bottom of the well.

Trish Sasani handed out a little case into which she had hurriedly thrown a few things. Stephanie put it on the lawn, told Trish to turn around and reach her hands out. "Just a minute," the woman said, and disappeared. She came back with a chair that had been out of sight, and then stood on it and bent backward, reaching her hands out into the night. Stephanie pulled as hard as she could, and they found Trish was seated in the well. A moment later they were both standing on the lawn, and Trish embraced Stephanie with the hug of all hugs. She then picked up her small bag, and said, "Where do we go?"

Stephanie said, "My car is right there, in the alley."

When they were both in the car, Stephanie felt around for her fob, and stepped on the brake. "This would be a marvelous time," she said, "for my car to start up like it usually does."

Which it did.

Trish Sasani was short and was somewhat thickly built. She had been a gymnast in high school, and was still full of that kind of bounce. After they had been in her company for a few days, Ace described her to Stephanie as an energetic rectangle.

She was brunette, with a few streaks of early gray. She appeared to have a cheerful disposition, and was quick to laugh, but she told Jon—as he was interviewing her prior to her possible testimony—that she was just trying to make up for all the crying she had done during her confinement.

The four of them, Jon, Stephanie, Ace, and Trish, had some extended discussions, one of them into the night, about whether they should have Trish go to the police to report her imprisonment. Trish wanted to report it, at least initially, but Jon was far more interested in springing her on the courtroom as a surprise witness. And after Ace and Stephanie explained the hassle they had to go through when they reported the attempted assassination to Colorado's finest, and how she would swiftly be made aware of the legal differences between Colorado and her native Arkansas (this awareness bringing much sorrow with it), she cheerfully acquiesced. "I am just happy to be out of there," she said.

CHAPTER 11

HINDU GOD OF WAR

FULL HEIGHT

Benson drew himself up to his full height, which was considerable. He felt himself becoming even taller on the inside, and he was feeling quite magisterial.

"Roberta, if Ace won't do the right thing, then we must step in on his behalf. I think in the long run it can only help him. Joanna Phelps with that big news clip service—they have millions following them—has asked me a number of times for an interview. We need to . . ."

"No," Roberta said.

Those who are knowledgeable about dams bursting will tell you that it can happen in different ways. Sometimes the cracks will appear years beforehand, and the Army Corps of Engineers will come out to look at the cracks, and they will scratch their heads, and put their hard hats back on, and write reports, and recommend certain courses of action. Sometime those courses of action are followed, and the towns below the dam breathe a sigh of relief. Other times the prudent course of action is shuffled around from department to department like a complicated game of "not it," and the department holding the report when the dam finally collapses is the department that employs the person who will soon become the fall guy. All this is a complicated way of saying that sometimes collapsing dams indicate to an intelligent observer that they are about to do so.

But other times they just think to themselves something like *why not now?* and simply do it.

Roberta was being more like that.

"No," Roberta had said.

Benson was startled, and looked up. "What?" he said.

"I said *no*," Roberta said again.

Benson had never dealt with anything of this nature from this quarter at all, and he was not quite sure how to respond. For Roberta had been taught, by her grandmother, and taught somewhat sharply, that submission was silence and silence was submission. She had diligently followed this outlook for the first half of her marriage to Benson, during which time he had developed *his* axiomatic and bedrock understanding that things were swell. It is fairly easy to believe you are an effective servant leader when you always get your way. When Roberta had been doing this in the first half of their marriage, she sincerely thought she was doing the right thing, and so she had just labored away at it industriously. It must be said that Benson had *sort* of a right to his misperceptions.

It was during Ace's junior high years that her real restiveness had begun. She had begun to suspect that something was off-kilter, and over the course of a few more years, she slowly came to the conviction that *everything* was off-kilter.

Right around the time when Ace first started taking his faith seriously and started doing all that reading, she had settled into the view that her marriage and her life were all messed up. But an object in motion tends to stay in motion, as Newton once observed for us, and her habits around the home were deeply ingrained by that point. As there was no new presenting source of conflict, she just continued to do what she knew, and what she had always done.

And so it was that Benson, who was oblivious to all of this, continued on with the serene understanding that he was being just the kind of man who is a godly husband, as described in the booklets distributed by his ministry. They hadn't used his picture on the covers, but they could have. He oozed servant leadership. Or at least that is how his thinking went.

He couldn't remember ever hearing Roberta say something like *no* to him. It was a novel sort of conversation for him, and he didn't know what he was supposed to say. He hemmed and stammered for a moment before he came up with, "Why no?" It wasn't much, but it was the best he had.

"Because you are wronging Ace by all of this, and because I have been wronging him by going along with it. And I am not going along with any of it anymore. I am done."

"Done?"

"Done. When we are finished here, which should be momentarily, I am going to give Ace a call and see if he wants to buy me a coffee so that we can catch up. You can come with me if you like."

"Honey, we have always agreed together that a heart for the lost entails . . ."

"The lost have little or nothing to do with this. Ace is not lost, although I suspect that we are. And we haven't always agreed on *anything*. You would just tell me things, and I would pretend to agree, even when I *did* agree. And I thought for some reason that it would be impolite or disrespectful to say what I thought, and you never thought it was curious that I didn't appear to have a thought in my sweet little head."

Benson was gaping. He didn't know what to do. He had no categories.

Roberta stood up. "I have no doubt that it feels to you now as though I am just letting you 'have it.' But I am mostly repenting of my own folly, my own laziness, and my own cowardice. I never wanted to stand up to you, and the possible benefits never seemed worth it, being very uncertain. But I miss Ace terribly, and I think it is worth it now. At any rate, I am going to go find out."

Benson stood up also. He was gesturing helplessly. "Roberta, we both love Ace. But his behavior in this whole tragic business has been tremendously off-putting to unbelievers. They range from disgusted to outraged—Jake showed me our latest internal polls—and so having a conversation about Jesus with unbelievers is nearly impossible in this climate. And that kind of disregard for the lost that Ace is showing is simply hypocritical, especially for someone who has been taught the way that he has."

Benson was not used to having to argue a case for anything—life at his ministry office was much like life at home—and so his objection came out somewhat jumbled. But he had used the word *hypocrisy*, and Roberta was rapidly discovering that bursting dams do not have a great deal of control over how much water goes downstream. All of it, usually.

"Hypocrisy?" she said. "Did you say *hypocrisy*? Did you forget that I was a computer tech when we met, and that I actually know how browsers work? And the limits of 'clear history'? I know what you do on your computer, and I know that it is a whole lot more *hypocritical*, to use your word here, than what Asahel is doing. Ace is taking a stand for righteousness, and at least he is going in the right direction, which is more than can be said for his father, who was going to suggest that we go be interviewed by that godawful reporter lady. And his father was doing this so that we could *act* godly in front of her, while we threw our godly son, our *actually* godly son, to those . . . sharks."

Roberta stopped, and her eyes got a little wide when she thought about what she had just said. Well, she was in it now.

"Go then," Benson said. "If that's what you want to do. Go."

And so she turned on her heel, and she went. She walked out to her car, which was parked in the driveway, sat down in the driver's seat, texted Ace, buckled her seat belt, and pulled out into the driveway. As she started down the road, her phone buzzed. Ace was free, and he would meet her there. As it happened she had suggested the same coffee shop where Ace's big conversation with Stephanie had happened.

HINDU GOD OF WAR

Benson was sitting on the edge of his office chair in his study. It was an understated study, with a handful of tastefully selected books on a few shelves, and an exhibition of tidiness itself on the top of his desk. Everything around him was in external order. The outside was completely and tastefully complete. But inside, his head felt like a baseball had just collided with a nest of Asian giant hornets, a nest that was on the large side, and all the hornets had just come outside to inquire about the baseball.

His initial emotion was anger, a sensation he had not felt for many years. How could this possibly be? How could she accuse him of being compromised? Without any warning? No warning at all? How *dare* she?

He sat there, cresting on the front of his anger, going over that conversation in his mind, again and again. After about a half hour of this, he stood up and grabbed his laptop, and sat down again to type. He was typing furiously, intent on telling Roberta exactly what he thought of her, her betrayal, and her desertion of him for Ace.

Ace . . . He thought about his son for a moment, and then shook himself. That thought had started him wondering if he really might be the compromiser that Roberta had said, and that was an unpleasant sensation. He shook himself a second time, and went back to the letter, and started to pour a little more heat into it.

He paused, hunting around for a riper adjective than the one he had started to type, and for some reason a long-forgotten comment of Ace's floated up into his mind. It was something about baptizing a sexbot. Why had *that* popped into his mind?

What had Ace said in their first discussions about all this? "About the only thing that could make things worse at that point would be if Pastor Rodriguez said that he *would*. And given that stinker of a sermon three weeks ago, he might just do it, too."

Just then Benson's phone buzzed at him. He picked it up and stared at it, staring at it as though a higher power had been at work, which it had. It was Pastor Benjamin Rodriguez. The subject line in the email was "Position Paper on Baptizing 'Alternative' Members Thoughts?"

Though Benson was sitting still, staring at his phone without even twitching, his internal sensations were quite different. He felt like a pilot on a low-level strafing mission who had flown straight into some power lines, and because of a remarkable display of God's creative use of the laws of physics, found himself within a matter of seconds flying at the same speed in the opposite direction. Not only was he flying in the opposite direction, but his finger was still on the trigger, and he was still shooting.

Ace had called this. He had, just as plain as day, *predicted* it. This had happened on a few other occasions as well. Benson knew that Ace did not believe that prophetic gifts were still operative today, and yet here was the third time when Ace had apparently taken an example at random, in pursuit of his argument, only to have that example come into an exquisite fruition a few months later. How did he *do* that?

Benson had been through enough conversations with Ace to know what he would say, but he still did not know how to make any sense of it. Ace would say that it was "worldview thinking," but to Benson it just seemed like lucky guessing. But when you start pulling hat tricks with such lucky guesses, it starts to seem like something other than guesswork.

Benson threw down his phone in exasperation, and stood up to pace around the room. His mind turned back to Roberta, and he started to heat up again. How could she just talk to him that way—out of a clear, blue sky too—without any warning at all? He started to warm to his subject again, but then the same thought stopped him short again. *How had Ace predicted the baptism of sexbots?*

He picked up his phone again as he was walking by his desk, and looked at the email again. There it was, still there, smirking at him. "Baptism of 'Alternative' Members."

The first time had been when Ace told his father three years before that incels were going to be allowed to use EBT cards for purchased sex. Benson had scoffed, and had scoffed like he had a true purchase on the facts, and then six months later what Ace had predicted just happened. And the second time was about a year ago, when Ace had said that brother-sister unions were going to be declared legit, as long as proof of sterilization was provided. And, he had added, that proof of sterilization is just for initial cover. Six months in, and nobody will care. After all, he had said, love is love. Just count on it, he had said. And then *that* had happened.

Benson walked out to the kitchen to get himself a glass of water. His head was buzzing at him angrily, and he was unaccountably parched. He was in his stocking feet, and because of his exasperation, he was walking a little faster than he usually did, and so when he turned the corner to come around to the front of the fridge, his right foot slipped out from underneath him, and his left followed immediately after. The glass in his hand shot straight up toward the ceiling, and Benson slammed flat on his back. A millisecond later, the back of his head struck the tile floor crisply, and with a *thwack* that would have sickened anyone who had heard it. But nobody did, and Benson said *ooofff*. A second later, the glass he had tossed toward the ceiling bounced off his forehead. *Ooofff*, he said again.

I should just lie here for a bit, he thought, before he lost consciousness.

He opened his eyes about three minutes later. But it seemed to him like it had been three hours, and he stared blankly at the kitchen ceiling for a few moments. *Where was I?* he was thinking. He thought, and then thought some more. *Roberta . . . Where was Roberta?*

And then it all came back to him in an incandescent rush, as his fury rose up before his eyes, before vanishing clean away. He remembered *all* his thoughts and arguments, and the letter he had been composing in the study, and all the heat that it contained, but the anger energy was just simply gone.

He stared at the ceiling for a few moments longer. He was thinking, but also gearing up for what he assumed would be the very painful exercise of trying to get up. He suspected that the back of his head might come off if he moved too quickly.

While lying there, one thought kept circling through his mind. *Ace is on trial for murder for crushing a mass of programmed metal and plastic. My son has been right about all of this.*

After that had occurred to him about thirty times, he decided to make a move. He painstakingly lifted his head from the floor, rolled onto his side, and then gingerly got onto his hands and knees. He looked down at the place where his head had been, expecting to see a puddle of blood. But there was nothing. Rising to his knees, he reached around to the back of his head to touch what he assumed would be a monster goose egg, and in this respect he was not mistaken. "Owww," he said, jerking his hand away.

Reaching up, he put his hands on the edge of the nearest counter, and slowly clambered to his feet. *Better go have a look at the old forehead*, he thought, and staggered down the hall. He was not mistaken about the state of his forehead either. An angry welt of a generally circular aspect stared back out at him from the mirror. He looked like a Hindu god of war.

He had recovered more of his equilibrium by this point, and so he walked back to his study. Without a glance at its contents, he closed out the letter to his wife that he had been writing, refusing to save the draft. *Farewell to all that*, he thought as he clicked the little x.

Now what? Roberta had said she was going to have coffee with Ace, and she said he could come. But did she really mean that? It was apparent to him now that he had not had any idea of what she had really been thinking for a number of years.

He had better ask.

THE ALMOST NAME

Roberta sat quietly in the coffee shop, waiting for Ace to arrive. She had been a few minutes early, and because Ace was on time, she was alone with her thoughts only briefly.

What thoughts she had were more or less peaceful. She felt serene, fully at rest for the first time in years. She had said what she thought, she had said all of it, and she hadn't taken any of it back. That had been her greatest fear—that she would walk it all back. She felt that a lifetime of lying and coward-ice were behind her. She didn't know what Benson would do. Would he leave her? Would he demand that she leave? She didn't know what she could possibly do to make a living if she had to leave, and so the fact that she felt so utterly peaceful was more than a little odd.

She had a pleasant face, with an oval shape and a small nose. She was a nondescript woman until you noticed her eyes. She glanced at things quickly, took them in completely, and was looking at something else immediately after. Her quick glances revealed her intelligence, for she was a very quiet woman.

She had known that Ace had great difficulties with his father, especially back in his high school years. She had almost said something then, for his sake, but had stopped when he started taking his faith so seriously. She wasn't sure enough of herself, and since Ace appeared to be dealing with his father much more effectively than before, she went back into her quiet mode. She had never had an open, heart-to-heart conversation with Ace about Benson. But she was about to.

"Hi, Mom," he said, coming up behind her. He had come through a side door. She got up, hugged him tightly for a moment, and then sat down.

"Have you ordered yet?" he asked.

"Waiting for you," she replied.

"What do you want?"

She told him, and he went up to the counter and was back, as Great-Grandma Hattie used to say, in two shakes of a lamb's tail.

Ace sat down across from her, and Roberta teared up right away.

"Ace, you are going to have to let me just gush for a moment. I have a lot to say, but the main part of it is right at the front, and if I don't get it out right away, we will be here all afternoon, what with me crying."

Ace said nothing, but put his hand out for her to hold.

"I told your father earlier today that I was going to come see you, regardless of what he thought about it. I need to apologize to you for going along with cutting you off, and I also need to apologize to you for not intervening on your behalf years ago, especially during that rough patch in high school. I am very sorry."

Ace nodded. He didn't need to say anything about forgiveness because it was all obviously there. The moment was full of forgiveness. The whole coffee shop was full of forgiveness.

She spoke rapidly, quietly, for about five minutes. When she was done, Ace said, "My turn?"

She said all right, and Ace brought up a few things that had troubled his conscience for some time—times when he had known his mother was suffering, but he hadn't brought the subject up because he knew he didn't have anything to say. "But I should have anyway," he said.

They talked for three hours. When the time came when it would be necessary to leave or to buy another set of drinks, Roberta's phone buzzed in her purse. She pulled it out, glanced at the screen, and paled slightly. "It's from your father," she said.

"Open it," he said. "I'm here."

"Please come home," she read aloud. "You were right about everything, and I have been a fool. You don't have to worry about coming home. Give Ace my love, and my respect. If you get here before eight, I won't be here, because Pastor has called a special meeting of the session. Given what I am planning to do, I don't think I will be there very long. Love, Benson."

Roberta looked up. "That reminds me. I don't know why it reminded me, but it did. When you were born, your father wanted to name you Phinehas. I really didn't want to, but I never told him why."

"Why?"

"Because I was afraid of what might happen. But it happened anyhow." And Roberta laughed, completely free. "And your father wants me at home. I should go."

EXCITEMENT ON THE SESSION

The session meeting opened with warmth, collegiality, and more warmth. It was like getting into an ecclesiastical hot tub.

Pastor Rodriguez gave a short devotional, which Benson recognized as coming from a popular website for busy pastors, and opened with prayer right after that. Benson had been entirely silent since he arrived, with the exception of shaking hands and greeting the others. Seven others, in fact, not counting the pastor.

In a very oblique way they had been talking for months about the presenting issue just underneath the pastor's position paper, the one he had sent out to them all just a few hours before. Someone in the church, name of Twisse, was requesting a special form of membership for his android partner, and according to the by-laws, *any* kind of membership required baptism, and because it was a sex doll, that meant a special form of baptism. And *that* meant a Greek word study of baptism!

Pastor Rodriguez thought he had hit on a verbal formulation that would keep Twisse, who was growing impatient, from blowing up in a white sheet of flame, and which would also not set the remaining traditionalists—about twenty-five in all—from reacting in *their* own way. Ordinarily one need not worry about twenty-five parishioners, but being traditionalists, they were almost the only tithers remaining. If they left, it would be the churchy equivalent of bean soup for a while.

But Benson had been looking at everything with a new set of eyes, ever since he had arrived. The laughter was hollow, the phoniness transparent, the warmth chilly. His forehead was looking, if that were possible, even gaudier than it had looked right after his fall. Right after the prayer, his pastor had looked at him quizzically, as if to invite Benson to share with everyone what he had been up to. Benson didn't feel like talking very much, and so he made a quick joke, of the you-should-see-the-other-guy variety, and then just added briefly, "Just took a tumble at home is all. Slippery tiles."

The world was covered over with slippery tiles. It was a metaphor. He had been cracking his head for *years*.

His phone buzzed. It was Roberta. "So happy. SO happy. See you shortly. Ace sends his respect and love."

Benson teared up, not knowing exactly why, and looked up as the pastor started the business portion of the meeting. "This is a called meeting, with only one agenda item, so let's jump right to that. Did everybody have a chance to read the position paper I sent around?"

Everybody nodded except for Benson. But this was not part of his rebellion—he *had* read it. It just hurt to nod.

As Benson sat quietly listening to the discussion, a plan started to form. There was one elder on the session who was a man of what appeared to be genuine conservative convictions. His name was Bruce Cassidy, and he was always voting *no*. Benson had wondered, for years actually, how he could be genuine in those convictions and still show up for the meetings, but that's the way it was. Benson thought that it was probably the fact that Cassidy's great-grandfather had founded the church and had been its first pastor over the course of thirty-five years. His picture was still hanging in the church library. Nobody went in there anymore anyhow.

Benson had also wondered why Pastor Rodriguez kept Bruce around, but over time he had realized that it was a big help with appearances. As long as Bruce was on the session getting rolled, there were traditionalists in the congregation who could reassure themselves with the mere fact of his presence. Bruce was a conservative, but he wasn't a cranky one. He always voted *no*, but he consistently took his inevitable losses in stride. It had been a long time since his voice mattered at all.

"I just don't know," Bruce was saying. "This really could be a bridge too far. I was talking to Mrs. Leiden after church on Sunday, and she somehow had gotten wind of all this. She asked me about it directly. *We aren't going to start baptizing those doll things, are we?* Her exact words."

Pastor Rodriguez cut in, soothingly. "That's just it, Bruce. The way I phrased it in my position paper allows us to use the language of baptism with respect to certain aspects of this, and the language of dedication or consecration in others. And this would be entirely in keeping with our evangelical heritage . . . as well as being in line with our rock-solid commitment to inerrancy. Not to mention the doctrine of sufficiency. And remember, once we start letting people legislate in areas where the Scriptures are entirely silent, we are on the fast track to legalism."

Gakkk, Benson thought, and was surprised to hear himself thinking that. Two weeks ago, he would have been nodding while the pastor talked like that. Two weeks ago, *he* would have been talking like that.

Plan, plan, he thought. He had one a minute ago. It was hard to think with the back of his head acting the way it was.

Bruce was obviously under some kind of strong emotion. He was swallowing repeatedly. It began to look like this one was not an issue where he would just "take it" like he routinely did. He was practiced at understating his actual convictions, and while the other elders knew he had convictions, it would have surprised them all to find out they were actual *convictions*. Benson was fascinated, in spite of the throb. From the way Bruce was talking, it was starting to look as though he might resign from the session over this.

A new plan rushed into Benson's head and ricocheted off the back of his skull, which made him wince, but then he smiled. A bit grimly, but it was a smile, and just for a moment he looked like Ace. Benson glanced around the table quickly, counting. Then he flipped to the church constitution on his phone, scrolled to the place where it discussed quorums, and just stared at it with deep satisfaction. If Bruce resigned, and then if Benson did, they would not have a quorum. They would be bound to limit all business to the task of elected additional elders. And if they tried to elect elders now, with the sex doll baptisms already an issue out in the congregation, the election might actually slide sideways on the majority.

"And so," Bruce quavered, "if this motion is placed before us, I am afraid that I would have to submit my resignation from the session." He said this out of conscience, having no expectation that it would have any influence of any kind. He had been functioning that way for years. And so we should try to imagine his surprise when Benson said, "And I would feel constrained to join him."

And then to the astonishment of pretty much everybody, Murphy, who never said anything about *anything*, said that he would resign also. Bruce was just staring, trying to get his mind around having some sort of showdown where he didn't lose. But he wasn't losing.

Then it got better. "If three of us resign," Benson was saying, "that would mean that the session would no longer have a quorum, and the only business the rump session would be authorized to take would be to approve new candidates for elder."

Pastor Rodriguez hadn't gotten over Benson's defection. "Benson, do you have a concussion?"

"Well," Benson said, licking his lips. "I would have to say *probably*. And if you were to ask me if that were related to this in any way, I would have to say, again, *probably*."

CHAPTER 12

GONZO LAW

SUGGESTION

Stephanie looked in at her father, scribbling furiously at his desk. She was on her way out for the evening, but she stopped for a moment at the door.

"Dad?"

He looked up and set his pen down, but was obviously still distracted.

"I haven't been to law school, or anything like that," she said. "But can I give you my two little bits on this case?"

Jon grinned. He loved it when Stephanie gave him free association legal input. He often walked away with something valuable. She had a good eye.

"What is it, sugar?"

"This is not a cultural system that honors the rule of law anymore. They honor the *appearance* of the rule of law, which is entirely different. But the world underneath that thin veneer is a world gone mad. And that means you need to give them their change in their own currency."

"Meaning?"

"Meaning that you must limber up a little bit, break out of your Aristotelean categories just slightly, and practice a little gonzo law."

"I see. Gonzo law."

"I will have to trust you to figure out what I am referring to."

Her father smiled at her. "So what makes you think that I am stuck, as you say, in my Aristotelean categories? What makes you think that I was not in here already, preparing the most gonzo of cases?"

Stephanie laughed. "Let us just say that you are very much 'A cannot be not A' around the house. But that kind of thing doesn't matter with these people, as admirable as that sentiment may be when dealing with so-called reality."

"Well, we haven't really done anything yet at all. It is all preliminary motions, gathering depositions, and whatnot. The first big real thing is jury selection, and we have all been posting up under the basket getting ready for that." Jon paused for a moment. "And I am a bit unsure as to how you would define gonzo jury selection . . . throw pens at the prospective jurors while asking them questions?"

"No, daddy dear." Stephanie came into the room and put both hands on his shoulders. "*This* is what I mean. If their crazy world-view were a car, you get into that car and drive it into a tree."

"You are speaking in dark parables."

"I will speak clearly then. Your first motion should be to require that a minimum of one third of the jury be made up of sex androids."

Jon lurched forward in his chair. *"What?"*

"A jury of peers. What *is* a peer exactly? Well, out of Asahel, Steven, and Sally, one third of that group was a sex android. So it seems to me that simple justice would require the jury to have that same composition."

Jon laughed. "But these jurors couldn't vote . . . Not unless somebody programmed them to vote. Ah, and that's just it, isn't it? Neither the defense nor the prosecution could be entrusted with that programming, the sex-droids would just sit there. A built-in hung jury."

Stephanie giggled. "That's the spirit."

Jon stopped. "But wait . . . If I were on the other team, I would use our willingness to have sex-droids on the jury as a concession that they *are* persons, and thus we have granted, in principle, the propriety of a murder charge."

"No," Stephanie replied. "You must anticipate them, as you just now have. But you have to make all these arguments while staying as solemn as the judge. All you have to say is that you are *not* conceding the point, but that you are in fact an open-minded man, and are prepared to see how they perform as jurors. We should all seek to remain as open-minded as possible, should we not? All while insisting that they not be programmed by anybody to vote for anything. That would be jury-tampering."

Jon sat back in his chair again. "So that is what you mean by *gonzo.*"

Stephanie nodded. "Yes, that kind of thing."

"I have to admit that your definition has somewhat exceeded the parameters of what I thought it might."

"Just being a dutiful daughter," she said, and disappeared out the door.

"Gonzo daughter," he said, after she had gone.

JURY OF PEERS

Judge Murray sat behind a dark, cherry-colored bench, crafted in another era. It was a work of artisanship and beauty, as if calculated to contrast sharply with the decisions that had been handed down from that same bench over the previous twenty years. The judicial decisions were mostly press wood with an oak veneer. The judge's chambers were immediately behind the bench, and they were ornate as well, and exquisitely done.

The jury box was on the right side of the court room, and the deliberation room for the jury was just behind their box, and, compared to the chambers of the judge, it was Spartan. The room contained twelve rickety metal folding chairs, and one long folding table that was doing its best to duplicate the posture of the old gray mare. It would appear to any dispassionate observer that the room was furnished and decorated as much as if to say to the jury that they ought to make their decision pronto and get the heck out of there. The judge had places to be, for at the Clifton Gardens Country Club, the scheduled tee times wait for no man.

Jon slowly rose to his feet, the roster of the jury pool in his hands, muttering to himself. "What is a peer exactly?"

"Your Honor, as I looked over this roster of names, it was hard to miss the fact that everyone on here is a bio. There are no androids in the jury pool."

Connorson jumped to his feet, as if he were about to object, but suddenly realized he had nothing to object to. What Hunt had just said was true. He just stood there, not sure what to say.

Jon looked over at him, as much as to say, *may I continue?*

Connorson said yes out loud, even though Jon hadn't asked anything.

"With the permission of the prosecution, I would like to petition the court, together with the prosecution, to have this unfortunate lapse rectified. I would propose that in a trial like this, at least three or four of the selected jurors should be android."

Connorson was frozen in place. This was a trap. It was clearly a trap. But what direction would the spiked poles come from? That it was a trap was clear. What *kind* of trap?

He eventually found his voice. "Your Honor, as pleased as the state of Colorado would be to join with the defense in advancing the cause of human rights like this, I find it hard to believe that this offer is being made in good faith."

Jon gestured handsomely to his opponent, and the judge said, "Proceed."

Connor ad-libbed. "As you know, Your Honor, this case is all about, er . . .the personhood of androids. The defense, unless I am guessing wrongly, is going to be arguing that Mr. Hartwick is not guilty of murder because Sally Sasani was, in effect, a doll, and not a person at all. Why would he concede the point at issue by, um, allowing androids—that he contends are not persons—onto the jury? That makes no sense." Connor took a step backward, largely pleased with himself. He generally couldn't think on his feet like that.

Judge Murray looked over at Jon, genuinely interested. He was ill-accustomed to relevant questions, given the kind of job he had.

"Your Honor, there would be no sleight of hand here. I am *not* conceding that androids are persons. I am simply saying that if you were to stipulate that a quarter or a third of the jury needed to be made up of androids, I would be content. I would not object."

Connorson was turning a bright red. "And why would you not object?"

"Because androids can't vote. I am willing, for the sake of the argument, to allow them the status of jurors. When it comes time for jury deliberation, the jury will retire, and will come back to us with the news that three of their number refused to vote."

Connorson sneered. "Androids can be programmed. *All* of them are programmed. It would be child's play to program them in a way that would enable them to vote."

"And if any of the android jurors vote either guilty *or* not guilty, then I will file a motion to have the case thrown out because of jury tampering. And I would recommend that the prosecutor's office go after the firm they hired to program the jurors, and throw the book at them. For jury tampering."

Everyone in the courtroom just sat there for a bit. In the back row one interested observer was carefully watching the ceiling fan. He hadn't had this much fun in years.

Eventually the judge cleared his throat, and said, "So where are we?"

Jon looked up at him and said, "I have made a request with regard to the jury pool. That androids be included, and that we select three or four of them to sit on the jury."

The judge looked at Connor, hoping for a way out. This time Connor did not disappoint.

"Your Honor, by telling us beforehand that he will file a complaint of jury tampering regardless of *which* way the jury decides, counsel has revealed to us that he is not operating in good faith. I would ask the court to deny the request, not because androids could not make suitable jurors, but rather because the sacred subject of human rights ought never to be made into a tactical football. Mr. Hunt is simply playing word games."

And so the judge went down the path of least resistance, and ruled against Jon. So Jon lost that round, but he had found Stephanie's advice exhilarating. Gonzo law had its appealing side. If you were going to argue cases before the Red Queen from Alice, you might as well enjoy yourself there.

And besides, the whole enterprise had given him an idea. "A doozy," he muttered to himself, "if it's myself what says it."

HERE GOES

The following day, the judge's bench was still the same color, and still solid wood. Everything was the same, except for Jon's internal outlook. Looking at the mirror that he had hung up in his brain, the place where he monitored how he was doing during trials, particularly when speaking to juries, he glanced up at himself, and grinned and waved.

He then opened his folder to his collection of invoices gathered during discovery. He stood slowly, and breathed out, just as slowly. *Okay, here goes.* After the jury selection skirmish, something had clicked, and he had gone back to his office and dug these out last night.

"Your Honor, in this case before us, my client is accused of murdering Mr. Sasani's concubine . . ."

"Objection!" the prosecutor was on his feet, his fists clenching and unclenching in a silent rage.

Jon looked over at him, as much as to inquire what the objection could possibly be now. The judge did the same, and the prosecutor sputtered helplessly for a moment.

"The defense is poisoning the well . . . What basis does he have for calling Sally Sasani a *concubine*?"

"Well, Steven and Sally Sasani were not legally married in Arkansas. In fact, in that state Steven is still married to a bio-woman named"—he looked down at his notes, just for show—"named Patricia. So the first thing is that he is married to someone else. Polygamy is against the law in Arkansas, and the legislature here in Colorado has its bill authorizing up to four wives still under consideration. That is the first issue."

"Go on," the judge said, interested in spite of himself.

"The second issue is that Sally went by the name Sasani, and so according to Colorado law, she is entitled to *some* sort of spousal status. I have at least three depositions here that testify to the fact that Steven introduced Sally to numerous people as his wife. The third thing is that a concubine is defined as a slave wife, and Steven Sasani bought Sally for about three thousand dollars early last year. If he purchased her—and I have the invoice right here—then that means that she is his property, duly purchased. And if she is a wife, as the prosecution claims, then the term for a wife who is also chattel property is concubine."

"Objection! Objection!"

"Your Honor," Jon said mildly, "we know *that* the prosecution objects. What we don't know is *why*. I have a copy of the warranty here, which clearly identifies Steven Sasani as the owner. The name for a wife that owned by her husband is concubine. I would be happy to use a synonym for concubine if the court will provide me with one."

The judge sat quietly for a moment, with a curious expression on his face. He turned and looked at the prosecutor. There had been nothing about any of this kind of thing in law school. And concubines were kind of kinky. "Objection overruled," he said eventually.

ISADORA FLAMES OUT

Once all the preliminary jockeying for position was done, the jury selection went surprisingly fast. And when that was over, on the morning of the first day of the trial, Jon sat at the breakfast table and tried to analyze how he felt. Trish and Stephanie and Ace were all chatting happily around him. He did have the jitters that he always had before a big trial, but down at the foundational level, he also felt settled.. He wasn't quite sure what was going on.

Connor Connorson began by calling Isadora Meadows to the stand, and he tried to do it in a subdued yet dramatic way.

And if you were already on his side, he succeeded. If you were Stephanie Hunt, you had to bite the fleshy part of your hand to keep from laughing out loud.

In her consultations with Thelma, a decision had been made to pull out all the stops. *Go big or go home* was the sentiment that arose between the two of them, and so Isadora made an intricate timeline of her hellish junior year at Denver Area Christian. As Thelma had asked leading questions, Isadora—a quick study in this department—acquiesced rapidly and inserted many new and increasingly lurid details. That timeline had entries that pertained to Ace on almost a daily basis, and Thelma would drill her on the facts of the timeline, and on the specifics of it.

"And how is it that your memory was sharp enough to write out a timeline like this?" Thelma had asked.

"Because I kept a journal during those times, the darkest of my life, and my therapist in the years that followed used the journal to get into the very darkest corners."

"And who was your therapist?" Thelma asked.

"Dr. Gundersen," Isadora replied.

Thelma had suggested this name because he was one who had a thriving practice in the area helping victims of molestation, and he had conveniently died the year before. Some thought it was a suicide, and some thought the suicide had something to do with allegations of improprieties that had been raised against *him*. But he wasn't available to testify in any case.

And so it was that Isadora felt more prepared for this moment than she had ever felt prepared for anything. Thelma had supplied the prosecutor with her list of questions, and he had nodded with satisfaction when he had first gone over that list.

"Ms. Meadows," Connor began, "what is your full name?"

"My full name is Isadora Absinthe Meadows."

"And where did you graduate from high school?"

"I graduated from Denver Area Christian."

"Can you tell me anything notable about your junior year?"

At this, Isadora faltered. She wouldn't have a Glastonbury legal aide to hand her tissues, but she had come prepared. She had brought her own.

"Yes . . . Yes. That was the year that Asahel Hartwick tormented me, on almost a daily basis."

"I see," Connor said. "And what did he do?"

"It would be better to ask," Isadora said savagely, "what *didn't* he do?"

"You said that he would do things on a daily basis. What sort of things might he have done on a daily basis?"

Isadora gulped, and managed to get the next words out with some difficulty, "We would pass each other in the hallway, at least twice every day. And he would leer at me as we passed, and he would undress me with his eyes. I could tell. Girls can always tell."

At this Stephanie closed her eyes, and massaged her temples with her forefingers.

"Anything else?"

"Yes. Occasionally he would walk up to me and whisper something to me, something obscene, something awful. I learned later in counseling that this is a grooming technique, and it was designed to keep me off balance."

"Our sympathies are with you, Ms. Meadows, and I think I can say that the sympathies of the court are with you as well?" At this Connor looked up at the judge, who promptly nodded. The sympathies of the court were legally mandated in cases like this. "Would you like a moment to compose yourself?"

At this Isadora nodded, and sat quietly for a minute or so, her shoulders shaking. Ace looked on impassively, but inside he was filled with amazement. The whole thing was so *brazen*.

After a time, her shoulders stopped, and she looked up at Connor, as though he might proceed, which he then did.

"What was the worst of your ordeal that year?"

"There were a handful of times that year, it was after the winter break, I recall, when he managed to get me alone. It was five or six times, something like that."

"What would he do?"

Isadora looked icily across the courtroom, not at Ace, but for some reason at Stephanie. "He raped me. He verbally abused me. He struck me in the face repeatedly. And he fat-shamed me." With this last, she bowed her head again, and her shoulders started up once more.

"One last question, as I know this is painful for you. In your knowledge of this part of Asahel Hartwick's character, is he the kind of person who could dispatch a man's companion droid in cold blood? Even though the man had repeatedly identified that droid as his wife?"

Isadora nodded, vehemently. "After that year," she said, "I could believe him to be capable of anything."

Connor turned and looked Jon Hunt square in the eye. "Your witness," he said, trying unsuccessfully not to sneer.

Jon appeared to be unfazed by the testimony, and approached the stand quietly.

"Ms. Meadows," he began "were you aware of the fact that Denver Area Christian had an honors program?"

"No, I didn't," she said.

"Objection!" Connor shouted. "I don't see the relevance!"

"If the judge will allow me to proceed, the relevance will be apparent in about two more questions."

"Overruled," the judge said, kind of curious in spite of himself, again. Jon kept doing that to him.

"And were you aware that Asahel was in that honors program for his entire senior year?"

"I never claimed that he wasn't smart. He is smart, all right. *Too* smart. He was devious. I don't doubt that he could have gotten into any honors program . . ."

"Just one more question, Ms. Meadows," Jon said smoothly, "and we can be done here."

Isadora Meadows nodded, and sat quietly, waiting for it.

"And were you aware that the honors seminars for Denver Area Christian were held in another location entirely? On a separate campus? And that Asahel was only on the main campus perhaps a total of five times that entire year?"

Isadora's eyes got big, and she froze, looking out over the courtroom for Thelma. She found her, and it was no help at all because Thelma's eyes were even bigger.

"Um," she said.

Jon had a particular technique for situations like this one. While some attorneys would press their advantage with follow-up questions, Jon would just let witnesses who had done this kind of thing to themselves twist slowly in the wind, air-drying as they spun. And so he just stood off to the side, hands behind his back, waiting.

"Um," Isadora said again.

Another thirty seconds passed, walking slowly by, arms outstretched like a zombie.

"Could you repeat the question again?" Isadora said, trying to keep a frantic note out of her voice. The sensation she was experiencing was not a new one; she had been here before. But she had not been here before while on the witness stand, under oath, with a courtroom full of interested faces looking at her. They all appeared to be tracking with the import of that infernal attorney's question.

Jon repeated his question. "Were you aware that the honors seminars for Denver Area Christian were held in another location entirely? On a separate campus?"

"Um . . . no, I was not aware of that."

"Given this fact, I was wondering how he could have passed you several times in a day between classes."

"Um, perhaps I was mistaken that he was getting out of class. Maybe he would come over to the main campus to see friends . . . and I just *thought* he was between classes. That must be it. An understandable mistake, given the circumstances."

"The honors students were not allowed to leave their campus, and it was forty minutes away, in any case. I have his attendance records in my folder there, if you would like to see them."

Isadora flushed red. "No, I don't need to see them."

Jon turned around. "Would the prosecutor like to see them?"

Connor scowled. "That will not be necessary."

"I have no further questions, Your Honor," Jon said, and went back to his table and sat down by Ace.

Ace leaned over and whispered to Jon, "You made that look easy."

Jon leaned back in his chair. "It *was* easy. I don't think these boys are as ready for prime time as they appear to think."

MOBY

Connorson was distraught with the Isadora Meadows flame-out, as well he ought to have been, and needed to get some points on the board fast, as he well knew. He knew—through back channels, he knew—that he was not going to lose the case, because Colorado was not going to *let* him lose the case. He was going to come out of this one a winner.

And yet, he somehow knew, down in his bones he somehow knew, that this was the kind of deal where he could wind up a loser kind of a winner. Like when the reffing is terrible in a game, and a touchdown is taken back by an outrageous call, and everybody in the country knows it, and the winners—or rather, the loser winners—go to the Super Bowl.

He was not interested in becoming a loser winner, especially in a competitive law office like his. And that meant putting points on the board, quick.

Dave Moby, Ace's old boss at the recycling plant, had been on his list of possible witnesses. When Isadora had come in with her story, he had almost determined to drop Dave as a background witness, but after Isadora's story turned out to be, well, a *story*, he had called Dave Moby and told him that he would need to be at the courtroom at eight a.m. sharp the next day. Nobody is ever really all that excited to testify in a trial, but Moby had somehow seemed even less excited than most.

After he took Connorson's call, Dave Moby walked back into the kitchen where his wife was, and sat down at the kitchen table. "He wants me to testify," he said, after a few moments.

Kathryn wiped a final dish, put it in the cupboard, and turned around.

"What is your thinking?" she said.

"I am thinking about the difference between watching them haul Ace off, when I didn't really have any means of stopping it, and when I *did* have the means of protecting you and the kids, which is all on the one hand, and then on the other, going into court tomorrow and being an active participant in doing a bad thing to a good guy."

"Go on," Kathryn Moby said.

"What I did when they arrested him was simply a diversion. I was protecting my family. My performance for the surveillance cameras was just defense. But this is different. They are asking me to join with them in perpetrating injustice. I can't do it."

Kathryn smiled, somewhat grimly, but obviously relieved. "I am so glad. I have been praying ever since the prosecutor first told you that you were on the witness list."

They were both quiet for a moment.

"Hand to the plow?" she said when the silence had gone on too long.

"Yes. This is the right thing. The only thing I worry about is what you and the kids can do if they come after me. They could get me fired, make me unemployable, and they *do* that kind of thing too, or worse, fine me for hate think at levels I couldn't pay, jail time . . ." he trailed off. "You do need a husband," he added.

"I most certainly do," she said. "But I need a *husband*, not a coward. If you went along with this evil, I would just be losing a husband in another way."

Dave Moby exhaled slowly, suddenly liberated. "Not even a little bit of cowardice is allowed?"

"Not around me," she said. "Not if you want to get past third base tonight."

At that he grinned, and ran his hands through his hair. "Oh, well, then. I feel the courage returning . . ."

The following morning, he was there at the courthouse at seven fifty a.m., sitting on a bench across from the courtroom. Connor was running late, and did not arrive until just before eight, and waved at Dave, signaling him to come in behind him, which Dave did.

Connor sat down at his table, and was fussing with some legal pads and his briefcase, and Dave sat behind him in the front row of the seats for the general public. Jon and Ace came in a moment later. Dave looked around at the spectators. He didn't recognize anybody except for Ace and Stephanie, who was always hard to miss. He was starting to feel the adrenaline.

That, and the double shot espresso he had picked up on the drive in. He was looking forward to the look on Connorson's face. He was actually looking forward to the look on everybody's face.

And in this respect, it has to be said that Connor did not disappoint.

After the preliminary questions that simply established the relationship—who he was, when he had hired Ace, what Dave's responsibilities at the recycling plant were—Connor moved to the point at issue.

"Given everything that has transpired, are you in a position to make a judgment about the character of Ace Hartwick?"

"Yes, sir, I believe I am," Dave said.

"And what would that evaluation be?" Connor said, swiveling around to look at Jon and Ace as he said it, but somehow looking at Stephanie instead. He was therefore in a position to see her eyes get wide as Dave answered the question, and then Connor's eyes got wide, and he swiveled back around the other way. "*What* did you say?" he said.

"I said that Ace is the finest young man I have ever met. I have three young boys, and if they turn out to be anything like him, I would be the proudest father in Colorado."

Dave's eyes met Connor's. Dave's were green, and very cool. Connor's eyes were not green, and they were also not cool. They were hot. Silence pervaded the courtroom. It was a cool silence in the witness box, and a hot silence around where Connor was standing. The rest of the courtroom was filled with more of an inquisitive silence, the kind that wonders what could possibly be coming next.

Connor cleared his throat abrasively, abruptly.

"Mr. Moby," he said. "I don't know how many times I watched the surveillance footage of the day at the recycling plant when you fired Asahel, but it was enough times to know that you did not seem interested in your sons becoming more like Asahel."

"That is correct. That was the intention," Dave replied.

Forgetting that he ought not to ask questions in open court when he was not entirely sure what the answer might be, Connor pressed ahead.

"And what possible reason might you have had for that intention?"

"I know that you boys know how to play rough. As I had no way of protecting Ace, I decided that I would protect my job and my family by making it look like I was angry with him on the way out. Ace was kind enough to play along—he is thoughtful like that and knew just what I was doing. And now you know."

"And what made you decide to come clean now?" Connor sneered at him.

"It is one thing to protect yourself when you have no way of helping the other guy protect himself. But it is another thing entirely to join in on the attack against him, to help destroy someone as fine as Ace is. That may be an arbitrary place to draw the line, but that's where I decided to draw it."

"Is that quite all?"

"That is all I have to say at this point. I would be happy to answer any questions you might have about Ace's integrity, work ethic, character, and so on."

"I don't need to ask you any questions about that." Connor pivoted and headed back to his seat. "Your witness," he said on the way to his table.

Jon rose to his feet, rejoicing in this unexpected grace, round two. First Isadora blew up in the way she did, and then Dave Moby *refused* to blow up. On his way over, Jon decided that one of his objectives in the questioning would be to provide Dave Moby with as much cover and protection as he could. It might not be much, but he thought he could do something.

"Mr. Moby, thank you for agreeing to testify. We appreciate it."

"You are welcome. Civic duty and all that."

"And I also am grateful for your very kind and unsolicited comments about my client."

"Nothing but the truth." Dave said.

"Now I want to begin by asking you a few questions about that surveillance tape . . ."

"Objection!" Connor said.

Jon stood quietly while the judge looked at Connor, waiting for the objection.

"The pretense and deception on his part that Mr. Moby has now admitted is hardly relevant . . ."

Jon responded. "If the prosecutor can ask about the surveillance footage, I do not see why I should not be able to. This gentleman is a character witness. We thought he was going to be a character witness for the prosecutor, but it turns out he is going to be a character witness for the defense. I do not see any reason why he cannot be allowed to do what a character witness does."

Connor snapped. "Yes, but he is here to talk about Asahel's character, not his own."

"His own character is relevant because if he is not a man of good character then why should we believe his testimony about the defendant?"

"Overruled," the judge said. Judge Murray saw that part of the defense strategy was going to be to try to make the proceedings look like a kangaroo trial, which it was, but he thought he should make some kind of display of evenhandedness, like siding with the defense from time to time, which he had just now done. He sat back in his chair, kind of pleased with himself.

"Mr. Moby, you said that these boys play rough. What did you mean by that?"

Dave Moby cleared his throat. "Well, look at where we are. A young man has acknowledged that he smashed a piece of machinery. For this destruction of property—and we can leave out of this the question of whether that could be justified—he is being charged with first-degree murder. That is ramping things up a bit, and would be a prime example of what I call 'playing rough.'"

"And how would this be relevant to you, such that you wouldn't want the surveillance cameras to capture you wishing Ace well, shaking his hand, and clapping him on the shoulder?"

"People who will charge a man with *murder* for wrecking an orgasmadoll would certainly be willing to fire a man from his position at the recycling plant for shaking hands with a so-called 'murderer.'"

"And yet you decided to testify this way here today anyway."

"Right thing to do," Moby said. "I fully expect to get the sack, because that is how these things go. But it was still the right thing to do."

CONVERSION

After Stephanie was sworn in—which was a convoluted process in itself, involving the Koran, the Jefferson Bible, and the UN Declaration of Human Rights—she settled herself in the seat and waited for Connor Connorson to approach the witness box.

As she watched him come up, for some reason she remembered what Ace had told her back in the coffee shop about how women do not have as *precise* a sixth sense about what men are doing as they sometimes think they do. They frequently know, he had said, but not as frequently or as accurately as they might assume. And Connorson was obviously a flamer, so she didn't quite know how to factor that in.

All that said, she was pretty certain he was strutting in front of her. Flamer or no, she was a really pretty girl, and he was still trying to show off some of his legal plumage.

When he had positioned himself in front of her, and when he had—she was pretty sure—flexed the muscles in his shoulders and neck for her edification, he turned and in his most solemn and courtroomy voice, said, "Ms. Hunt, are you a Christian?"

Her father was on his feet like a shot. "Objection! I can't imagine the relevance here."

Stephanie's mind was racing wildly. She was grateful for her father's objection because she needed a few seconds to think.

Think, think. *Think*, woman. Somehow she knew that this was it. This was the moment of decision. If she said no . . . it was unthinkable to her that she might say no. But if she said yes, here, under oath and everything, then that was it. It would be almost like a baptism. She would be committed. Committed. *That* had a nice ring.

The judge turned to her somewhat solicitously, but before he had a chance to say anything, Stephanie said, "I don't mind answering the question, if that is the concern."

"Objection withdrawn," Jon said.

The judge nodded. "You may proceed then."

"Are you a Christian?" Connorson repeated.

"Yes, I am," Stephanie said. Her father's eyebrows shot up, and Ace sat up straighter in his chair.

"And how long have you been a Christian?"

"Well, I have been considering it for almost a year. I have read the Bible several times during that year, and have given the whole subject a lot of thought. I have been going back and forth in my mind about the whole thing. I have not been baptized yet but, taking one thing with another, I would estimate that I have been a Christian for about two minutes. Your question just pushed me off the fence. So yes, I am a Christian."

She glanced at Ace, not really wanting to, but needing to, and their eyes met. He was looking at her with a great deal of interest. He nodded, and she felt warm all over. There it was again, *her* conflict of interest and *his* dimple. It was a well-worn path for her, and so she walked down it again as she waited for the prosecutor to get himself together again.

Connorson, for his part, was more than a little bit flummoxed. He had assumed from her behavior at the Dismantling of Dwight news conference that she had to have been a Christian, and a somewhat radical one. And then the episode with Lionel had reinforced his view that she was a radical Christian, an extremist. His line of questioning had assumed all of that, and he was going to seek to show how Ace was receiving aid, comfort, and encouragement from such radical elements.

"Umm," he said, floundering, "what had you been before this? Before a few moments ago?"

"When it came to theological issues, I would have called myself an agnostic. Positively, I was a libertarian."

At this, a sibilant whisper ran around the courtroom. Libertarians were almost as bad as radical Christian elements. At least that was the public line to take.

Connorson jumped on that, somewhat eagerly. "And are you still a libertarian?"

"I suppose."

"What was it, if I may ask, that pushed you off the fence? Why did you decide to become a Christian mere moments ago?"

Stephanie looked at him, beaming, and then looked the judge.

"It became clear to me in that moment, right when you asked that question, that everything is coming to a point. Everybody is becoming more and more what they have been becoming all along. And I decided . . ."

Stephanie suddenly halted.

"Please continue, Ms. Hartwick."

"I have no desire to be rude, and if I say what I was thinking, it might come across as rude."

"I believe we can risk that. What pushed you off the fence?"

"I realized that, as much as I disliked all the people who are trying to get Ace, if I didn't come to Christ, I had more in common with them than I did with Ace and the other real Christians I have met."

Connorson sneered. "So you did it because you didn't want to become like *me*?"

Stephanie nodded. "Yes, that's right. I wouldn't have put it so bluntly though."

Connorson turned away, flexing his neck muscles as he did so. He was not heading back to his table, but instead turned to the judge. "Your Honor, may I ask for a fifteen-minute recess before I finish questioning this witness?"

The judge nodded, and tapped his gavel sharply. "Fifteen-minute recess." It was a little soon for a recess, but the judge had a small bladder.

When Stephanie came down from the stand, her father stood up and gave her a hug, brief but warm. Jon followed her to her seat in the first row. After she sat down, he leaned over to whisper a question to her, and she nodded, and smiled.

Jon went back to his table, and sat down, busily texting. He was texting his pastor, a former Navy SEAL named Troy Gilbert, inviting him to come over that evening, if he would be so kind, in order to baptize his daughter. Normally he would have wanted to wait for the nearest available Sunday, but he didn't like the look his legal adversaries had on their faces, and he had also gotten a very interesting letter from the governor of Wyoming. A Sunday baptism might not be in the works.

Troy understood the dilemma, and didn't ask too many questions. And, as it happened, the Gilberts were free that night and would be delighted to come over. Troy's wife Julia said she could come with him, along with their older daughter Rebecca. Jon and Ace were also going to be there, and then Stephanie made six.

When the recess was over, Stephanie resumed her place on the stand. During the recess, Connor had been whispering furiously with Steven and scribbling notes on his legal pad.

When the courtroom was graveled together, he approached Stephanie again. "I have a line of questions," he said, "that have to do with the episode at the Isadora Meadows press conference."

Stephanie smiled and nodded. Her father was on the edge of his seat, leaning forward in anticipation of his next objection.

"Ms. Hunt, why did you accuse Dwight Glastonbury III of raping you?"

Stephanie's eyes got wider, and they were usually pretty wide, as Ace had noticed more than once. Wide, and lustrous. Her voice had a mild and slightly shocked tone. "Are you maintaining that he didn't?"

Connor was not expecting anything like this, and rocked on his heels slightly. "Um," he said, and stood there. After a moment, he collected himself, and said, "Is it *true* that Dwight Glastonbury assaulted you in the manner that you described?"

Jon was about to object, but he could also tell that his daughter was up to something. He hesitated, and then didn't object. She *was* up to something.

Stephanie, for her part, looked at the judge. "Your Honor, I am being asked if something is true or not, and I need to know whether the State of Colorado wants these questions answered with a correspondence view of truth in mind, or with a coherence view of truth in mind."

The judge had barely passed an intro philosophy course his freshman year, and he hazily remembered something about all that. So he punted. "Please tell us what *you* mean by those terms, Ms. Hunt."

"The correspondence view says that if I say that my purse is on the chair there," and she pointed, "then if the statement corresponds to the purse actually being there, then the statement would be true."

"Of course," said Connorson, wanting to get back into the action.

Stephanie continued. "Another example would be if Mr. Sasani said that Sally Sasani was his wife, and if she actually was, then that statement would be true. Otherwise, if she was just a sex android, for example, the statement would be false."

Connor stared at her, seething. Ace, with increasing admiration.

"And the coherence view?" asked the judge.

"Well, there the story just has to be internally consistent. The person is telling the story which is true for him or her or it, and the details of the story line up and are coherent internally."

"And so," Connorson said, seizing the reins again, "was it *true* that Dwight Glastonbury sexually assaulted you in the way you described?"

"According to which view?" she asked innocently.

"Both," Connor almost snarled. "What would your answer be under the correspondence view, and what would it be under the coherence view?"

"Well," Stephanie began sweetly, "if you are asking me under the correspondence view, I would have to say *no*. I never laid eyes on the man until that morning at the press conference. But if you ask me according to the coherence view of truth, I would have to say *yes*. Yes, yes—he was terribly abusive to me. It is still very painful to talk about."

Stephanie had encouraged her father to go in for a little gonzo law, and she had now decided to model it for him on the witness stand.

"It has to be one or the other," Connor said to her grimly.

"Does it?" she said. With that she looked at the judge, and decided to play it cute and dumb. "I would assume that in a court of law, the approach would be the correspondence view. But the whole prosecution is assuming the coherence view—Sally Sasani must be a woman and a wife because that's how Steven Sasani identifies her. So I thought I better ask which one you wanted."

She waited. The judge looked at Connor, and Connor looked at the judge.

BAPTISM

Troy stood at the head of the living room, up by the fireplace, and Stephanie was invited to sit in a chair near him. He gave a brief explanation of what they were about to do from Romans 6, and then read the first half of the baptismal service from a small battered book he had with him. Then he gestured to Stephanie to come up and stand by him, and began to ask her the questions. Her head was bowed, and she answered yes, quietly, to each of them.

When the questions were completed, he baptized her by cupping water in the palm of his right hand, and placing it on the top of her head. "In the name of the Father, Son, and Holy Spirit, amen," he said.

"Amen," Stephanie said.

Tory then gestured for everyone to stand, and he raised his arms in the benediction. When he was done, there was a momentary hush. Ace stepped over to Jon, and whispered a question. Jon's eyes went wide in surprise, although he admitted later that he wasn't *that* surprised. The question was "May I kiss your daughter?" Jon recovered himself quickly, abruptly nodded, and said, "Quite right. Under the circumstances, quite right. Proper, in fact."

And so Ace walked over to where Stephanie was standing, and said, "May I be the first to congratulate you?" She nodded, smiling, expecting a small courteous exchange, but then he bent over immediately and kissed her full on the mouth. Her mouth was warm and startled and every bit as lovely as he had expected. It was beyond fine.

He stepped back and looked straight into her wide eyes. "Well," she said. "Am I to conclude from these, um, advances that we are now an item?"

"You may, girlfriend," he said, and held out his left hand, which she took. She had been expecting his interest to be expressed at some point, and earlier she had worried a great deal about this staining the motives for her conversion, but now in the event, she was at peace. Her father had been right. When she had surrendered to Christ, other things fell into place also.

Pastor Troy was laughing, and extended his hand to Ace. "So this is the young man who has all of Colorado almost on a full boil."

Ace smiled, shook his hand, and said, "I am afraid so. Good to meet you. I must also thank you for removing one of my central temptations. Just like that, you did it."

"Central temptations?" Pastor Troy and Stephanie both spoke at the same time.

Ace nodded solemnly. "My central temptation for the last month or more has been that of wanting to kiss a non-Christian. I have been manfully restraining myself. You should have seen it."

"It sounds quite manly of you," Stephanie said.

"So I gather that was your first kiss that I witnessed," Pastor Troy said.

Stephanie said yes at the same time that Ace said no. Then they both laughed.

"What do you mean?" she asked. "That was too our first kiss."

"But only if you limit it to what actually happens. You know, the correspondence view of things. But if you factor in the intent of the heart, as Jesus instructed us to . . ."

"So how many times?" she said, her eyes shining.

"Oh, a couple thousand," Ace replied. "Like I said, a central and ongoing temptation." He looked at Pastor Troy. "She would just walk up to me and *talk* to me with that mouth. And it was just two feet away."

"It must have been quite the trial," Pastor Troy replied.

They all laughed, and Stephanie colored just a bit. Then she stood up on her tiptoes and kissed Ace's cheek. "There," she said. "All better?"

"Almost," he said.

WILL YOU BE . . .?

The next day in court was much the same kind of thing, which led to a conversation that evening.

"If legal success can be measured in how unhappy you have made the other side," Jon said, "then we have had a few successful days. But this should not be confused with actual success, as when you win the case."

Jon and Ace and Stephanie were sitting around in Jon's living room, discussing the events of the previous couple days.

Ace suddenly turned to Stephanie and said, "Well, we're good friends now, right?"

"Right," she said. "An *item* was the expression I believe we used."

"I just had an idea. Another gonzo thing your father can throw into the mix."

"Let's hear it," Jon said. Stephanie nodded.

"Will you be my concubine?"

"Friends or not, I am pretty sure that is supposed to go 'Will you be my Valentine?' . . ."

"No, I am thinking of the case, and how we can continue to mess with Connorson's categories. We are at the courthouse every day, and Colorado just changed their marriage license forms a few months ago. Remember that hubbub? Lines for up to five people, and no preprinted husband/wife stuff? You fill in what you think you are doing yourself? Remember all that?"

Stephanie nodded, and Jon did also, a second after.

"So we go up there tomorrow early and apply for a marriage license. We fill in the blanks—I would write in something like *suzerain* and Stephanie would write in *concubine*. If they issue the license, then we have a legal document with *concubine* on it. If they don't, then we can make some hay out of that—it appears that Colorado still has a long way to go in fighting the hate."

Stephanie laughed. "And if they say no to *concubine* in their bigoted ways, then I will ask for another one, and write in *dusky Nubian slave*."

"But you aren't Nubian, and you are not even a little bit dusky . . ."

"This was your idea, Ace. I would have expected that you would understand it. I am not a slave either. But while applying for that marriage license, I am *identifying* as a slave. And as a Nubian. And as dusky."

"Huh," Jon said.

"And if they make up a rule on the spot that you cannot identify as anything more oppressed than you currently are, then I will ask for a third license, and identify as a captured Nubian princess. You will, of course, be secretly recording all of this. That way we can capture everything they say, especially about that legally important category *concubine*. Because if I can be a concubine, then there is no reason that Sally Sasani can't have been one."

Jon had been rapidly flipping through one of his law books. "And if they say no to concubine, then they are in plain violation of the law. It says here that *no negative judgments whatever will be made by the issuing clerk.*"

Ace said, "So I will be secretly recording this, eh? So you have apparently not gotten tired of being an internet sensation?"

Stephanie smiled. "Maybe it is because the fan mail is starting to dwindle, and I need to juice it again." She paused for a minute. "No, actually, we wouldn't post it. We would submit it to the court as evidence, and we can use it whichever way it goes."

Ace started to say something else, but then stopped.

"What?" Stephanie said.

"This is too good to be true. Chances are we'll never get to use it."

And that is exactly what happened. Together they gave the clerk who issues licenses one of the most difficult hours in her entire career, and came away with no license, but with some very interesting footage on Stephanie's phone. Jon thought a great deal of hay could be made from it, but as events began to pick up speed, they never got the chance.

TRISH TAKES THE STAND

Jon assumed that the prosecutor would be prepared for it if he were to call Trish Sasani to the stand to testify, and in this he assumed incorrectly.

Steven Sasani, of course, knew that his imprisoned wife was gone from his house, but his hope was that she was long gone, and he also thought that if he told Connor about it, it would only complicate things. Jon assumed that Sasani knew how devastating it would be to his cause if his wife came forward to testify, and that naturally he would want the prosecutor to know this beforehand. But in this Jon had failed to reckon on the depth of Steven Sasani's selfishness and self-absorption.

And so when Jon called her to the stand, the prosecutor was just scribbling notes, on the assumption that this was some cousin twice removed, brought in to testify about how Steven had taken too many barbecued ribs at a family reunion once. Steven Sasani, for his part, sat there quietly in the front row, staring straight ahead at the Colorado state flag, looking as solemn as a judge. In fact, since we had an actual judge in there for purposes of comparison, he looked even more solemn than the judge.

When Jon approached her and asked for her name, Connor kept scribbling. When Jon asked what her relationship was to Steven Sasani, and Trish said she was his wife, Connor's head snapped up. And when Jon asked where she had been living since she arrived in Colorado, and she said, "Locked in the basement of my husband's house," Connor swiveled around in his chair and glared some hot hatred at Steven Sasani, who appeared to be effortlessly keeping his composure, regardless of this remarkable turn of events. He found the large blue stripes on the flag to be quite soothing.

But the trial was proceeding onward, and Connor could not afford any therapeutic hatred. Testimony was unfolding behind him, and so he swiveled around again, and stared at Trish.

Jon was in the middle of his follow-up question. "Are you saying that you were being held prisoner at your husband's house? Against your will?"

Connor didn't know what his objection was exactly, but he knew that he had to have one. "Objection!" he shouted. It came out like the *cawwk* of a distant crow because his mouth was inexplicably dry. He was on his feet, playing with his pencil. He broke it in two.

The judge looked at him expectantly, as did Jon. "I . . . I fail to see the relevance of this witness's testimony . . ." He trailed off.

The judge looked at Jon. He already knew how the trial was going to end, having already been given some ungarbled instructions from the governor. It was therefore in his interest to let Jon do his thing, so long as he didn't do anything that made the fix against his client too obvious. And the judge wasn't sure what category this new development was in.

Judge Murray leaned forward, trying to seem wise. "What do you intend to show by this line of questions, Mr. Hunt?"

"I intend to show that Steven Sasani was not divorced from his bio-wife, and that his identification of Sally Sasani as his wife was being undertaken at the expense of someone who really was his wife."

The judge nodded. "Overruled," he said.

Jon turned back to Trish, and resumed. "Mrs. Sasani, how long had you been held as a prisoner, and what led up to it?"

Trish sat up straight in the chair, and was looking directly at her husband, who continued to be fixated on the flag. "I was kept in the basement of our home here in Colorado since we moved here, which was about five months ago. And I was restrained in a similar way back in Arkansas, for about a year before we moved here."

"Thank you." Jon's questions were well placed, thoughtful and deliberate. "Would you mind describing for us what led to your imprisonment?"

Connor was on his feet again, having had a moment to think about what was going on. "I do not see the relevance of this. I submit that the defense is simply trying to poison the well. He is simply trying to get the jury to think ill of Mr. Sasani."

Jon turned smoothly toward the bench. "Your Honor, this line of questioning is directly relevant to whether Sally Sasani should be considered to be a wife, and is also directly relevant to whether or not Steven Sasani was genuine in identifying her as his wife."

"Overruled," the judge said again. He was beginning to wonder how he was going to get out of this mess.

Jon turned back to Trish a second time and repeated his question. "What was it that led to your imprisonment?"

"When we were first married, about ten years ago, we were very like-minded, with both of us describing ourselves as freethinkers. We had actually met at a freethinkers conference. So when we were first married, we were, as we described it to ourselves, sexually liberated. Open marriage, fetishes, S&M, the works. I was as bad as he was, and in some respects, I would say I was worse. But after some years of this, I found myself growing discontented with it, and the discontent gradually grew deeper and deeper."

Jon nodded. "And what then?"

"One day something snapped inside me, and I found myself saying that I did not want to be treated that way any longer. It had gotten really old. And his treatment of me in that way had gotten less kinky, if you know what I mean, and increasingly petty, and vindictive, and personal. When we started, we were both chasing our kicks. But over time, I found that there wasn't any kick anymore. And he didn't seem to be chasing kicks either—he just started to seem plain old mean. And so one day I admitted to myself that I simply didn't want that, not at all. The next time it came up, I told Steven what I had decided, and that I didn't want to be treated that way."

"What did you expect when you told him that?"

"Well, to be honest, I expected him to get angry and to just file for divorce. And I think I expected that because on a human level it made perfect sense why he would. We had gotten married with that shared commitment to transgress all boundaries, and I was the one who was changing. And yet, at the same time, I felt like I was coming home."

Jon nodded again. "I see. And what happened?"

"He got angry, just as I had anticipated. And things went stone cold between us for about three weeks. And one evening at dinner, I found myself weaving back and forth in my chair, and when I woke up, I was in a bedroom in the basement, with reinforced locks and bolts on the outside of the bedroom, in the hall. There was an attached bathroom, and so the whole thing was self-contained. Once a day, he would bring me a bowl of tepid oatmeal to eat."

Jon turned around and looked at Steven Sasani, still staring at the flag. Connor was furiously scribbling. The judge was staring at the back of the courtroom, trying to figure out what he could do with this testimony. It appeared that it was going to be a lot more damaging to the prosecution than he had initially guessed.

Jon turned back. "During the months that he held you captive, did he communicate with you at all?"

"Not really. Nothing to speak of. I asked him three times to let me go, said that I would just leave and we could divorce, and that would be the end of it. I promised him I wouldn't try to press charges against him if he would just let me go. He would laugh, and leave the oatmeal in a little slot he had built in the wall."

"Is that all?"

"No. Periodically he would come down to the hall outside my room, and would bring that doll thing down with him, and would do things there."

"What sort of things?"

"Sexual things. Degraded things. I would rather not talk about the details."

"About how many times did he do that?"

"I am not quite sure. About three or four."

"So he never offered to negotiate anything?"

Trish shook her head. "No, he did not. He simply wanted to torment me."

"All right, then," Jon said. "Just three more questions. Did anything else of significance happen to you during your captivity?"

At this question, Trish lit up. "Yes, yes, I would have to say so. It actually made everything worthwhile, at least in retrospect. When I called a halt to the way we were living, that was actually just me being tired of it all. But about two months in, by which time I had plenty of time to reflect on my life, my choices, my complicity in having married Steven in the way I did, I was given an unexpected gift. One morning I woke up in my little bed there, and as I was lying quietly, trying to get up the nerve to face another day of solitude, I found that I had a new heart. I wasn't just tired of the way I had been before, I was now repentant."

"Did Steven ever find out about this?"

"I think he figured it out. He got a lot meaner, at any rate. And I think he must have heard me singing from time to time. I went to a Christian school for a few years when I was a girl, and all I knew were a few stupid little songs from their chapel program. But I sang them as though I wanted to wear them out."

"Last question. How did he manage to get you from Arkansas to Colorado?"

"I have a very hazy memory of being stretched out in the back seat of the car. Steven's a pharmacist, so he would have had no trouble figuring out how to lace my oatmeal with something potent. But even so, I think he must have driven straight through. When I woke up in the house here, it was a very similar set-up to the way it had been before, only a little bigger. And I was very grateful for that, I can tell you."

Jon turned to the judge. "No more questions, Your Honor."

As Connor approached the witness stand, Trish looked at him and just smiled. Here was an adversary, coming to attack her, and her heart just sang. She wasn't locked up in a bedroom anymore. And even though it was an adversary coming to ask her questions, she was being allowed to answer. She felt like she had a lifetime of answers in her. After Stephanie had gotten her out, the Hunts had put her up at their home, in a little guest room in the attic. "No more basements for me, thanks," she had said.

They had wanted her to lie low, which she was happy to do. Her only request had been for a Bible, which she had read through twice over the course of the last month. *Do not prepare what you are going to say beforehand*, she remembered.

"Trish . . ." He began.

"I would prefer to be called Mrs. Sasani," she said.

Connor cleared his throat. "Very well," he said. "Any reason for that preference?"

"It is my name," she said. "And as I understand all this, it is more or less the point at issue."

Connor nodded, reluctantly. "My questions largely have to do with timelines."

"Very well," Trish said.

"About when was Sally introduced into your, um, family?"

"The doll was introduced into our house about two months before I first told Steven that I was done with our games." Trish was praying furiously, hoping that he would open up a particular line of thought . . .

And that is precisely what he did.

"And you went along with this, at least initially?"

Trish nodded. "Yes, I most certainly did. Much to my shame."

"Did Steven ever refer to Sally as a *wife*?"

Again Trish nodded. "Yes, he most certainly did."

Connor had begun to swell, imperceptibly to most, but he had begun to swell. Stephanie noticed it right off.

"And what did you think of this? What do you make of this fact now?"

Trish leaned forward. "There are two aspects to it. The first is the legal side. It was not possible to have two wives in Arkansas. I was his only legal wife. And in Colorado, the new law that will allow up to four wives still requires the consent of the previous wife or wives. I never gave that consent, and so I think it has to be said that the doll was in no sense a wife. Ever."

And Trish would never refer to the doll as Sally.

"I see. And the second aspect of this was what?"

"It was the emotional side of it, what it meant to me."

"Meaning?"

"I testified earlier that Steven's behavior toward me had turned from kinky or naughty to cruel or just plain mean. This was part of that."

"Sally was part of that?"

"Well, it was the last sex android. There were three others before that."

"*Three?*" Connor turned around and stared at Steven, who was still studying the flag. Connor was starting to develop similar views to Jon's on unexpected courtroom surprises. Almost against his better judgment, he turned back around and asked, "Where are they now?"

"Steven made a point of introducing each one of them to me as his next *wife*. Then they would become a bad wife. The next stage was when they were deemed rebellious. After that, Steven would destroy them."

The spectators in the courtroom all gasped, as did Connor. "No further questions," he muttered fiercely.

The judge looked at Jon, who had already risen and was approaching the witness box. He was smiling grimly. "How did he destroy them, Mrs. Sasani?"

"He tied a cinder block to the first one, and threw her into a lake that was just down the road from us. The second one was burned in a big trash pile we had—we lived on a few acres. The third one he took to the recycling plant." At this last bit of news, all the courtroom gasped again.

"So that I have it right, you are saying that Steven demolished, in some way or other, the three dolls prior to Sally, and he did it having identified them to you as his *wives*? Is that right?"

"That is right. And the subtext, aimed straight at me, was not at all subtle: *This is what happens to disobedient wives.* That is part of what I meant by his cruelty."

MESSING WITH THE JURY

The judge had ordered that the jury be sequestered, and so it was that they could only eat in a smallish back room of the courthouse cafeteria. A couple of bailiffs would stop the regular line that was wending through, the jury would come through, pick up their chow, and head off back to the back room. Several of them were not looking forward to the deliberation process at all. They predicted all kinds of snarls, both kinds, meaning tangled threads and the kind where teeth are bared.

But they were actually spared *all* of that. This was the point where the judge thoughtfully decided to play the situation with an open hand. No sense beating around the bush. He picked one of his underlings there at the courthouse, a man from the sheriff's department assigned to the judge, a man who carried himself with a thuggish demeanor. He was a man Judge Murray trusted as much as he trusted anybody, which wasn't very much, but he had plenty of goods on him, and so he felt comfortable with his insurance levels. One afternoon, he had a heart-to-heart conversation with this man in his chambers. The man was named Wayne Foote, and he would find a sweet bonus in next month's paycheck if he would be willing to conduct a little mission for the judge.

"What's the job?" Wayne said, his eyes brightening. It was generally hard to tell when his eyes brightened because they were mostly enclosed in fat, and looked like little black raisins that had been pushed down into the porridge, almost complete-ly under. But you could still tell they were *there*, and in this case the judge could actually tell that they brightened. Wayne liked little bonuses in his paycheck.

"I would like you to have a word with the jury. When they go down to lunch today, I would like you to follow them into that little room about ten minutes after they are all in there. The bailiff will be in there with them for lunch—I think it is Morris today, insufferable little man—and I would like you to tell Morris that I have asked to see him about a most urgent matter in my chambers. You will take the duty for him until he comes back, which should be about fifteen minutes. I have a little errand for him to do, which he will bring back to me before he comes back down to lunch."

"Alone with the jury, got it."

"When he is fully out of the picture, I would like you to explain a few practical matters to the jury. Actually, just one thing. I would like you to explain to them that if anything other than Ace's conviction for murder comes back to me from them, all of them will be very, very sorry. Not only will they be sorry, but so also will their wives and/or husbands be sorry, and their sweet little daughters will be sorry, and if any of their daughters have cute little puppies or bunny rabbit pets, they too will be sorry."

"I am getting the picture." Wayne loved this kind of work. He had a cruel bone, and on *top* of that he was going to get a bonus. He would do it just for the bonus, of course, but he loved it when his work had that little extra kick in it. "Let me make sure I get it," Wayne said. "Of course, you know nothing of my visit with them, or of my words, and you would deny it all if anyone were stupid enough to talk about it. And if they talked about it to someone, and the story started to get around, they could enjoy those feelings that come from being good, but they would have to enjoy them in the fifteen-minutes prior to being very, very sorry."

"I like you, Wayne. What happens to this Ace is no concern of mine, although I do have to say that it takes all kinds. What matters is that the governor has given *me* the ungarbled word. In fact, he told me something like 'anything shy of a murder conviction,' and *I* would be 'very, very sorry.' I am just passing the costs on to the customer, the way big business always does."

"Got it, boss," Wayne said. He glanced at the clock. It was eleven thirty. "As in, today?"

"No time like the present," the judge said. "I am happy to let the jurors have a little time to get their minds around the necessary concept of guilty-as-charged."

And so it was that a very short time later, Wayne was delivering this message to the jury, and they all just sat there in silence for a moment. Seven of them were mightily relieved. It turned out that they would not have to think, or argue, or even pay attention in the rest of the trial. The path of duty lay open before them, and they could just vote "guilty" and be done. But a sense of citizenship was still alive in five of them, and out of those five, three had active consciences, and did not like what Wayne was delivering, not at all.

One of them raised his hand. "What if we have a hung jury? No conviction, no acquittal, no nothing?"

Wayne was happy to go over the outlines of his message again. "Anything other than a 'guilty as charged' and all twelve of you get the treatment."

The juror, whose name was Travis, said that he didn't think that was fair or just, or anything remotely resembling fair or just. "If three jurors won't vote for 'guilty,' you or parties unnamed are going to punish all twelve?"

"You've got it, boyo."

A woman named Sheila, numbered among the compliant seven, protested. "That's not fair. Why would those who complied with what you said be punished? We tried to do what you said."

"Tried isn't good enough. The state of Colorado needs a guilty verdict, and the mistake in your reasoning is based on the idea that any of this has anything to do with justice or fairness."

"But why should all twelve get the same treatment for what just three did?"

Wayne grinned, and it was kind of slimy. "Oh, it won't be the same treatment. Everybody in here will be very, very sorry. But you will know the names and faces of the three—if it is three—who rained this trouble down on you all. And you can be my guest if you want to make them very, very, *very* sorry."

With that, he turned to go. When he was most of the way out the door, he turned back in and said, "Results, that's all. I'll just wait here outside the door until the nice bailiff comes back. You can have a moment to yourselves to discuss the situation."

The door clicked shut, and the jurors all just stared at one another. Some of them had heard Wayne's first statement with deep relief, but now a vague horror was descending upon them. Sheila, white in the face, glared at Travis.

"Are you seriously thinking about doing anything other than what has been required of us?"

Travis nodded. "We aren't supposed to be deliberating yet, but yes. An honest vote is on the table."

Sheila started to hyperventilate, in the way that usually got her what she wanted at home with her husband and kids, but Travis seemed unaffected by it. And before she got too far into the routine, the bailiff came in.

"All done with lunch already?" he asked.

CHAPTER 13

EXTRACTION AND AFTERMATH

INVITATION

Jon opened his briefcase and pulled out the blank envelope that he kept there, and quickly scanned it again. He looked across the table at Stephanie and Ace.

"So here is a letter I have from Rory McCullough, governor of Wyoming."

"Or," Stephanie added cautiously, "a letter *claiming* to be from the governor of Wyoming."

"No," Jon said. "I've had it for a couple of weeks now, and my friends at CLD confirmed for me that he did send one to me."

"What's it say?" Ace asked.

"Let me read the whole thing to you."

That reasonable task took only a few moments, as the letter came right to the point.

Jon looked up when he was done. "Basically, the governor says that their intelligence agency says that the fix is in on our case. It doesn't matter what anybody says or does, you," and here he glanced at Ace, "are going to be convicted of murder."

"What does he want us to do?"

"He wants us to let him extract us from our danger. Very nice of him, I call it. The general populace in the free states are in kind of a froth about your case. They are almost ready for war just because the trial is even going on. What they will do if you are convicted, the governor does not like to imagine."

"Wishing to extract us and actually doing it are two different things," Stephanie said.

"He apparently has that covered. I am supposed to go down to see Maria in the marriage license office here, and tell her that 'in olden days a glimpse of stocking.' She will say 'shocking,' and will thereupon give us a key that will get us up on the roof of this building. We don't have much time to decide. He wants us up there at five this afternoon. He will have a helicopter from the Wyoming National Guard appear promptly at five. That's just a couple of hours from now."

"Wyoming has secret agents in Colorado? And Maria is *one* of them?"

"It would appear so. And if Rory McCullough is on that helicopter himself, I would venture to guess that he is running for president of what's left of these United States."

"Why didn't you tell us before now?"

"Didn't want to worry anybody but myself. But now we all have to decide."

HELICOPTER EX MACHINA

Jon drummed his fingers on the desk. "So here we are," he said, "waiting for our moment to fly out of here. It all seems too simple, because I think it is."

He suddenly reached into his bag, and pulled out the letter from the governor of Wyoming again. Looking it over, he nodded, and folded the letter back up again.

"There are three of us here," he said, "but I think there needs to be four total, not counting me."

Ace looked up at him sharply. "What do you mean, not counting you?"

"I have every intention of getting out of here, don't you worry," Jon said. "My future in these parts would definitely be bleak. But I am thinking of two others, and the governor's note here says that the helicopter coming for us has room for four, and no more."

This time it was Stephanie's turn to look at him sharply. "I don't get it."

Jon drummed his fingers again, this time more loudly and decisively. "Well, the fourth in our party should be Trish Sasani. I think she needs to get out of here, almost more than the rest of us. Once we are gone, and there is no cover provided by our circus of a trial, I think she would be really vulnerable."

Everyone nodded at that, and Stephanie said, "And so she's our fourth."

"Agreed. She's our fourth. Stephanie, can you text her, and ask if she has a way to make it here in the next hour?"

"Can do," and everyone stopped while Stephanie sent the message. They had just started to talk again when Stephanie's phone buzzed with a reply. "Downtown now. Will be over there in a few minutes. Curious."

"Good, good," Jon said.

"Okay, and there's our four," Ace said.

"Maybe," Jon said. "Stephanie, how far is your mother's office from here?"

Stephanie's eyes got wide, but she said, "Fifteen minutes. Why?"

"I think you should drive over there. Talk to her in person. If she is there, could you please invite her, for me, to take my place on the helicopter? I have my own way of getting out of Colorado, all lined up and ready to go, and can follow you all within a week or so. Everyone will just assume that I was on that helicopter anyway, and I can arrange to 'disappear' myself."

Stephanie's eyes, already wide, filled up with tears, and she hugged her father around the neck, just before she disappeared out the door and down the hall. Ace started to follow her, but she pushed him back. "*You* need to stay here. They will be watching for you."

Ace nodded reluctantly and walked back into the room to sit down. "I will be back, quick as I can," Stephanie said, over her shoulder.

As she drove to the realty office where her mother worked, Stephanie tapped on the steering wheel impatiently. The traffic was normal, but she felt like all the streets were crawling and crowded. The lights conspired against her, turning red as often as they could. But even with all that, she found herself pulling into the parking lot of the office after just twenty minutes. Not *that* bad. It just felt that bad.

It was Stephanie's first big exercise in trusting God. Her mom was out, showing a house to a client. The receptionist greeted Stephanie warmly, and said that Victoria Hunt had said that she would be back by the top of the hour. It was ten till.

"Are you Vickie's daughter?" The receptionist asked. "She talks so much about you."

Stephanie nodded, and sat down in the reception area, concealing her exasperation well. How was she supposed to wait for ten entire minutes? And then another thought filled her with horror. Suppose her mom was late? Suppose her mom was late enough that she had to decide whether or not to leave without talking to her? The minute hand climbed painstakingly up to the top of the hour, and then began to go down again. The next two minutes, the worst of Stephanie's life, came to a bright and cheerful end when the little bell on the doorway rang, and it was Vickie.

"Stephanie!" she said in surprise. "So good to see you!"

Stephanie was on her feet. "Do you have an office where we could talk for a minute?"

"Certainly, dear. Right down this hall."

As soon as the door closed behind them, Stephanie began to talk. "Mom, I can't go into all the backstory explanations, but there is a helicopter coming to rescue us, to get us out of here."

"Who is *us*, dear?"

"Ace, and me, and Mrs. Sasani. And Dad. But Dad says that he has prepared another way for him to get out of Colorado, which he is going to do right away. He asked me to come and ask you if you would like to take his place on the helicopter. Would you, please?"

Victoria stood still for a moment. "*He* wanted that?"

"Yes," Stephanie said, almost dancing in place. "It was his idea."

"Well, I told the Lord this morning that I was ready for whatever adventure he sent me today, although I have to admit that this is a bit larger than what I had in mind. But I did *say* that to Him. I'll go."

Stephanie kissed her mom on the cheek. "So we have to go right now."

"Well, it is a good thing that there is nothing back at my apartment that is worth anything at all."

For some reason, on the drive back to the courthouse the car seemed to fly. They pulled into the parking lot with forty-five minutes to spare. Stephanie led her mother back to the conference room they had been using, and burst in, with her mother right behind her. Ace was sitting there at the head of the table, waiting, and Trish Sasani was across the table.

"Where's Dad?" Stephanie said.

"He decided to reconnoiter. He is just past the locked door to the heliport. He will get a message when the chopper is five minutes out, and he will text us. He will meet us by that door, one of us will run the key back to the water fountain, where Maria can pick it up and get it back to the supervisor's office in the land title office, the one she swiped it from. He is on vacation apparently, and she couldn't use her key because they can tell which key it was."

Ace had stood up while he was explaining. "And this is your mom?" he said.

"Oh, yes," Stephanie said, embarrassed. "This is my mom. Victoria Hunt, this is the infamous Asahel. We call him Ace."

Ace and Vickie shook hands. Stephanie then turned to Trish, and introduced her mother again. When those pleasantries were done, they all sat down again. Ace texted Jon that all of them were assembled and ready. *Good, good,* the reply came back.

After about ten minutes, Ace broke the silence. "I *hate* waiting," he said. "And I always have to wait for stuff."

The four of them then sat quietly, wondering what they could possibly talk about, casting glances at the clock on the wall. Ace was doing math problems in his head. Stephanie was thinking about her mom and dad. Trish Sasani was wondering how she could make a living in Wyoming, but was desperately eager to try. And Vickie Hunt was trying to deal with her dry mouth. She was going to see Jon again. Jon was going to be back in her life in just a few minutes. Unless he didn't want to be back in her life.

Suddenly Ace's phone buzzed on the table. "Come," it said.

They filed out of the room, walking deliberately, slowly, and in a way calculated to attract no attention at all. The hallway was somewhat crowded, and everybody appeared to have somewhere else to go, and so it was not difficult to seem just like the rest of them. They walked to the back of the courthouse, took a hard left down toward the restrooms, and then turned right at a door marked "Employees Only." It was open just a crack, and Ace pushed.

Jon pulled the door open, let them all in, and stepped out into the hall himself. "Stay right here. I will be back in two shakes." He was good to his word, although it might have been three shakes. They opened the door for him, and he quickly said, "This way," and trotted up the stairs. Trish was behind him, then Stephanie, then Vickie, and then Ace.

Vickie's heart was pounding, and it was only partly the brisk climb up the stairs. Would she have a moment to say something to Jon? What could she say?

They popped out onto the roof, quickly, suddenly. It was a fair day, blue sky, and Stephanie pointed toward a big expanse of blue. "There's the helicopter." It was a largish dot, coming straight toward them.

Her father said, "The hospital is just past us, and the bogus flight plan that was filed has them flying there. The people in the hospital think they are bringing in a patient from a car wreck that happened near the Wyoming border. They are going to divert at the last minute and land here. We don't have to worry about any reactions until you are off again. I will be off as soon as the helicopter diverts. I don't want to run into anybody coming up the stairs."

Vickie reached up to her neck, as though to pull her heart back down into her chest. She stepped over to Jon and said, "We have just a minute then. Could I speak to you for a moment?"

Jon nodded, and they walked over away from the group, about twenty feet off. The other three turned to talk with each other as a way of giving them space. The helicopter had begun its descent, and the pilot was trying to make it look as though he was heading for the hospital.

Vickie looked straight up at Jon's face, and said, "I wish we had more time. I have so much to seek forgiveness for."

Jon raised a hand in silent protest. "We are both in the same position. I have much to seek your forgiveness for as well, more than can be covered here." He glanced at the helicopter, which had suddenly veered toward the courthouse. "Let's do it this way. Let's forgive one another, generally, in an all-encompassing way, here and now. I know there are particulars that we each have to mention—I know I have a list—and I would like to ask you out to dinner in just a couple of weeks. I know a restaurant in Laramie. Will you go with me?"

Vickie's eyes filled with tears. "I would love to. Thank you."

Jon suddenly bent over and kissed the top of her head. "See you in a week or so, sport."

With that, he trotted over to the door that led down below, waving to the other three as he passed them. The helicopter touched down just as he opened the door, and three armed soldiers jumped out, covering the whole rooftop with their weapons. The governor of Wyoming was right behind them, briskly beckoning the four to come, come now, come *now*. The small group quickly made their way over, and clambered up in the chopper—Vickie first, then Trish, then Stephanie, and Ace last. The governor was right behind them. The soldiers backed up to the helicopter, and then turned around swiftly to jump in— as though all three were one single organism. As soon as the third soldier was in, the pilot hit it, and the helicopter abruptly launched like it was a skeet in a shooting exercise.

Across the way, the receiving crew on the top of the hospital had started gesturing violently as the chopper roared off the way it had come.

A few minutes later, the courthouse crew that usually received helicopters burst through the door that Jon had gone down, and ran over to the edge of the building. The helicopter was a small black dot on the horizon.

Back in the helicopter, there was some initial excitement when an explosives expert, a Sgt. Minor, motioned Ace to the tail of the chopper. "Let us have a look at that ankle bracelet, friend," he said. He had Ace lie down and insert his right leg and foot into a steel box that appeared to have been constructed for just this operation, which it had.

"We need to get this baby off," Sgt. Minor said. "But before doing that, we need to determine what kind of ankle bracelet it might be."

"What are my options?" Ace asked.

"There are many variations, but the two basic ones are these. One goes off like a siren and just won't quit. It is the kind that helps cops chase down someone who decided to hop out of their van. That's the standard issue. The other is the kind that will blow your foot off if you get outside a specified radius from downtown Denver. And because this is not a slow helicopter, we thought we ought to check. It would be just like those johnnies to not tell you if that is the kind it is . . . yep, that's the kind it is."

Stephanie's eyes widened. "Can you tell the pilot to fly slower?"

"Not really, because the bad guys behind us are no doubt scrambling some planes to chase us—even now as we speak. But we still have a good fifty miles before we have to worry about anything, and I did really good in this class in explosives school."

"Define 'really good,'" Ace said.

"B, B-plus, I forget," Sgt. Minor grinned. "Now lie still."

"How long will this take?" Stephanie asked.

"Not long. Five minutes, if you know what you are doing."

Seven minutes later, the sergeant chuckled, and lifted the bracelet over the rim of the metal skirt where Ace's leg had been, and placed it gently in a heavy steel container that looked like it could handle anything. He closed the container softly, and flipped a couple of latches, and set it off to the side.

"Back to your friends," he said, gesturing to Ace, who grinned back at him, and clambered back up front, and sat down next to Stephanie again.

For the rest of the ride, all four evacuees sat facing each other. Trish was across from Ace, and Vickie was across from her daughter. The vibration of the chopper felt like it ought to be able to put them all to sleep, but they were too excited and too happy to sleep. Stephanie was happy because she leaned over and laid her head on Ace's left shoulder, and because he let her. Ace was happy because Stephanie had laid her head on his shoulder. Trish Sasani was free, she was not locked up in a basement anymore, and her sins were a thing of the past. Vickie was alternating between the realization that Jon was fully prepared to forgive her, and had asked her on a date, on the one hand, and the fact that he had called her *sport* on the other. He hadn't called her that since about their third year of marriage. She kept wanting to lean over to tell Stephanie, "He called me *sport*," but she also kept thinking that it wouldn't mean the same thing to Stephanie.

About twenty minutes later, they all heard a muffled *whhum-mppff* from the little container where the ankle bracelet was. Sgt. Minor's eyes brightened, and he looked at them all with a thumbs up. "B-plus, bah!" he said.

THE WAR WAS BRIEF

After the four were whisked safely away to Wyoming, a number of other things happened in rapid succession. Jon, true to his word, was able to leave the courthouse successfully—because everybody just assumed that he had been on that helicopter, and nobody was looking for him yet, at least not on the ground. Standing out in the courthouse parking lot next to his car, he grinned widely, and threw his briefcase full of notes about Ace's case into a pick-up truck full of garbage that was parked next to his. He wouldn't need those papers anymore, and the briefcase was getting old.

He started the car up and headed out. He was going north, and was going to make just a quick stop at home to pick up a few valuables. He hadn't planned on making a bolt for it today, but he always kept a flight bag ready to go, one that had all his essentials in it. He thought he could risk a brief visit home to grab the flight bag.

And they *did* assume that he was on the helicopter, but they almost got Jon in spite of themselves. For some reason, the police came to his house almost right away to collect the evidence they would need for the (no doubt) vain extradition request. Jon was actually driving away from his house, down by the nearest intersection to his house, when he saw three cop cars hurtling down the other way, back toward his home. *Thank you, Lord*, Jon thought, and turned left.

He immediately contacted his hunting guide and partner, a good friend named Caleb, and told him that he had a sudden itch to go hunting near the Wyoming border, where there were plenty of back trails. "Okay," Caleb said. He was free to leave any time.

Jon had actually sold his house about six months before, and had also managed to get almost all of the proceeds from that sale into cryptocurrency. He would be just fine if he could get anywhere with an internet connection—which about two days later, he did.

So when the governor of Wyoming held his press conference, explaining why he had sent in the helicopter, and released the intelligence reports that decision was based on, the dam burst. The trial of Asahel Hartwick had almost been a *casus belli* in itself, but the way the trial had ended—or not ended—had made everyone angry. Judge Murray needed to do something to keep the governor off his back, and so he simply declared Ace guilty *in absentia*. The jury never had to fight it out, and Travis breathed a big sigh of relief. So did the other jurors. But the guilty verdict was immediately swallowed up by subsequent events across the nation, and on top of that, the fact that Ace was walking around free in Wyoming, acting as though he was very much *not guilty,* took some of the shine off.

The heartland states were angry at the mere fact of the trial, and fully believed the governor's evidence, which was sound enough, that the fix really had been in on the verdict. The blue states were angry at Wyoming's obvious violation of the "rule of law," as they defined it, and understood the rescue as a deliberate provocation, which it actually was.

And so California seceded from the Union almost immediately, giving the raspberry to the slow-motion process they had been following before. Other states like Oregon and Washington followed in rapid succession. As soon as they did so, and just before the fighting started, Connor Connorson decided that Colorado was not going to be a suitable place for his glorious future. He decided, and fairly promptly, that California was far more to his liking. If he had been pursuing that move out of a new-found humility, it might have done him some spiritual good to start over. But he wasn't, and it didn't. But whether he was pursuing obscurity for the sake of wisdom or not, obscurity came to him anyway. It came to him unbidden, and we never heard from him again.

Unlike the first Civil War, the fighting that broke out immediately was *not* fighting in order to keep the Union together—all parties being now equally enthusiastic about going their separate ways. But there *were* some conflicts that had to do with boundaries and borders and outlets to the sea. Everyone was fine with being apart, but which parts should go with which parts, exactly? It was not an easy question.

The two main military actions were taken by the red states. After Colorado seceded, the first move was to seize eastern Colorado, up to the continental divide. The rest of Colorado was annexed about six months later. It was felt that blue encroachment that far east should be considered intolerable.

A man named Porter Jameson was appointed to be the interim governor of Colorado, and he was a man who had a keen sense of poetic justice. During Ace's trial, he had been riveted by the televised courtroom antics and shenanigans, and had actually been quite moved by the testimony of Dave Moby, Ace's old boss at the recycling plant. Gov. Jameson had actually been moved by pretty much everything that had happened in that courtroom, but by Dave most of all. Porter was a native Coloradoan, sixth generation, but he had been living (in exile, as he put it) in Chevy Chase, Maryland. He had been Secretary of the Interior twice, under different presidents, and was the obvious choice for interim governor. Despite being the obvious choice, he was somehow selected by the president's head hunter committee anyway, and he was promptly installed.

His first act as interim governor was to sign an executive order pardoning Dave Moby for his contempt of court conviction, and his second was to offer Dave his choice of a seat on his cabinet, which Dave gratefully took. This was a double vindication when it came to the extended Moby clan. His wife had been "so proud" of her husband after his testimony, and yet dealing with the loss of his job, and the contempt of court decision, which was a felony, was a real challenge to her faith. This challenge lasted for about three weeks, which is just about how long the old Colorado regime lasted after Ace's trial. Then when her husband was promoted beyond her wildest dreams, and at triple the salary, she told her children that she felt like a plot pivot right out of the book of Esther. The second point of vindication regarded her brother, who had not had a steady job for about fifteen years, who had been part of the mob at the Glastonbury press debacle, and who pronounced his brother-in-law the "king of the morons" after his testimony. He did not take Dave's elevation with any kind of grace, and conversations at family Thanksgivings were tense for some years to follow.

In another matter of poetic justice, Dave promptly hired a young man named Travis to be his administrative secretary, and didn't find out until three months later that Travis had been the juror who was preparing to revolt against the judge's instructions. The helicopter extraction had meant that Travis was the opposite of very, very sorry. Dave and Travis found out about it sharing a beer after work, and Travis observed that it was "almost as though a higher power was at work." Which it was.

Steven Sasani made his way to California, where he was a minor celebrity for a few years. After that, it was a downhill glide into what he and the other tenants of his apartment complex considered abject poverty.

And when Washington state seceded, the eastern part of that state turned around and did the same thing, asking to be annexed to Idaho. And in an interesting twist that precisely no one saw coming, Alberta seceded from Canada, and applied for statehood.

The legislatures of Oregon and Washington responded to these things by closing off Portland to all trade coming down the river from Lewiston, Idaho. The landlocked states of the inland Northwest reacted to this by sending troops to capture Portland, which they were able to do in about three days. Lewiston was an inland seaport, and the red states were not about to tolerate any restrictions on their direct access for shipping grain to China. This move astonished the legislators of Oregon and Washington, who had been pacifists long enough that they were not exactly savvy about military affairs. They filed suit in a now virtually non-existent federal district court—the *building* was still there—and so it should have been no surprise to them that nothing ever came of that.

The heartland USA put Denver and Portland under martial law until they were "detoxified," as one commentator put it. Six months after that, the same thing happened to Chicago after Illinois was annexed. *Annexed* sounded more polite.

CHAPTER 14

HONEYMOON ADVENTURES

QUITE THE WEDDING

While all the martial excitement was unfolding across the country, which only took a few weeks, various forms of marital excitement were developing in Laramie.

Jon actually made it out of Colorado with no drama or excitement. His promised date with Vickie happened in the first week after he was there, and despite the fact that both of them had a splendid case of the jitters, it did go smoothly.

Before he came to pick her up, Vickie was pacing back and forth in the suite of the hotel that the state of Wyoming had reserved and set apart for Vickie and Stephanie. She suddenly wheeled around and looked intently at Stephanie.

"Stephanie, what if he is just being nice? Suppose he just wants to say that since we are both Christians now, we need to

271

put everything on a more amicable footing? And then he drops me back off here, hoping that I enjoyed my steak?"

Stephanie put her magazine down. "Mother, you are being silly. First, there is a mirror right over there. Go look at yourself. Even if that were Dad's plan, which it isn't, he would fail to execute that plan. He would be looking across a candlelit table at you, and given what you look like tonight, he would fall in love with you again on the spot. And that is what would happen if he were driving here fully resolved to do the amicable and best-of-friends routine. Which I can assure you he is not."

Vickie's phone buzzed in her purse. "He's in the lobby," she said. She took a moment to text back, "Coming." And then she turned back at the door before going out. "Stephanie, pray for me. I am nervous, nervous, nervous."

"Just like he is, no doubt. So I will pray for *both* of you."

Jon was in the lobby, pacing back and forth near the elevators, checking his watch, checking his wallet, checking the cuffs on his shirt, and checking his heart rate. The elevator doors opened, and he swallowed hard and smiled. She smiled also, and he fell in right away.

Victoria Hunt was not taller than her ex-husband, but she only missed it by about half an inch. This meant that whenever she wore heels, she *was* taller than he was. At the beginning of their marriage, this hadn't bothered Jon at all, but later on when things began to go south, Vickie had taken to wearing ankle-buster stilettos with a kind of "take that" attitude, and Jon had not been at his finest in taking, as she appeared to be saying, *that*.

She was a ginger, and with a temperament to match. Her maiden name had been O'Hara, and the Irish cascading into her veins from both sides was almost undiluted. The only exception had been a Greek great-grandmother on her mother's side, and *she* had been as fiery as anybody else there. She had fit right in. She had blended well. Her presence in the family tree, as far as it went with Vickie's general demeanor and outlook on life, had been more of the same.

And so Jon and Vickie's marriage had been stormy, but it had been a one-way kind of stormy. It had been like a rock on a promontory on a turbulent coastline, one that had waves crashing around it all the time. Vickie had been really volatile, and Jon hadn't responded to her at all. He had thought that he was being gracious by not reacting, and she thought that he was being the ultimate in ungracious by not caring. He didn't react at all, really, until after she had left him. But of course, she wasn't there to see that part of it.

She was tall, full-figured, and had hazel eyes. She was impetuous—one example was when she had left college one semester before graduation, after having maintained a four-point average for the first three and a half years. She left because they were starting to bore her, and she made this unexpected move to the consternation of her mother, and the delight of her father. In short, she was a pistol.

Vickie came out of the elevator, and Jon approached her with his arm extended for her to take. Suddenly he stopped. "You're wearing flats," he said.

She nodded.

"Do you have heels here? That go with that lovely dress?"

She nodded again.

"Would you do me a big favor, and go put them on? I want everybody to see who I get to come into the restaurant with me."

She hesitated. "Are you sure?"

"Positive."

She didn't tear up about *that* until she was in the elevator.

When she made her second entrance to the hotel lobby, he was more prepared, as was she. He walked up to her, and presented his left arm. "Shall we go?" he said. "The car is right out front." She took his arm, remembering it fondly, and walked with him. This was a good sign.

*   *   *

That first week was also a time when Ace had very few responsibilities, and so he used up all of his free time acquainting himself with the ins and outs of engagement and wedding rings. He had saved a good bit of money back in Colorado, even though he had been in school. The bad news was, because of the political turmoil, he was not able to withdraw that money. But a number of generous people in the free states were thrilled with what he had done for the country and what had resulted from it. They were willing to give him money or lend him money, whatever he needed. Ace refused the gifts but was willing to have donors front him some money until the banks in Colorado were open for business again.

Ace and Stephanie spent a great deal of time together, and the day after Jon and Vickie's date, he obtained Jon's blessing to propose. Ace asked this right after lunch, and Jon told him that he should go right on ahead, but that he and Stephanie would have to do something in exchange for it.

After Jon and Vickie had both confessed their sins to one another, and each had extended a full and complete forgiveness, Jon had reached across the table with his palm up. Vickie had put her hand in his, immediately, and they had looked at each other.

"Would you be willing to marry me again?" Jon asked.

"Yes, I would. More than willing. Eager. And I would be a dutiful wife this time."

"Well, we would be a matching set then, because I would be a decent human being this time."

They talked another hour or so, and discovered that neither of them really wanted to make any fuss about the ceremony. "I still have my ring," Jon said, reaching into his pocket. Vickie held up her purse. "And I still have mine," she said.

And so it was that Ace found out that in exchange for Jon's blessing on a proposal, he and Stephanie would need to accompany Jon and Vickie down to the courthouse in order for a justice of the peace to marry them. "I called them this morning," Jon said. "It's all set up. I just need you two to witness it."

And that was how Ace and Stephanie found themselves standing off to the side, holding hands, while they watched Jon and Vickie exchange their vows.

When the brief and very solemn ceremony was done, the judge—who had been subbed in for the justice of the peace—told Jon that he could kiss the bride, which he did.

Ace looked at Stephanie and nodded toward the hallway. "I am feeling inspired and need to speak to you privately for a minute," he whispered. She nodded back and they slipped out into the hall.

"Motivated by the wonderful example of your parents, I wanted to point out that if I had an engagement ring with me, and if you were to say yes, we could go right back into the office here, and get our very own marriage license. Will you marry me?"

"Nothing could persuade me to do anything else," she said.

"You weren't expecting this, were you?" he asked.

"I was totally expecting it," she replied.

The truth is that they had both known from the evening of Stephanie's baptism that they were going to be married, though they hadn't spoken of it together. They just knew.

* * *

Three days after their engagement, Stephanie received what can only be regarded as the profoundest of shocks, at least for her. Ace had asked her parents to accompany them for dinner to The Golden Bee, and they agreed without checking with each other, saying *yes* right away. They responded as though it was planned beforehand, although Stephanie couldn't put her finger on why it felt that way. And Ace was very particular about the time, about going there right at seven p.m. Stephanie wondered, but then forgot about it.

As they made their way into the restaurant, Jon and Vickie went in first, and Ace held back, holding the door for Stephanie. She was starting to like that. The four of them started walking to the right, as though the restaurant host were leading them—but no restaurant host was there. They came around a corner and found a large table with a couple already seated there. Jon was holding a chair for Vickie, and so they were apparently meeting someone Stephanie didn't know.

Her eyes met the woman's—who was strikingly pretty—and she nodded briefly. The woman smiled. Because she was expecting someone she didn't know, it took her a couple seconds. When it hit her, she erupted with joy. "Sara!"

And then her eyes moved over to Sara's escort and she froze. "Lionel!" And then a moment later, "*Lionel?*" There was a table across the way, and Stephanie grabbed at a chair and sat down. She didn't know what to do, say, or think.

The others were all laughing, and so Stephanie knew something was up. Something had to be up. Now Ace was seating her directly across from Sara. When they were all seated, she glared at her father affectionately. "Okay," she said. "Something is up, but I have no idea what it could possibly be."

Jon cleared his throat. "Well, for starters, we have only known about this for two days, when Lionel asked us if we could arrange for a meeting where he could clear something up with you. We just got the final clearance from his authorities this afternoon."

"His authorities?"

So Stephanie turned to look at Lionel, with a look of quizzical amazement on her face. She was delighted to see Sara again, but there was also something indefinably different about him. She wasn't sure what it was. But as soon as he began to talk, she identified it right off. He was being masculine, with that undertow of a lisp completely gone. And the hand gestures, they were clean gone also.

"Stephanie, if I might, I will come straight to the point."

"Please," she said.

"For the last two years, I have been in the employ of Nebraska's secret service—the AGI, we call it. In short, I was a spy for the free state of Nebraska. Most of it was pretty boring, attending conferences and trying to network with important Coloradoans. But there were also moments where things could get pretty dicey . . ."

"Go on," Stephanie managed to say.

"Well, the main thing I wanted to tell you was that I was in character during all our interactions, and out of *all* the piffle that came out of my mouth, I would like to ask you not to believe a word of it. But the most important thing is this—in that crowded room after the press conference, when you got your black eye, even though I was there in character, I really wanted you to know that I didn't really ditch you. Right when you were punched, someone on the floor grabbed my trouser leg and pulled me right down. It was completely unrelated to what was happening to you, and to this day I don't know what that guy's issue was. So I was involved in a five-minute wrestling match down there, and when I finally prevailed and stood up, Ace had already gotten you safely out."

Stephanie suddenly went white in the face, and put her hands over her mouth. "The video! Oh, I am *sorry* . . ." Then she looked at Sara. "I am *so* sorry."

At this, Sara laughed out loud. "Given what you had to go on, I don't really think any apologies are necessary. But if there were to be one, it should go to Lionel, who was the direct recipient of your ire. But in my view, the whole thing serves him right because he decided to go the Scarlet Pimpernel route. Act like a wuss, get treated like a wuss. As for me, that video solved all my problems. I was the happiest girl in Denver for two weeks afterward."

Vickie leaned forward. "Why is that?"

Sara recounted the story of how Lionel had saved her in the parking garage. "And then we went on what I like to call our first date. He explained that he couldn't explain everything, but that he was not really working with Connorson or any of that vile gang. Although Lionel didn't talk to me in detail about his 'missions,' I managed to guess at a general idea of what he was doing, though I didn't know the exact reasons for it. I guessed that he was showing attention to you because he had been watching out for your father, and that outlawed legal outfit he was working with. So I knew what he was doing, and I trusted him completely. But trusting him completely did not prevent me from being fabulously jealous of you, especially as I had been blessed with the privilege of becoming your friend. You, my dear, are gorgeous, and when Lionel told me that you had dated a few times, I was fit to be tied."

"She *is* gorgeous," Ace said.

"Takes after her mother," Jon said.

"Stop it, both of you," Stephanie said, turning back to Sara. "But I really don't understand."

"Well, whenever I caught myself getting jealous of the fact that he had gone out with you those times, all I had to do was think of that video, and it would make me happy again. Before I knew about Lionel, that video just made me proud of you. After I knew him, it made me proud of you, sorry for Lionel, and elated over the general situation. And now that the fighting is over and Lionel has told me everything, you can be as gorgeous as you want without causing me a twinge."

"Sounds like a plan," Ace said.

"Even so," Stephanie said, "even if you really had been what I thought, I had no business talking that way to you. My conscience really got to me on that one. Please forgive me."

Lionel nodded, and then laughed, confident and relaxed. He put his hand on Sara's hand. "As soon as it became apparent that the Free States were going to annex Colorado, I was able to get out. And because that particular video made me, um, somewhat *famous*, my superiors in Nebraska decided to retire me from their service—that department can be disbanded anyway now that the union is disbanded—and they kindly agreed to a public rehabilitation of my reputation. A few news profiles are going to be coming out over the next few months, and we thought that we should tell you about it first. Also, as soon as I am no longer the internationally recognized p-word, I will be able to give Sara this ring I have been carrying around, without all her friends taking her aside to talk about the big mistake she has to be making."

"I see," Jon said.

"But don't tell Sara about the ring. I want it to be a surprise."

Stephanie looked at Sara, who just sat there, deadpan but thoroughly happy. "Don't mind him," Sara said. "He's just being funny. I helped him pick the ring out."

"One more thing," said Lionel. "Guess who is paying for this dinner, and is going to be making an extremely generous donation to each of your wedding funds?"

"Who?" Stephanie asked.

Lionel smiled. "Connor Connorson. His practice paid me handsomely for you all's personal information. It's a pity you'll never read the reports. I put some good stuff in there. All fake, of course."

*   *   *

It was after this dinner that the other big surprises for both Ace and Stephanie began in earnest. They had talked it over with Jon and Vickie and set a date about a month and a half out. "I don't have a job here yet," Vickie had said. "This will give me something to do." The annexation of Colorado had already happened, and so Ace had checked to make sure his parents would be able to make it up. They had already booked a church, and Pastor Troy said that he would be available to conduct the service.

The hairpin curves began when Jon called Ace up and asked him if he was sitting down. "No, but I could sit down easily enough," he said, sitting down. Stephanie was with him and looked at him quizzically. "Okay, shoot," he then said.

"You know that modest little guest list you two had put together?" They had spent a couple hours on it a few nights before, and they thought they might break a hundred guests.

"Yes?" Ace said.

"I have been talking to a few people, and it looks to me like we are going to have to revisit our plans. I was talking to the governor today, and it came out that the *president* is expecting to be invited."

"What?!" Ace lurched forward in his chair, and Stephanie jumped. He looked up at her and said, "The president is expecting an invitation to our wedding . . ."

Her eyes widened.

He went back to Jon on the phone. "You mean the president of the local Kiwanis chapter, right?"

"No," Jon said. "I mean the president of the US of A. Or maybe the reorganized US of Free A. I don't know what we are going to call it yet. But I am referring to the leader of the free world."

Ace sat silently. After a moment, Jon resumed. "You still there? You understand the import of this, right?"

"No, I don't," Ace said.

"I am confident that this is only because you haven't had time to reflect on all of this. I have been mulling on it for about an hour now. What it means is that you are going to have a *big* wedding, and not a small one. There is no way that you can invite just the president, and not have that entail a host of other dignitaries."

Ace rubbed his forehead.

"I took the liberty," Jon said, "of calling St. Matthew's Cathedral here in Laramie to see if they would be willing to rent their facilities, and if the date you settled on was available. They do, and it is."

"Okay," Ace croaked. "Let me talk to Stiffy here, and I will get right back to you." He ended the call, and stared at Stephanie. "Jeepers," he said.

* * *

The next night, Benson and Roberta arrived by car. Ace had rented a house for them, and he and Stephanie met them there. The plan was to unload their baggage from the car and then go out for a quick bite before they came back to get settled. They wound up spending six hours at the restaurant.

The first twenty minutes was full of awkward laughter, but after that it straightened out and became completely normal. The awkwardness evaporated right after they had ordered, and Benson broke out an elephant gun in order to kill the elephant that was in the—as they say—room. What he did was apologize to Ace as fully and as completely as anybody in the history of the world, or at least in the history of Colorado and Wyoming, had ever done. While talking, he would regularly look at Stephanie, directly in the eyes, as much as to seek her forgiveness as well.

"Ace," he said, "you already know all the ways I have sinned against you, and over a number of years. I misconstrued your arguments, tried to mentor you in ways that I knew would aggravate you, and a whole host of other similar things. But after I got things right with God a few weeks ago, thanks to your mother, I had to come to grips with the central sin that was driving all of it. The thing I have confessed to God, and the thing I need to seek your forgiveness for now is this. I have been envious of you and of your abilities for quite a number of years now. The hand of God was on you for blessing, and I could really *see* it, and it was eating me up inside because it did not appear to be mediated through me. I was being bypassed. And it appeared that the blessing was going to far surpass anything I could ever give you. Which it now has. But now that it has come to pass, the grace of repentance means that the whole thing delights me now."

And so they talked, and talked some more. Ace and Stephanie told them the entire story, leaving nothing out—including Camila, and the way Stephanie had been converted. They also told the story about how Stephanie's parents were now back together. They also delivered the news of the president coming, along with a number of international dignitaries.

After about three hours, they each ordered a second dessert in order to justify taking up a table for so long.

* * *

It took Ace and Stephanie twenty-four hours after that to get acclimated to the idea of a cathedral wedding. It was hardest for Stephanie, who had an almost pathological fear of people thinking that she had always carried around a secret desire to be a princess. The reverse was actually the case, and she was beginning to suspect that perhaps the Lord was thinking that being a princess for a day might do her some spiritual good. The thought filled her with horror.

And so there was an internal war going on within Stephanie, one that actually *was* doing her some spiritual good. There was one Stephanie who was simply in love with Ace. Then there was a second Stephanie who was beginning to suspect that being married to Ace was going to be a much bigger deal than either of them had anticipated. He was obviously a prince among men, and if she were to marry him, what did that make *her?* She wanted to be with him, but was entirely uneasy about what that would entail about her status. She was a confident girl, but did not want to be confident in any kind of high-polish aristocratic way. She didn't mind what others thought of her, just so long as they didn't think that she was striving for something like *that.* The third Stephanie was diligently poking holes in the faux-humility of the second Stephanie. She could see right through it and could also see that this was the basic issue lying underneath her conversion, and that meant that it was already settled. It *was* settled, right? But she also knew she had to do *something* that would be the equivalent of crossing her marital Rubicon. The fourth Stephanie was supremely happy, and looked down on the emotional tumult of the other three Stephanies with a sense of detached satisfaction. Nothing touched her.

But she still had to figure out what to *do.* Her internal chatter wasn't bothering her, but she also figured that it would start to bother her sometime if she didn't do something about it. And one day the word *curtsy* came into her mind.

And so it was, when the day arrived, when the doors in the back of the sanctuary slowly opened, and her father stepped into the aisle with her, she looked with joy down the length of the church and saw Ace standing there next to Pastor Troy, she resolved that she would just do it. On the right, she could see the VIP section where the president, and the governor, and other dignitaries were. On the left, behind the front rows for family, were three rows reserved for the press. Their wedding was a thing. It was an international *thing.*

When the organ music stopped, the question was asked, "Who gives this woman to marry this man?" Another layer of joy was added when her father said, "Her mother and I." Her *mother* and I.

Ace came slowly down the steps of the dais, and suddenly stopped when he saw the look in Stephanie's eye. She let go of her father's arm, and in a deep fluid motion, she curtsied to Ace. He told her later that he was startled, but he didn't act as though he was. In return, he solemnly bowed, as though he had been doing that his entire life, which we all know he hadn't. She had been watching videos online and had been practicing in her bedroom for weeks. The effect, working together with her dress, was spectacular. Rather, the effect, together with her dress, and about twenty-five cameras in the press corps capturing the moment, created a sensation.

Time magazine had been purchased by a concern in Omaha about ten years before this, and had been returned to some of its former prestige and glory. And this is mentioned because it was their cameraman who got the best shot, and that is how Stephanie wound up on the cover of the next issue of *Time*, over a heading that said, simply, "The Curtsy."

And so it was, over the years that followed, the curtsy and the bow became an essential part of wedding ceremonies. But not in California.

A BIT OF EXCITEMENT

Ryker had been pretty chafed ever since the failed assassination attempt. He had taken it poorly, as it was a point of personal pride. That pothole at the wrong moment had ruined a string of assassination successes, and so he had taken the whole thing with a singular ill-grace.

His only previous assassination failure had been about ten years before. There had been a pastor in Sacramento who had been preaching an expository series through Leviticus, and chapter 18 had entailed any number of hate crimes and illegalities. All the complaints had been filed, but the mills of the gods appeared to be jammed, and Governor Felix, then in his first year of office, had shown that he had *always* been appreciative of direct action. He had requested the hit.

The pastor in question, a man named Hagan Gilbert, as it turned out, was the older brother of Troy Gilbert, the pastor who had conducted the ceremony for Ace and Stephanie. He also had been a Navy SEAL, and that was before he was a Rhodes Scholar, which was before he had made it through Princeton Seminary with his faith intact. All the brothers were dudes, and they were all brilliant. It was *that* kind of family. Their younger brother, bringing up the rear, was the starting quarterback for Louisiana State, attending there on an academic scholarship. He was studying physics. *That* kind of family.

In this earlier failed hit, the failure was another matter of bad luck, just like the pothole. Ryker had decided to take Hagan out during one of his worship services, for the sensation effect, and so he had taken his place on the aisle, right in front of where the balcony was. He would wait for the pastoral prayer, squeeze off a couple of rounds while every head was bowed, every eye closed, and then blow out of there. The make-up people had arranged for him to look about twenty years older than he actually was, and he had a walrus mustache that actually looked genuine. He would be able to hotfoot out of there, and if anybody tried to stop him, well, he would still have some rounds left. The plan was watertight, and somehow, once the first thing went wrong, almost everything after that went wrong also.

When Hagan was just a minute or so into his prayer, Ryker looked around and saw his chance. Nobody was looking, all were deep in prayer to their imaginary god. He stood up into the aisle, and took careful aim, silencer on.

Well, it would not be strictly accurate to say that *all* were at their prayers. There was a five-year-old in the balcony, name of Mason, who was fidgeting in his seat. As the prayer was apparently going to be one of those long ones, he had begun to experiment with how long he could balance a psalter on his index finger. As his parents were down at the other end of a large family, and because he was experimenting quietly, his conduct was unobserved. He was generally doing well, but then his brother next to him distracted him by whispering that he needed to knock it off. This caused him to glance away for just a moment, but that was enough. He lost the balance, and the psalter fell away from him. He leaned forward to compensate, overdid it, and the psalter, taking on a mind of its own, slid over the railing that lined the front of the balcony.

This happened just as Ryker was going to fire off his first round, and the psalter—almost like the thing was fated—grazed Ryker's arm at the very moment he fired. The bullet missed Hagan by about a foot and a half, splintering the side of the pulpit, and making a loud clang as it struck the metal cross on the wall behind the pulpit. A man two rows ahead jumped up, apparently a member of the security team, pulling a gun out of suit coat as he came. There was no time for a second attempt, so Ryker turned and fled. As it transpired, he got clean away, and there never was a solution to that case.

But in the meantime, Hagan had not even flinched. He had been under fire before, and he had looked up languidly from his prayer, touched the splintered pulpit, and said, "Those guys are so gay they won't even shoot straight." All of this was caught on video, and the celebrity that grew up around him as a result was a central part of the reason he'd had to escape from California, lowered from the city wall in a basket, as it were. He became a pastor in Tulsa.

That was Ryker's one earlier failure, and the pothole failure rankled him in a similar way. So his plan had been to wait out the trial, and if the conclusion of the trial was satisfactory to Governor Felix, then he would just let it go, personal pride notwithstanding. But if the verdict was in any way a disappointment to the governor, then his plan was to finish the job. He had spent several days casing the place where Ace was then staying—with his attorney apparently—and considering the roads into and out of that neighborhood. He had a pretty good plan established—and he thought he could probably get that girl too, which would be a bonus. She was altogether too good-looking to be on the other side. They didn't need any more good-looking chicks. They were already running a surplus.

And then that helicopter had flown off to Wyoming with all of them.

This is how it came about that Ryker was now staying in Laramie, fuming to himself, while he was watching for news of the very happy wedding and maintaining close contact with Governor Felix's team of hackers as they tracked the likely trail of the future honeymooners. And that is why he was able to drive on ahead of them, one day ahead of them, getting a room on the ground floor of the motel where they would be staying on their third night.

His hackers had told him that, judging from the reservations, they were planning on driving all the way through to Banff that next day, which told him they were likely to get an early start. So from six a.m. on, he just sat in the breakfast lounge that was adjacent to the motel lobby, and nursed a long series of coffees. About six thirty, the two lovebirds, *bah*, came down for breakfast, indicating that it was in fact going to be an early start for them. Ryker just sat, staring into his coffee cup. For all his sinister intentions, he just looked like a trucker gearing up for a long day. After about fifteen minutes, they disappeared again. They must have packed before breakfast because they were back down in the lobby again just a few minutes after that.

At the bottom of the stairs—they had not used the elevator because they were only on the second floor—Stephanie clapped her forehead, and said, "Oh, what a ninnyhammer! I forgot something." Ace handed her the room key, and she dashed up the stairs again.

Ryker really was good at what he did, and he knew that while planning beforehand was always a good thing, clean opportunities were always better. As it happened, the clerk had disappeared back into his cubbyhole, the breakfast room was completely empty, and Ace was just standing there, staring out the front door with his hands in his pockets. The place was deserted. And Ryker had his gun with him, all ready to go, inside his coat. His earlier plan had been to follow them out to the parking lot and take care of business there. But his car was parked in the front row, right next to the motel, and this looked to be just as good. The girl would be spared, but she would be messed up plenty with a dead groom on her honeymoon. Make hay while the sun shines. Always a man of action, Ryker stood up, pulling his gun out as he came.

He knew how to walk like a cat, which he was doing, arm, hand, and pistol extended, and pointed straight at the back of Ace's head.

And that is what Stephanie saw when she came out of their hotel room, a room that looked over the rail of the mezzanine down into the lobby, with her forgotten hardshell traveling case in hand. All in one fluid motion, she reacted. She had no time to think anything through, and so she just did what seemed right at the time. And what she did was raise both hands above her head, and she *hurled* the case at Ryker. As she did so, her first thought was that she should have screamed instead, and her second thought was that it looked like she might be a pretty good shot. Maybe screaming wasn't the best option—that would have just resulted in Ace being thrown into a fistfight with a man with a gun.

And she *was* a good shot. The traveling case was spinning around like an overweight discus, and it sailed down out of the mezzanine like a hard green plastic angel of death. And so, right before Ryker pulled the trigger, one corner of the spinning case hit him squarely on the back of the head. The stars fought from their courses against Sisera, and Jael the wife of Heber looked down from the balcony. He staggered forward, saying something akin to *uuuhhh*, and as he fell he remembered that he was supposed to be pulling the trigger for some reason, and so he shot himself in the leg. It was an ignominious end to a storied career as a hit man.

The state of Montana took a dim view of all of these proceedings, especially as it involved our two distinguished heroes, and Ryker wound up spending the rest of his life contemplating how the various faults of others had landed him in the penitentiary.

Stephanie careened down the stairs three at a time, no doubt setting records for that establishment, but by the time she got to Ace he had already retrieved the gun. Ryker was face down, out cold, and bleeding on the motel carpet. The clerk was back at his station, whiter than one of the motel's towels.

HEADED HOME

The last formal day of their two-week honeymoon, before the beginning of their leisurely three-day drive back home, Ace and Stephanie came out of their five-star hotel in Banff.

Their plan was to drive back down to Wyoming, gather up what little stuff they had there, and move to Idaho. Both of them had about two years left of college to complete, and as Ace and

Stephanie had each been offered a full-ride scholarship at New Saint Andrews College, and because NSA had been making prophetic noises about all the coming Troubles back before they had actually happened, the new Hartwick clan decided to reboot there.

But for the present, they both stopped at the top of the steps and stood there for a moment. They each had a hot cup of coffee to go, steaming in the cool of the morning. The hotel behind them was enormous—a great lodge built out of logs that were about as wide around as trash cans. The grounds around the hotel were landscaped wonderfully, and behind the scattered tamarack, they could just make out the highway behind the trees, with an occasional car flashing by.

Up behind the highway there was a steep slope, almost a mountain, covered in a thick, piney fur. The sky was an early morning blue, the trees were an evergreen sort of green, two colors that should never go together, and yet they somehow did. But the most beautiful sight in all of this morning splendor was the parking lot. It had rained sometime well after midnight, and the moisture was now evaporating off the asphalt, curling up in little miniature spiral staircases of vapor. The parking lot was new, so the asphalt was jet black, the yellow lines were radiant, and all the cars looked like they were covered with diamonds.

Their car was already loaded up, they had enjoyed a glorious breakfast at the hotel, and they both felt almost ready for the drive home. The sun had just come up over the roofline of their lodge and had settled on their car, as if to warm it up for them.

After they walked down to the car, they both stopped, somehow reluctant to start a trip they were both eager to complete.

"Let's just stand in the sunshine for a minute," Stephanie said. She put her coffee on the hood of car, and put her arms around Ace's neck. He put down his coffee also, and just held her.

After a few moments, he said, "Ready?"

She nodded, and remained right where she was. He waited another few moments, and then she stepped back, and put both hands up on his shoulders.

"Ace, dearest, remember our first important conversation, in that coffee shop? And my crack about the testosterone?"

Ace nodded.

"I apologized back then, as I should have done, for my bad manners. I really was sorry, as I should have been, and I remain sorry. I remain sorry down to this very day. But now I need to approach that entire question from another angle, as I am now in a position to address it on the basis of ascertained facts, scientifically determined. Being now *something* of an expert witness, I am compelled to withdraw the jibe entirely, on every level. I have not had many math or science courses, but I do believe it is statistically improbable and biologically impossible for me *not* to be pregnant. I mean, golly."

Ace opened the door for her, and kissed the top of her head. "Well, the only way for us to do anything about *that* problem, if you want to call it a problem, which it isn't for *me*, is for you to stop being so darn cute."

"Not gonna," she said. And Asahel closed her door.

THE END